INTIMATE RELATIONS

Finn O'Brien Book Four

REBECCA FORSTER

**WOLFPACK
PUBLISHING**
— EST 2013 —

WOLFPACK PUBLISHING
— EST 2013 —

Intimate Relations
Paperback Edition
Copyright © 2021 Rebecca Forster

Wolfpack Publishing
6032 Wheat Penny Avenue
Las Vegas, NV 89122

Paperback ISBN: 978-1-64734-656-0
Ebook ISBN: 978-1-64734-998-1
LCCN 2021932171

Cover Design by Hadleigh O. Charles
Cover Photo by Joshua Case on Unsplash

INTIMATE RELATIONS

It is so easy for a woman to become what the man she
loves believes her to be!
The House of Mirth by Edith Wharton

For the loves of my life: Steve, Alex, Eric

ACKNOWLEDGEMENTS

As always, thank you to those who help me along the road from the moment I have the barest kernel of an idea for a new book to the final word. Their patience and good humor is always appreciated. My incredible editor, Jenny Jensen is simply brilliant, kind with criticism and generous with kudos. The fabulously brilliant Bruce Raterink who reads faster than a human being should be able to. The ever hilarious Glenn Gallo whose little notes make my day. Thanks to my husband who becomes chief cook and bottle washer during the process, my kids who distract me with their own adventures, and all the readers who pop me a note asking when there will be a next book. A special shout out to the strange pockets of Los Angeles that inspire the Finn O'Brien Thrillers, and to Wolfpack Publishing for giving Finn and so many other characters of mine a new home.

PREFACE

The night it happened, the City of Angels was quiet in the odd way a big city can be. It was a deceptive silence, an illusory calm, and no more sustainable than holding one's breath. Eventually Los Angeles would exhale and blow out the hot air of discontent, and it would not go unnoticed.

Night owls, insomniacs, creatures cloaked in human skin who lay in wait in dark corners would hear it. Their ears would prick, and their heads would cock as they tried to interpret the sound. Was it the lazy lament of a metropolis settling? Was it the sound of resignation? Had this city, the one that crowned itself with a celestial moniker, always been a hellish place? Or was that little click and whir— that sound of a worn piece of the city giving way—a precursor to something foul. Whatever it was, the sounds that disturbed the peace only mattered to half the population.

The rich half didn't have a care in the world. Those privileged folks were long gone. They had buttoned themselves up in chic Westside condos. They lounged in glass houses perched on stilts in the Hollywood Hills. The wealthy barricaded themselves in their faux villas in Bel-Air. They were safe behind guarded gates, in huge homes rooted on acres of precious land. They rested in condos on Wilshire, a doorman on watch to guard them through the long night. Each day these folks returned to the city, made their fortunes, and scurried back to safety as the sun went down.

Yes, all was right with half the world.

It was the other half who wakened to the sound of the city exhaling. It was the people in Chinatown, Koreatown, Compton, and East LA whose sleep was fitful. The sound disturbed the homeless who seeded the sidewalks, were scattered over empty lots, and took shelter in the doorways of government buildings. The illegals, day laborers, and displaced heard it. The abandoned elderly housed in crumbling apartments heard it. The sometimes creative, seldom successful, often-a-bit-mad freaks, actors, and artists; they heard it.

That night, the sound seemed to come from the frayed edges of the city. In East Los Angeles where livings were eked out in hole-in-the-wall *taquerias and* gangs replaced government something was stirring. In this part of town there are homes and businesses, but few of them are of any note or consequence. There is one place, however, that stands out. A strange castle of sorts. A compound. A dystopian sound stage of a place. It houses some rich folks and some poor; some on the verge of 'making it', some who never will. Still, this place is magical. To live there means that you belong, that you are acceptable, and that you deserve to be safe behind gates and walls.

In another life this place was a brewery that employed thousands of people. Then it fell victim to microbrewery fashion and California regulation. The people who owned the brewery dismissed their workers and abandoned their buildings. For a long while the compound stood empty; a looming, grey blight built on footprints of concrete poured on cheap land.

But one man's crumbling empire is another's opportunity. In this case, the opportunist was a man and his three daughters. The man and his daughters saw a pot of gold in the brewery's industrial chic buildings. They partnered with the city of Los Angeles, and developed the property into the world's largest artist community. Their pitch was brilliant. Only those who lived and died by the arts could live there. The stipulation immediately made the address desirable. After all, who in Los Angeles did not believe they were a star in the making?

Now The Brewery address was as good as a sprinkle of stardust. Either you would fashion your own galaxy from the glittery stuff or it would bury you. The creative folks had free rein over their individual spaces. They built out bedrooms, and kitchens, and galleries. They painted, sculpted, wrote, and invented stuff. Musicians were the least favored, and trumpeters were not allowed. Even the most creative among them could not bear the sound of a trumpet in these concrete quarters. Soon The Brewery was a thriving concern. The city got its philanthropic jollies, the man and his three daughters got rich, and the artists got a very cool place to live.

The night it happened, the city and The Brewery were peaceful with one exception. There was a party in the three-story unit that was the envy of every artist in the colony. Even by L.A. standards, the party was an exclusive gathering and the guest list rarified.

The guests arrived without fanfare, disappearing into the building so quickly few took notice. There were no windows on the first floor of the unit and minimal windows on the second. On the third floor the windows were cathedral-worthy. On a clear day the people who lived there could see all the way to the ocean. But this was not a clear day, and the people who lived there had not invited those who attended the party. They were but a little cog in the night's wheel of business. They understood the nature of the gathering, but they were not part of it. They hoped the men and women in their home would soon be gone. They hoped the night would end as it had begun: quietly.

They should have known better. This small part of the city was about to exhale.

CHAPTER 1

The handpicked guests were at the party for two reasons. The first was to indulge themselves as only the very wealthy can. The second was to witness the unveiling of something they hoped would make them richer still. They had no idea what that 'something' might be, but it didn't matter. The man who invited them was a god, and when God called you answered, 'Yes, Lord.' While they waited for the unveiling they were thoroughly entertained, barely noting the passage of time. Two men, however, stood apart from the rest, unnoticed in the shadowy alcove near the narrow staircase.

The first man was the artist who lived in the space. He created works of such beauty grown men were brought to their knees. His talent lay in his precision and attention to detail and his delicate touch with a paintbrush. It seemed a strange talent for a man with such an unpleasant look about him. He was tall, broad shouldered, and barrel chested; his long legs and arms were skinny ropes of muscle. The artist's hands were big, his fingers gnarled. The man's head was too large for his body, his face was long and worn. He was not young nor did he seem old, and yet women found him intriguing, even sexy. Men tried to analyze his strange appeal. Eventually they decided that it was the artist's energy, focus, and, above all, his unbridled passion for the female form that made him so unique. Women who inspired him knew their beauty was unimpeachable. He was a man who could make fantasy reality, and that was quite a talent.

The artist was foreign. Czech many thought although no one knew for certain. They wondered about the man and his wife and how they had come to make their living in such a unique way. It was simple, the wife would explain: he was the artist, and she was the engineer. She said this each time the question was asked, even though this was not what people wanted to know. They wanted to know how the artist and his wife felt about what they created. Neither of them ever answered. Eventually their clients decided that it didn't matter what they thought. All that mattered was that they got what they paid for. The artist and his wife and their feelings, in the end, were of no concern.

That night, had the guests noticed the big man in the alcove, they might not have realized he wasn't alone. The person with him did not so much join the artist as appear like a shadow with the movement of the light. He was slight, Asian, and of an indiscernible age. Unlike the artist, his face was as smooth as a young boy's. His eyes were strangely blank and moist behind his thick glasses. His coarse hair was short all around, but longer on top. His ears were small and low. His teeth were not the best, but few people knew this because he never smiled and when he spoke his lips hardly moved.

As they talked, the artist's fists opened and closed with an angry rhythm; his body undulated with frustration. The Asian man stood with his arms to his side and his shoulders hunched over a pathetically narrow chest. His feet were close together. He wore soft shoes, pants the shade of putty, a shirt with short sleeves that was neither white nor beige. His pants rode too high on his thin frame; his shirt was buttoned up tight. The only bright thing about him was the silver buckle on his belt. If anyone had taken note of this man and then blinked they would have no memory of him. They would not have recognized him for who he was, but the artist knew. The artist was on intimate terms with him, but like many relationships it was complicated.

What they shared was a passion for beauty and, above all, challenge. The purpose of that challenge had changed in the last few months, so now they argued fiercely. Rather the artist did. The shade-of-a-man was as silent as the city. The artist didn't hear the small sounds that signaled his displeasure.

"It is over now," the artist said, his vowels distorted by his accent. "Do you hear me? I am done."

"I have paid. We have a contract," the man said.

"I give it back. Every penny. Back in your pocket." The artist raised his hands. He threw his big head to the side as his eyes rolled toward the people in the great room. "Tell them to go. I will not have you exploit her. It's different now. It is all different."

"She is mine." The man did not blink. He did not raise his voice. He did not smile or frown. His words were a mantra, a statement of fact, audio on a loop. "I have paid you. She belongs to me."

The artist slammed the palm of his hand against the wall behind the man's head. The strike missed by an inch; the Asian man didn't flinch. He wasn't brave. He simply lacked the ability to understand anger in the same way he was unable to experience joy. Desire he understood, but that lesson had been long in coming.

The artist's wife often spoke of the man as she and her husband worked. She liked to talk whether her husband was listening or not. The Asian man, she decided, was actually a jellyfish. He had big head full of brains, but his body was useless and unconnected to the brain. She neither liked nor disliked him. He did not make the hairs on the back of her neck stand up. He was not dangerous or lascivious. He was, she said, wealthy, strange, and harmless.

The artist's wife liked that he had chosen them for his grand project. She dreamed of how famous they would become because of this man. The work made her feel alive, and the money was something she had never dreamed of. The artist's wife laughed at their good fortune, the man, and the commission he was paying. Each laugh was different. She giggled at their good luck, chuckled at the man himself, and belly laughed at the ridiculous money he showered on them.

At first the artist laughed with her, but as their work went on he wearied of her talk. There came a day when he didn't pay attention to her at all. The wife understood this. It was his way to withdraw when his art reached a critical stage. She took no offense at first. When he crossed a line, she regretted not having paid more attention.

The night of the party, the artist's wife came down the stairwell intending to take her husband away. They would run from all the people in their home. They would run from the Asian man because now this business was bad. It was horrible. It was hell. But when she saw the two of them arguing she stopped and put her back against the stairwell wall before they saw her. Her chest rose and fell. Her breath was shallow and quick. She was frightened as she listened to her husband growl. He sounded like an animal; she had never heard such passion from him. Her eyes darted to her smock and she saw two buttons were undone. She buttoned one only to jump when she heard her husband's hand strike the wall. Her fingers were shaking as she fastened the second button. When he hit the wall again, she almost cried out. Twice more her husband tried to make his point to the jellyfish man. Twice more she heard their patron's flat voice as he reminded the artist that he had been paid. Twice more the man demanded to see her, his property.

The artist's wife raised her eyes as if she could see through the ceiling to the floors above. She shook her head, lowered her eyes, and leaned forward in time to see her husband make a fist. When he raised it, she rushed down the last two steps and put herself between them. The Asian man would not understand that he was now truly in danger. She was sure that her husband had not thought of the consequences of hurting this man.

Her backside was against the jellyfish man. He had no sense of personal space and didn't move. There was so little room that her behind pressed into his private parts. The contact disgusted her

"Get out of my way, Emi."

The artist took her shoulders and tried to move her aside, but she was not a small woman. She stood her ground, put her hand on her husband's chest, and tried to push him back. He, too, was unmovable.

"What is going on? Stop this fighting. It's almost time. The people—"

Her head inclined toward the open room. She whispered though the guests could not have heard her even if she raised her voice. She put her fingertips to her husband's face to make him look at her, but he shook her off. She tried again.

"*Ju lutem.* Please. They are waiting. You have promised. I will go get her. Let me go up to get her, Enver. It would be best."

Emi looked behind her. The jellyfish man still pressed against her. She shivered. She understood. Were it not for his money he would be alone to the end of his days. Emi turned, and now her backside was against her husband. He stepped back. The Asian man was shorter than she by only an inch, so their eyes met: her frantic dark ones, his moist and black.

"Move. You must move away."

It took all her self control to keep her voice soft and kind, but firm. He blinked and did as she asked. Emi turned back to her husband.

"Enver."

Emi spoke to him in their own language. She told him that he must get through the night. That was all. She told him there was too much at stake to anger this man. She told him that she knew what to do. She, Emi, would go upstairs and bring her down. That way the man would get what he wanted and the artist would not have to watch.

Her husband waggled his head. His large hands went to his face and when he looked again it wasn't at her. His wife turned her head. She saw nothing but empty space. It took her a moment to understand what that meant. The Asian man was gone, stealing up the stairs. Emi pushed her husband, but there was no controlling him now. He knew what was happening. If the artist wasn't going to give the man what was his, that man would take it.

"No. No. No," she whispered, baring her teeth. "Let him have her."

"No. Never."

The artist's voice rose until the wail of it caught the attention of more than one guest. Women paused, men's heads turned. A few smiled thinking that this was the sound of pleasure. Others were annoyed at the disruption of their own.

"Hush," Emi pleaded, near tears as she took his arm. He shook her off. She fell back against the wall, but scrambled up before her husband could give chase.

"I'll get him," she said. "You stay here. Please, Enver. Let me."

"Do not interfere." The artist took his wife by the shoulders, and looked at her as if seeing her for the first time. "Go change your clothes. You shame us looking like a peasant in your work clothes. Take that scarf off your hair; that smock off your body."

"No," she said. "I will not."

He paused when Emi snapped at him. She seldom angered. Now she was full of fury, shaking with it. Still, it wasn't enough to stop him.

"You're right. It doesn't matter what you look like. Leave me alone. Throw those people out."

With that he pushed past her and bounded up the stairs. Emi's fury became panic; just as suddenly panic passed to calm. The wheels had been set in motion long ago, and to make a scene now would ruin everything. Still it would be even worse if she didn't stop both men from going upstairs. She gathered her energy. She would do what she could.

Emi had her foot on the second riser as she thought through her plan. The sound of her husband's footsteps as he pounded up the stairs became fainter the farther he climbed. He stopped on the first landing taking enough time to lean over and look at his wife.

"It is over. She stays."

With that he was gone, and Emi collapsed against the wall. She was exhausted in body and soul; she was terrified in her heart. She thought of the Asian man already steps ahead of her husband, and was almost sorry for him. She was sorrier still for Enver, and herself, and for whatever would come after this. Then she started to laugh. It was a tragedy, yes, but it was also tragically funny. This Asian man didn't know she existed, her husband didn't care that she did, and all because of *her*.

Emi looked up, but there was nothing to see. Her ears pricked but there was nothing to hear. Her eyes went to the strange and beautiful people in her living room, people whose names she didn't know. She should tell them to go, but before she could gather her strength a sound came from above that turned her blood to ice.

The concrete walls did not absorb it, the narrow stairwells did not bottle it up. Heads went up. The guest's eyes darted here and there as they tried to identify where it had come from, this muted howl of agony. Women moved closer to men who hoped they would not be called upon to be heroic.

The sound was like the roar of a distant train carrying a cargo of insanity. Emi took two steps down. She pushed herself into a dark corner of the alcove where moments ago she had tried to assuage her husband. One of the guests rose from his chair. He smiled as if the sound thrilled him, but his anticipation soon dissolved into a look of confusion.

Worse than the inhuman cry, was the silence that followed. That quiet was huge and filled with something so horrible there was no name for it. Before the wealthy people could decide what to do, the artist rushed down the stairs, ran past his wife, and threw himself into the big room. He fell against one wall and rolled onto another before standing tall and raising his arms to heaven. In that instant, he issued another abominable cry. This one was so deep and long that the guests froze with their eyes wide and their mouths open.

Someone dropped a glass, and it shattered on the hard floor. Collectively, the guests fell back one step. Wild-eyed, the artist staggered around the room. All the fancy folks scurried away. His size cowed them. The look in his eyes spooked them. And the fact that his shirt was red with blood terrorized them.

Clearly the party was over.

CHAPTER 2

Finn O'Brien caught the call at 2:26 a.m. On a normal day he would be dressed, armed, and out the door on his own. This morning his partner, Cori Anderson, was by his side. She had been in Finn's bed when the call came. She slept alone, grateful that her partner had offered his roof while her home was being tented.

The night before she had arrived with Chinese, an overnight bag, and a litany of complaints about the little buggers eating her out of house and home. It was costing her a small fortune to kill them dead, not to mention putting everyone out. Thomas Lapinski had offered her shelter, but she declined. She and Lapinski — attorney at law, brilliant, and lovesick —were on the edge of a relationship. Cori wasn't sure if she wanted to leap into the abyss or retreat, so spending the night at his place seemed unfair. The fact that she and Finn were on call settled the matter.

The sleep-over had been a success. Cori and Finn worked a little, followed up the Chinese with ice cream Cori found smashed in the back of Finn's freezer, managed the bathroom without a fuss, and went off to bed at a reasonable hour. Cori was sleeping like a baby when Finn yanked her awake with a shake and a shout out that there was 'business to be done'. Now here they were, headed out to a dust up.

"Are you going to sit there wasting your best scowl or will you talk to me, woman?" Finn cast her an amused glance as they sped through the dark on deserted streets.

"Contrary to the great male wisdom, O'Brien, almost nobody likes to be thrown out of a warm bed with a 'get up, woman'. No wonder you're single if that's the best you got."

She slid her eyes his way and almost smiled. The man looked the same no matter what time of day. Granted that wasn't much of a challenge when you shaved your head, your T-shirt and jeans were a uniform, and your square jawed face was pretty damn perfect.

"Sure, didn't I say it nicely, Cori? Woke you like a princess, all soft spoken and everything." He exaggerated the Irish in him as he tried to make her smile, but Cori didn't give in easy.

"Yeah, you were sweet as honey," she said. "But you're one noisy guy in the morning when you're rushing around."

"'Tis is the dead of night in my book. I'm quieter when it's not work I'm dressing for," Finn said.

Now Cori did smile. Her partner had settled into the man she knew well. Finn O'Brien was a hybrid of the seventeen year-old Irish immigrant he had been, and the red-white-and blue American he had become. It was such a pleasing mash-up that she settled down too. It wasn't his fault the call came, nor that they were on unfamiliar footing.

"I never liked a call like this," Cori said. "It's a neither-here-nor-there time. Wake up after two in the morning you never get back to sleep. You toss and turn and work yourself up into a lather, so you're a witch all day. That's what I hated when Amber was a baby. I would get up, feed her, she sleeps, and I'm left staring at the test pattern on the TV."

"Television hasn't had test patterns since 1963," Finn said.

"Have you watched TV in the last ten years? It's all as good as a test pattern," Cori said. "No matter. I hate this time, and I'm none too fond of this part of town either."

"Anything else?" Finn asked. Cori chuckled, and it was a sad little sound.

"Sorry. I'm just worn slap out, O'Brien. Amber's taking classes, and it's a scramble between us to see to Tucker. And if you don't think a two year old can be like a bat out of hell, you don't know much. Now I've got problems with the house." She waved her fingers, tapping the backs of her nails against the window. "Pretty soon I'll be gnawing on the beams with the termites 'cause I won't be able to afford food."

"Pity, they don't pay us by the call," Finn said.

"We'd be in high cotton if they did." Cori rested her elbow on the window's edge, then put her brow against her open palm. "I never knew how much I liked Wilshire Division before they lent us out. I know this assignment isn't a forever thing, but this part of town is friggin' depressing."

"It does feel like people never leave once they land," Finn said.

"Don't say that. I mean what if they reassign us permanently? You don't think they could make us stay, do you?"

Cori dropped her hand, ran it under her long hair, and tossed it back. Finn smiled. Cori should be strutting a runway with a beauty queen sash on her shoulder instead of a holster. Even yanked out of a sound sleep she managed to tease her hair Texas-high, and shade her eyes with her favored blue eyeshadow.

"It's possible we might have to stay here," Finn said.

"You don't think Captain Fowler is punishing us for something, do you? I thought things were going pretty good for us at Wilshire," she said. "Why didn't he send Sanders and Lopez over here? Or Black. Steve Black could have come. Why not send him? He's between partners."

When Cori paused long enough to let him know she wanted him to speak, Finn said:

"Captain Fowler gave us the nod, and here we are. East L.A. for at least a month. Truly it's as simple as that, Cori," Finn said. "And if it weren't that simple, there's nothing we could do about it right this minute."

"Well, it sucks," Cori said.

"That it does."

Finn blew through a red light at North Main and Caesar Chavez, staying tight on Main. They had passed Olivera Street a mile and half back. The birthplace of Los Angeles was quiet now, but by noon every restaurant and souvenir store would be packed with tourists. San Antonio Winery was a darkened blur. Later in the day lawyers and judges, clerks and bailiff's would find their way to the place for lunch. In the near distance was the UPS fulfillment center sprawling over a good half a mile of land. Their destination, The Brewery, was a mile and a half beyond that.

"I hope we can wrap this up PDQ. I've got to check in with the ME on that old guy later today. The one the insurance company wanted autopsied? You're supposed to follow up with the Martinez family, too. I swear, this captain's been dumping more than our share on us."

"The captains have their work, we have ours," Finn answered. "Truly I wouldn't want theirs, so let's be grateful we're not the ones doing the assigning."

Cori started to laugh, but immediately sobered. It wasn't as much that the sour mood had passed as the time for fun and games was gone. They were close to whatever had called them out in the dead of night.

Finn leaned forward; Cori leaned back so he could look past her. The geography of this division was a far cry from Wilshire. Since they would be traveling it at least another six weeks, Finn looked for landmarks to map it out in his mind. There wasn't much of merit. To Finn the whole place looked like real estate Morse Code: dots and dashes of open spaces and structures. The open spaces were the dots — few and far between. The low slung buildings that housed small manufacturing businesses, offices, and duplexes were strung together like architectural dashes. The message it spelled out was that this was L.A.'s version of fly-over country.

Here and there single-family homes popped up. Some of the houses were abandoned and some not, but all bore wounds. Paint peeled off window sashes, house numbers were faded, and weeds sprouted from the cracks in the crumbling sidewalks. Now and again a patch of greenery struggled to survive in a tiny fenced yard or an errant sunflower reached for the sky.

Bars covered all the windows, the metal bolted to the exterior walls. It was clear there were no interior release mechanisms. A spark from a barbeque, a space heater, an illegal firework, and the buildings would go up in flames. There would be no way out for the people inside, and no way in for the fire crews.

In this city, release bars were the law. Still the politicians could pass a million laws to protect their citizens, but without enough people to enforce them ormoney to comply the laws meant nothing. The marginalized populations would have to take their chances.

"There."

At Cori's call Finn slowed the car. He didn't see the entrance to property. He did see a landmark he would not soon forget. Up ahead, towering thirty-feet off the ground, was a fiberglass statue of a cowboy astride a gargantuan horse. It was the kind of thing one would see at the entrance to an amusement park. In the darkness of the early morning, though, the cowboy looked like the guardian of Hades.

Dark patches marred the horse's white flanks where the California sun had taken its toll. The cowboy's blue pants and red shirt were faded. His face was pock-marked, a chunk of plaster had been taken out of his chin; one eye was worn away. But none of this bothered the cowboy. He grinned, ready with a how-dee-do. The horse reared with gusto. The cowboy's arm was raised and he held his ten gallon hat skyward, beckoning all to enter.

This way.

Come on, y'all.

Wonders to be seen; adventure to be had.

This way, suckers.

Finn gave a soft snort, a whinny if you please. It wasn't likely that there was anything wonderful to be had this night. Still, he accepted the cowboy's invitation and pulled a hard right through a wide gate. The gate was part of an impressive iron fence that stood ten feet counting the curls of barbed wire on top. He rolled through a parking lot. Each space was occupied. Some of the cars were fine; others looked as if they were ready for the junk heap. Finn stopped. Both detectives scanned the grounds. There seemed to be no direct path to the interior. Cori got on the horn with dispatch to confirm the exact location, but before she finished her query Finn said:

"We're good, Cori. I see."

He backed up and made a tight turn and another turn quickly after that. They were on a wide walkway that ran between two buildings, heading toward a pulsing halo of red light. Cori popped her belt. They had arrived at their destination, but two black and whites beat them to it. Finn inched past an ambulance and came to a stop between the two cherry tops. He and Cori opened their doors and closed them as if their movements were choreographed. They hitched their jackets: Finn to confirm his weapon was at the small of his back, Cori that hers was in the holster under her arm. They took note of their surroundings as they went toward a young officer.

Two EMTs were in the back of their vehicle, sheltering in place, waiting to be called. One, a woman who looked more like a girl, hopped to the ground. She held onto the open door of the van and watched them. The detective's arrival signaled that something would be happening soon. Finn would remember what she looked like in the same way he would remember the odd layout of the property. It was always this way when he arrived at a scene. It was a skill and a blessing, his hyper vigilance.

They walked across a concrete slab that looked like a village square. There were no vehicles other than those of law enforcement. The utilitarian buildings surrounding the area were of varying heights. Some had a great deal of space between them; others were so close together they shared walls. Picture windows punctuated the taller buildings; squat buildings had no windows at all. Every concrete block had a door and over that door was a number. Industrial fans were embedded high in the walls for ventilation. Raised concrete walkways framed the lower structures. Wooden railings that looked like hitching posts studded the length. The spaces in front of some units were swept clean; others were a riot of potted plants, furniture, and toys.

People had come out of their apartments, awakened by the flash of the lights and the sound of cars where no cars should be. They were a motley crew. Leaning over the wooden railing in front of one of the units was a couple who had come straight from their bed. The girl wore a T-shirt; Finn wished her boyfriend had been as modest. He wore something like a thong and nothing else. From the looks of his middle, he was a man who enjoyed his Guinness. They seemed neither amused nor alarmed by the goings on and were minimally curious.

A young girl with a thatch of hair growing out of the top of her otherwise shaved head, was filming on her phone. She would get nothing more than the red glare of the light from atop the police car since she was shooting into it. No payday for catching a cop-doing-wrong on video.

Another woman - gorgeous and tall, dressed in a flowing kimono-like robe - leaned against a post smoking. It was only when Finn passed that he realized it was a young man with glorious hair and not a woman at all. He eyed Finn, did the same to Cori, and dismissed them both as not worthy of his notice.

"We've got a guy recording at four o'clock, too."

Finn swung his eyes up at the person Cori had tagged.

"We'll be on the nightly news if we cross our eyes," he said.

"How do I look?" Cori said.

"Prime time worthy," Finn said.

"You are a class act, O'Brien."

"I try," Finn said.

He picked up the pace. Cori matched it. When they got where they were going they positioned themselves on either side of the uniformed cop who only had eyes for his partner's back. That man faced off with a woman in the doorway of the large unit. She stood alone, frozen in the glare of the car's headlights.

"Detective O'Brien." The officer glanced Finn's way when he introduced himself. He looked the other way when Finn said, "Detective Anderson."

"Hunter," the cop answered.

"And him?" Finn said, indicating the officer in no-man's land.

"Douglas," Hunter said. "Senior officer."

"What have you got?" Finn asked.

"Dispatch sent us out on an assault call."

"From?" Finn asked.

Hunter pointed to an old man with very long hair.

"His name is George. He says he has insomnia, so he walks this place at night. Likes to think of himself as security. He stopped for a smoke, was checking out the stars, and he sees some stuff he didn't like. There had been a woman in the window." Officer Hunter pointed to the third floor of the unit in question. "When she disappeared he figured she had gone to bed. Then he saw someone else in the room. He thought it looked like that person had a weapon. A club or something. He worried about an assault on the woman. That's all we got."

"No description of the one with the club?"

Hunter shook his head.

"He's old. He couldn't even tell if the second person was a man or a woman. We didn't think much of the whole story until we got here. It's not the first time the old guy has cried wolf. As soon as we try to check it out, that one freaked." He indicated the woman in the doorway. "That's when we called for detectives."

"It would seem Officer Douglas is taking the lazy river, now isn't he?"

Cori's Texas drawl drew out the words like a smear of butter across a biscuit. Officer Hunter wasn't the swiftest. Before Cori could make her contempt clear, Finn stepped in.

"Officer Hunter, why haven't you gone in and established the nature of the crime? Or even if one was committed?"

"Douglas said the situation was hinky. He said we needed to wait." Finn muttered something under his breath, and Officer Hunter took exception.

"Hey, I'm seven months on the job." Officer Hunter sounded like a five year old whining that none of this was his fault. "If he says wait, I wait."

Cori snorted and started for Officer Douglas. Finn stopped her.

"I go, Cori."

If there was trouble to be had, he wanted to field it first. Cori had no problem with that. They each had their strengths. One of Finn's was testing the waters, and Cori's was to be ever watchful. She knew that a lot of people didn't particularly warm to her partner given his history on the force. After he had taken out one of his brothers in blue, shot him dead, Finn became an outcast. It didn't matter that he fired his weapon in self-defense, it mattered that he had fired it at all.

The man Finn approached was tall and in good shape. He was equally impressive from the front though he was older than Finn had imagined. Given that Officer Douglas had mileage on him, Finn gave the man the benefit of the doubt. His instincts would be honed, and his call would be informed. Finn stood beside the officer so that he, too, could keep an eye on the woman in the doorway. She had not moved and she looked no more dangerous up close than she had from afar. She was middle aged, distressed, but not hurt.

"Officer Douglas," he said. "Detective O'Brien. With me is Detective Anderson. Your partner says you've been standing down."

"The woman says everything is fine, and she wants us to leave," Douglas said.

Finn admired the baritone. The voice fit the man, but there was something in the words that didn't fit the situation.

"And your thinking is?" Finn said.

"My thinking is that I don't want my ass or my rookie partner's in a sling 'till I know what we're walking into. Look at that thing." He gestured toward the building with one hand, the other stayed on his hip. "Three stories, outdoor staircases, rooftop access, the interior isn't linear. We could be walking into an ambush."

Finn did a double take: a glance at the man, at the building, and back again. Even though the assessment was correct, the inaction seemed cowardly.

"Am I to understand that you're waiting eventhough there might be a person in need of medical attention in there?" Finn said. "You signed on to serve and protect, did you not, Officer Douglas?"

The man turned his head and ran his eyes over Finn. His small smile was not one of camaraderie.

"In case you haven't noticed, cops have targets on their backs these days. I wasn't going to put my officer or the EMTs at risk." Douglas said. He chucked his chin at the woman in the doorway. "She could be anything. She could be a decoy."

"And she could have a vest full of dynamite strapped to her, but I'm thinking not," Finn said.

Douglas shuffled. He took his eyes off the woman in the doorway, and turned slightly to make sure Finn heard hm.

"I got three years 'till retirement, and I'm going to make it there all in one piece. I'd like to go home to my wife and kids every night for the next three years. Now that I know you caught the call, I think I made the right choice. I'd rather you walk in ahead of me 'cause I sure don't want to be target practice for you either."

Finn pulled up his bottom lip. He put a hand on Douglas's shoulder. Finn gave him a smile that never reached his eyes.

"That bit's getting old 'tisn't it, Officer Douglas?"

The man stiffened, his hand clenched. He wanted a piece of Finn, but he wouldn't try to take it. As the officer said, he would do nothing to jeopardize his retirement. Officer Douglas was disappointed that his slur had not been the gut punch he intended. Before either spoke again, Cori came between them.

"What's going on?" she asked.

"Officer Douglas has declined to make his way inside that building. He wants assurances no harm will come to him," Finn said.

"Isn't that nice, Officer Douglas." Cori smiled at the man and then turned to Finn. "What shall we do about that, Detective O'Brien?"

"I'm thinking we should leave Officer Douglas here, and call him when it is safe," Finn said.

Finn and Cori did not wait for agreement from Officer Douglas. They walked away quickly enough that they did not hear the curses muttered by the uniformed man. They only had eyes for the woman who clutched her high-necked, loose dress to her throat. Finn held her gaze hoping she would see that he meant her no harm. The eyes that looked back were not beautiful, but they were expressive: pained, confused, and distrustful. Finn stopped a few feet from her. Cori came up behind him and stood on his left so that she could hear what transpired.

"Missus, I am Detective O'Brien and this is Detective Anderson. We are responding to a call for assistance. We understand that you have denied our officers access to this building. We cannot leave without looking into the matter. Do you understand that?"

The woman's head bobbled. Her lips parted, the muscles in her throat contracted, but there was no sound. Finn nodded slowly, hoping she would understand his sympathy and catch his calm.

"Fine, then. No need to speak. We are here to help you." He extended a hand, palm up. "Please stand away from the door. 'Tis for your own protection."

Finn waited, but the woman didn't move aside. Her hand twisted the fabric of her smock so tight that it appeared she might strangle herself.

"This is bull, O'Brien," Cori mumbled. "Those clowns wasted too much time already."

Finn nodded. He raised his voice so the woman could make no mistake as to what would happen next.

"We are going to come to you now. Detective Anderson will move you aside. Do you understand?"

The detectives moved in. The woman's eyes darted between them until the moment Cori took her hand. She held it long enough for Finn to note the wedding ring on her finger. When he nodded, Cori turned the woman to the wall.

"I'm going to make sure you haven't got any weapons."

Cori adjusted the woman's hands and feet, and then ran her own over the woman's head scarf, her smock, and down her legs. She shook her head at Finn. She turned the woman around and asked. "What's your name?"

The woman's eyes never stopped moving. It was as if she was struggling to understand them. Finn checked out the entrance to the unit. It appeared that this woman was alone. Having a firm hold on her arm, Cori had a line of sight past the corner of the building. There were no unexplained shadows or movement. She gave her partner a thumbs up and asked again:

"What's your name?"

"Emi," she said.

"Okay, Emi. Is this your place?"

She nodded.

"Are you under duress?" Cori said, but the woman looked at her blankly. Cori tried again. "Is anyone threatening you?"

"Please, please don't go inside. It is only a mistake. Please. Go away."

She pleaded with them. She begged them. She covered Cori's hand with one of her own, looking for understanding. Cori's eyes flicked to Finn, and they exchanged a look over the woman's head.

"Is your husband upstairs?" Finn asked.

Her head jerked as if she couldn't decide between a shake or a nod. When she hung it low, he knew it was a sign of defeat and agreement.

"Where exactly is he?" Cori asked.

"I don't know now," she said. "He was in the big room. The first room."

"And where is that?" Finn asked.

She pointed up the short flight of stairs.

"And above that? Up there?"

The woman's eyes went up. "Where we work."

"And the top?" He persisted.

"Where we work. We work, that is all."

"Is there anyone else with your husband?" Cori asked as she waved Officer Douglas over.

He in turn signaled Officer Hunter who came to take the woman. Finn pitied Officer Douglas's wife. She only had three years until he retired. Then he would be ordering her about for the rest of her life.

"Yes. Eight people I think," the woman said. "Maybe more."

"Who are they, missus?"

"Guests. I don't know them." She started to cry.

"Are they in the first room, too?" Finn asked.

"I don't know now. Please, please. Don't hurt my husband. He is sick now. He is sick only."

Emi grabbed Finn's arm as she begged, but the detective set her aside. Officer Hunter took ahold of her. She strained to get out of his grasp. She appealed to Cori, swearing over and over again that her husband was ill.

"We'll take care, ma'am. Does he have a gun? We need to know that," Cori said. Again the woman signaled the negative. "Do any of them?"

"Not my husband. No, no one. I don't think there are guns." As Officer Douglas pulled her to him, she focused on Cori. "Let me go in. Let me go. I will tell him you need to speak. He will come out here if I ask him... Please...I am his wife. A woman can do this."

Cori and Finn weren't listening. Hunter was taking the woman away and her voice was nothing but a cry in the wind. The detectives moved toward one another. Finn reached behind and took out his gun. Cori's hand disappeared under her jacket. Suddenly, they heard Emi's voice raised in a cry of absolute despair.

"Don't hurt him."

The detectives ignored her because there was no promise they could give. As Cori and Finn took the first step inside the building, the woman's voice rose again.

"Enver! Enver!" Finn and Cori looked back to see she was struggling and howling with every step she took away from the building. "You don't understand."

"I'm thinking it won't be a tea party we find in there," Finn said.

"You reckon?" Cori answered and gave him a nod.

They released the safety on their weapons.

CHAPTER 3

"O'Brien," Cori said.

"I hear it."

He took one more step up, and put his back to the wall. Cori took two steps and mirrored him against the opposite one. They were almost at the top of the short flight of metal stairs. It ran through a narrow entrance to the front door of the unit. The door was a work of art. Voluptuous, naked women cavorted on a pale blue background. Brass Art Deco sconces fashioned into graceful, scantily clad women hung on either side of the door. Their faces were raised toward the globes of crackle glass that they held above their heads. The light from the fixtures glowed deep yellow against the grey walls.

While the concrete was soundproof, the door was not. Through it the detectives heard muffled sounds of rage followed by muted responses of collective terror. Whatever was going on inside was not being played out up against the door, and that was a good break. Still, Cori kept her voice low when she asked:

"Locked?"

Finn shook his head. Given the woman's distress when they confronted her, it was unlikely she had stopped to lock the door. Letting go of his gun with one hand, he held up three fingers on his other, and pointed at the door. Cori nodded, but he paused and waited through a sudden stretch of quiet. It was only when they heard the angry sounds again, that Finn started his countdown.

One finger...

Two fingers...

Three...

In one motion he took hold of the knob and swung the door open. Bursting through first, he went right; Cori, on his heels, went left. Both raised their voices, identifying themselves as officer of the law, only to fall silent in the next instant. They had fallen down a magical rabbit hole into an alternate universe: exotic, erotic, eccentric.

They were in a giant box of a room that was half the size of a football field. The concrete floor had been shellacked to a high shine. The walls were left rough and met a ceiling that rose a good twelve feet off the ground.

Where Finn and Cori made their stand was empty space. At the far end of the huge room there seemed to be living quarters, and in the middle sweeping sofas upholstered in silvery grey silk created two halves of a big circle. Deep, high-backed chairs covered in white and black leather were scattered about. A glass coffee table as clear as arctic ice and as big as a skating pond was in the middle of it all. On top of the table, Cori's consciousness noted bowls of fruit, chocolate, and condoms. Wine glasses were tipped over and broken.

Finn only had eyes for the people scattered throughout the room. Men in tuxedos, women half naked, and everyone masked. It was a macabre collage of faces that looked like golden goats and silver bulls. The women's eyes appeared wicked behind swaths of lace. One naked lady wore a headdress of purple plumes and diamonds. Four men and six women cowered and cried, starting forward as they tried to escape only to scurry back when the raging man in their midst took note.

The giant of a man cried out in a language Finn had never heard before. He paced right and left, his hands flew to the side of his head, pulling at his long, grey hair. He swooped down and cleared the table with a swipe of his long arm, sending the crystal flying. But it was the next moment when the room spiraled into a hellish cacophony of screams and pleas, that Finn saw what was coming.

"Knife!" Finn called and pushed off from his crouch.

He crab-walked, keeping his back to the wall, arms extended, the crazed man in his sights. Cori did the same on her side of the room. But the angry man, the insane man, had no care for anything or anyone. Before either detective could get a clear shot, he grabbed a woman off the couch by her hair and threw her to the ground. In that split second, the people in the room went from fear to panic. The men stumbled over the furniture, saving themselves in the face of danger. The barely dressed ladies fled leaving the woman on the floor to her fate.

"Hands up! Drop it!"

Finn locked on to his target, but each time he thought he had a clean shot the man moved. Finn was aware of the other people in the room, but saw them only as blurs of flesh and feathers, golden masks and black jackets. He holstered his weapon, knowing he could not afford to make a mistake by firing and hitting someone who made an unexpected move. He had barely positioned himself for the attack, when the big man fell to his knees, raised the knife above his head, brought it down, and gutted the woman on the floor.

A naked woman screamed and covered her mouth with her hands. Two more flung themselves into one another's arms. Someone came out of a room in the back only to duck away again. Finn saw everything and nothing as he launched himself over the couch, and hit the big man with the full force of his body.

Finn felt a jolt in his shoulder as sharp as if he had hit a rock wall. While the man had an advantage in height, Finn had the element of surprise and the leverage of a rational man. They rolled, grappling on the floor. Finn's advantage almost evaporated as the man fought back, but it was the detective who had the training and the will to bring this to a proper end. Finally Finn got him down, put his knee between the man's shoulder blades, yanked the man's right arm behind his back, took the knife, and threw it aside. The man's head rose up as he tried to buck the detective off. Finn pushed the man's face hard onto the concrete floor even knowing that the man would look beaten after this was all over, and he might be called to account.

"Stay down. Down! Down," Finn cried.

"Back. Everybody back!" Cori ordered, stalking a half circle to herd the scattering people.

Satisfied their fear and the paralysis of shock would keep them in place. Cori holstered her weapon, and fell to her knees beside the victim. No one spoke; no one seemed to breathe. All eyes were on her. All ears were primed for a call for a doctor or a wail of pain, but there was only an eerie silence. Cori's shoulders slumped. Her head dropped, her long blonde hair fell over one shoulder shielding her face. With both hands, Cori rolled the woman over. Slowly her head waggled back and forth.

"Detective Anderson?" Finn said, and then louder: "Detective."

Cori started. She raised a hand to him, and it took Finn a moment to understand why she would do such a thing. Then he realized that Cori's hand was not bloody. Finn swung his eyes to the knife on the floor. The blade was clean. Cori shook back her hair and got to her feet. With a grunt, she dragged the woman up and plopped her on the couch. The body slumped sideways. Cori turned toward Finn and held up something that looked like a rib cage.

"It's plastic," she said and then patted the woman's head. "She's just a big doll."

CHAPTER 4

It didn't matter to Finn that the man on the floor had his hands cuffed behind him. It didn't matter that Finn might have pressed a bit too hard on the man's head as he subdued him. He had no care for this person. Mutilating a doll was not a crime. Threatening people in the room was one easily dealt with. What mattered was that the man was bloodied. Finn flipped him over like a side of beef, and ran his hands over the man's chest and down his legs looking for weapons or wounds. He found neither.

"Whose blood is this?" Finn barked. "Whose blood?"

The man shook his head. Finn yanked him into a sitting position, threw him against the wall, splayed his own legs, leaned over, and put his face close to the man's. The vein on the detective's neck bulged, the color in his cheeks was high, and his right hand was on the butt of his gun. He gave the man one more chance.

"You're not hurt. Who is it that's hurt?"

The man said nothing.Finn took him by the collar, intending to shake the information out of him when he heard Cori snap.

"You stay put."

Finn looked over his shoulder and saw a fancy dressed man move a step closer to her.

"Do you know who I am?" he said.

Whatever Cori answered, the man was both surprised and cowed by it. He fell back, into the safety of the group. Finn got up and strode across the room to the front door. He called to the officers outside, telling them to bring the woman inside. Finn had only just returned to the prisoner when he heard:

"Enver! Enver."

The woman in the smock rushed across the room, flinging herself at her husband. She landed on her knees and threw her arms around his neck. She seemed not to care that he was covered in blood. The face she turned up to Finn was angry and accusatory.

"You have hurt him." Her accent was the same as her husband's, but her English was better.

Finn ignored her. He only had eyes for the big man with the grey hair, the one whose rampage had kept the people in this room hostage, the man whose big head lolled from side-to-side, and whose glassy eyes saw nothing. He could be drugged, drunk, a fine actor, mad, or guilty as hell of a viscious crime, but that would be for others to determine. Finn had only one job. To find this man's victim.

"I won't be asking again. Whose blood?" Finn's patience was gone. "You're a dead man unless you speak now."

"Enver," the wife begged.

Finn swung her way.

"There is trouble on both of you. Best you tell me what you know."

Finn, more than anyone else in this room, understood the desperation of the moment. There was evidence of violence. There seemed to be a clear perpetrator. Once he had been on the wrong side of such a situation, but understanding it did not mean he had sympathy.

"Listen to me." Finn said. "Mistakes can be made right, or they can destroy you. Which will it be?"

The woman let go of her husband. She slumped against the wall. Once again her hands were entwined in the fabric of her smock. This time she hung her head, unable to look at Finn.

"Missus." Finn snapped at her. Her head jerked up. Her lips trembled.

"I... She..." The woman tried to speak but seemed to have lost the ability. Her body started to shake.

"She's dead because of what I've done." The man found his voice and it was hollow.

"Enver." His wife whimpered. His name could have been a warning to say no more, or encouragement to bring this to an end.

"Who? Who is dead?" Finn asked.

The man shook his head. "I don't know."

"Where is she?" he demanded.

Finn swooped down and took the man by the shoulders. The woman fell away from her husband, uttering a small cry.

"Where?"

Finn was prepared to do what he must, but there would be no fight. The woman put one hand over Finn's. It was the soft touch of surrender.

"Upstairs. She is upstairs."

CHAPTER 5

Officer Douglas was taking a statement from a lady who now wore a tuxedo jacket wrapped around her nakedness. Her legs were very long, her heels very high. Without her mask she seemed less a temptress than a tired, frightened young woman.

The jacketless man who had been chivalrous enough to cover her caught Finn's eye as the detective went by. The fancy man raised his chin. Finn would have laughed at the mano-a-mano gesture of solidarity had it not been so vile. He understood what that look meant.

We are men of the world. We both know that this is easily swept under the rug. He understood Finn was doing his job, but...

Finn gave him no more than a glance, thinking him a fool. Spreading tail feathers and chucking chins meant nothing to him. He was the most powerful man in the world at that moment.If this fellow needed to be taken down, Finn would be happy to oblige. But if it came to that, it would be done for cause and not ego. Nothing, though, was going to be done any time soon. Upon leaving the grand room where everything could be seen in one look, Finn and Cori found themselves in a Rubik's Cube of a building, a place that rightly gave Officer Douglas reason for concern.

This house would be a perfect place to stage an ambush with its jagged architecture and unlit passageways. As a working brewery the layout might have some rhyme or reason, but now the outcroppings of concrete, the ledges, the strange hardware embedded in the walls seemed to have no purpose. Most of all, the twists and turns of the corridors and the narrow stairways made Finn wary.

There was little room for one person going up the first flight of stairs much less two-way traffic. Lighting was minimal. Tight spaces were dark and open spaces shadowy. The steps were metal and constructed with a rise and angle that made climbing them difficult. The miserly depth kept Finn's booted feet from getting solid purchase, but at least they were tightly affixed to the wall. They could be climbed quietly if one were careful. Finn counted twenty-three steps to the first landing. That space was deep, but a wall on the left made it impossible to see everything.

Finn glanced at Cori. When she gave him a nod he stepped onto the landing, swung himself around the wall, and found himself in a space no bigger than a large closet. No one lay in wait. There was no blood. There was no body. He was looking at three walls and a door cut out of the one he was facing. Mincing his steps, he put one hand on the knob, aware that Cori was on watch, hugging the wall where it met the stairs.

"Okay?" she whispered.

Finn nodded once, licked his lips, and reached for the closet door. It didn't shame him that his heart skipped a beat when he found it locked. He had no love of surprise, especially in a space this small.

"'Tis clear."

He stepped away.They started up the next flight of stairs. Slivers of window reminiscent of the castles Finn had climbed as a boy in Ireland gave him a glimpse of the compound below. No one on the ground could have seen through the narrow glass.

Finn ducked his head, and Cori did the same. The ceilings lowered for a few feet before rising again over the next landing. There they soared over a square turret-like structure. Above them was a latticework of copper pipes. It was cold here, cold like a tomb.

This landing was twice the size of the one below, but there were no doors only two small spaces tunneled out at the bottom of one wall. They measured three-by-three by Finn's guess. He put his hand to one and felt air, confirming that it connected to the outside. A small man or a slight woman might squeeze through, but not without causing a commotion below. Near the ceiling, metal plates were screwed high into the wall. The screws were rusted, so there was no cause for concern. Finn started off with Cori a half a step behind. When they reached the end of the hall, the detectives pulled up short. Cori let out a low whistle.

"Sure it seems we've found God's workroom," Finn said.

"No God that I know," Cori whispered.

Finn went ahead while Cori looked for signs that there was a living person in the room. When Finn turned his head one way, Cori's eyes went the other. When he looked up, she looked down. When her partner paused to touch one of the things hanging from the ceiling, a chill ran through her. When he stopped to face one of the bodies propped upright, Cori wanted to look away. When Finn motioned her to follow, Cori complied with care.

Human body parts clogged the long, narrow room. Legs and arms hung from the ceiling like Spanish moss, others had been packed in crates on the floor. Full-size dolls were skewered from the small of their backs to their shoulder blades with metal rods that kept them upright. All the dolls were female, naked, and anatomically correct. They leaned forward in stances that were both expressive and unsettling. One held her arms out as if begging for help. Another's legs were bent as if to run. A third had one hand over her chest and the other over her private parts, hiding her nakedness.

There were blondes with pale skin, and Asians with exotic eyes; dark skinned lovelies with corn-row braids, redheads, and brunettes. Their eyes had a depth of expression so that the dolls seemed near tears or lost in the throes of passion. They looked across the room at the faces of their disembodied counterparts.

The unfinished heads were attached to the wall like game trophies. One's expression was hard and tough, another's wholesome and pleasant. Their lips were full, their eyes long lashed, and their cheekbones high. Finn half expected one of them to speak, but the thought was fleeting. There was no life here and no death either. What was in this room was worse than death. Those beautiful faces were attached to skulls that were laid bare, sculpted from metal and plastic. These were empty things. No brains in these heads, no hearts in the beautiful breasts of their assembled sisters.

"Holy Mother," Finn muttered. "They look so real."

"They feel real." Cori ran three fingers down a leg hanging near her head, and then rubbed them together as if trying to rid herself of the feel of the 'skin'.

"I don't know what game those two are playing, but I'm not liking any bit of it," Finn said.

"What kind of game could it be? That man was covered in blood," Cori said.

"Paint?" Finn made a ridiculous stab at an explanation. "Play acting? You saw those people downstairs."

"If it was performance art he would have said so, and sent us on our way,"Cori said.

"Except he said that *she* was dead," Finn reminded his partner.

"And *she* could have been the doll he sliced and diced."

"It does no good to speculate," Finn said. "Let's go back and sort it out before the sun rises."

"I'm going to have nightmares for weeks. This stuff really creeps m..."

Cori adjusted her holster as she complained only to find that she was talking to herself. When she looked for her partner she saw him disappear through the mass of body parts at the other end of the long room. The doll torsos were still swaying when she got there, so she pushed her way through, fighting off a pair of extraordinarily large boobs. Finn stood in a wide opening in the wall and she took her place beside him.

The room they were looking at was smaller than the one on the first floor, and larger than the workroom. Three towering, arched windows graced the outside wall. Dawn's pale pink and grey light illuminated what seemed to be an apartment.

There was a long gleaming dining room table with eight intricately carved chairs surrounding it. It was set for two with crystal and china. A chandelier hung above it. On the far wall was a free-standing tub, a toilet, and bidet. Outdoor lounges and tables were set in a semi-circle as if around a pool, but there was only the cement floor. There were drapes across the room near the windows, but no breeze to billow them. Finn flipped the switch on a light panel. The track lighting was illuminated, but not the chandelier.

"The table lamps aren't hooked up either," he said.

"There's no plumbing." Cori pointed to the tub and the bidet that were positioned away from the wall. "Maybe this was one of those plays that got out of hand. You know those murder mystery theater deals?"

"And all the world's a stage," Finn said .

Cori leaned into him, knocking his shoulder, and raising a hand to the curtains on the far wall. The light had changed, and now they could see the silhouettes of a high dresser, a chair, and a luxurious bed. They also saw a woman lying atop it. Her legs were together, her bare feet pointed upward, and her arms were at her side. The detectives looked at one another. Finn inclined his head, asking a question Cori couldn't answer. Real or a doll? There was only one way to find out.

"Police," Finn called as they made their way across the room.

Cori got there first and reached for the curtains only to stop cold. She lowered her eyes. Finn did the same. Blood stained the bottom of the white curtains where they touched the floor. Cori pulled aside the curtains. The woman on the bed didn't stir. She couldn't even if she wanted to. She was real, dead, and where her face had been there was only a bloody pulp.

"Call the ME," Finn said. "Get a forensics team out here. And tell officers Hunter and Douglas that everyone in the God forsaken place is to be taken in. No exceptions."

Cori had her phone out to start the process, but she

never dialed. A woman was headed their way and she was mad.

"Where are you, you bitch? Where are you?"

The sound of her heels on the stairs was deafening. The sound of her shrieking was grating. Finn and Cori stood shoulder to shoulder, at the ready, but neither was prepared for the tall woman who burst into the room. Her white blonde hair was short in the back, and fell long over one eye in the front. She wore a leather corset and stiletto heels. A studded leather collar circled her throat. When she saw Finn and Cori her surprise was as great as theirs. It took no more than a second for her eyes to deepen with disgust.

"Well, well. Look who's here," she said.

Finn didn't respond. That didn't surprise Cori. Seeing your ex-wife half naked in a room with a dead body was definitely a shockeroo.

CHAPTER 6

"Cover up, woman. People are seeing you half dressed."

Finn tried once more to put his jacket over Beverly's shoulders. Again, she threw it off.

"Have you looked around this zoo, Finn?" Bev laughed, and it was an ugly sound. "I'm the classiest thing they're ever going to see, so let them look."

"I don't understand this. Hard as nails. No shame. What has happened to you?"

Finn grabbed up his jacket from the ground, and shook it out all the while keeping his eyes on his ex. On a movie screen she would have been a goddess. But they were in an artist's compound in a rough part of Los Angeles. In the clear morning light his ex-wife looked like a stripper or worse.

"Nothing has happened to me." Bev grabbed the top of her corset and pulled up, re-adjusting her fine breasts. "We're divorced, Finn, so don't go pulling your righteous Irish act on me. I'm not your mother, and I never was. That was the trouble, you know. Who could compete with your saintly, long suffering mother?"

"Beverly," Finn said, and she understood the warning.

Finn's family was off limits. That was fine, because there really wasn't anything to complain about. The O'Brien clan was as close to saintly as they come—all nine of them —but especially the long-dead, forever-child Alexander. It had been a predator, a murderer, that picked Finn's brother up from school when Finn had forgotten to fetch the little boy. Finn would never stop doing penance for that sin, and God help the person who suggested the mystery of Alexander's death should be put to rest.

Bev crossed her arms and threw herself against the wall like a petulant child. Moments ago Finn had taken her by the wrist and pulled her behind a latticework of rotting wood. It was overgrown with a vine that thrived in spite of neglect. The shelter was minimal, but it was the best he could do. He wanted to keep their meeting private. When he took Bev from the building she had stumbled after him, those ridiculous heels of hers clacking on the metal stairs and concrete floors. She took two steps to every one of his. Now through the wooden lattice, he could see the team going about their business. The EMTs were gone; the Medical Examiner's people and a forensic team were there. Two more black and whites had come to help Officer Hunter and Officer Douglas. Cori would be seeing to the artist and his wife. He attended to his ex.

"Sure, Beverly, I'm not judging because I've got no idea what it is I've been looking at in that place."

Finn ran his hand over his head as he turned away from her only to turn back again. This time he had both hands out, and he used them to rake the air.

"And this. What is this you're wearing among strangers?"

"These people aren't strangers," she snapped.

"You're telling me those are your friends?" Finn asked,

his Irish spiking as it did when emotions ran high. "I'm thinking you can do better, Beverly, my girl."

"Yeah, like all those cops you thought were your friends?" she said. "Those good guys who turned their backs on you when you needed them most. God, is it any wonder I left you?"

'Tis a wonder now that you mention it." Finn tried to lighten the mood, but Bev shot him a withering look.

"Oh, please. How could I stay when your trials would never end, Finn?" Bev threw up her hands. "Alexander was one thing. We were kids when he got killed. I knew I could help you through that, but the thing with the cop? I wasn't going to live my whole life under that cloud. You could have come with me, quit the force, and had a better life. I needed you to say screw 'em all."

Beverly shook her head. She put her palms flat against the wall. Her stance made her look as if she were resigned to a firing squad and the truth would make no difference to the bullet.

"You're such a boy scout. I admire that, but not on my time. We got married too young, and I never had a chance to see what else was out there."

"I knew what was out there, and it wasn't pretty," Finn said. "I would have kept you safe."

"I am safe." Beverly pushed away, chastened a bit when she saw that she could still hurt him."Nobody can live with a saint. People don't even like saints."

"I've never said that I was one," Finn said.

"You didn't have to." Bev tossed her head. "Saints love being tortured, and if you live with one you can't be more tortured than they are. I needed to have some fun and—"

"And that's fun?" Finn pointed to the building. "Men dressed up like animals in fancy dress, women on their knees before them without their clothes on?"

"I don't have to explain myself, Finn," she said. "And you don't need to save me from anything. So thank you very much, I'm out of here."

She did a ridiculous two-step in shoes that weren't meant for walking much less dancing. Finn took her arm and pulled her back until they were chest-to-chest, eye-to-eye. He felt none of the love he once had, but he still felt for her. What he felt was pity.

This woman was beautiful, but not pretty like his Beverly. This woman spoke her mind, but she didn't seem to have a rational thought in it. This one was desirable, but not to him. In that moment Finn realized it was finally done between them. He let her go. Feeling he still owed her something, he would try to save her from herself.

"Sit. It hurts me to look at you in those shoes." Bev raised her chin, but he'd have none of it. "There is a murdered woman inside, and you rampaged through that place looking for her. Everyone took note, and if there is suspicion on you it's well deserved. Now sit."

Bev sat down on a small wooden bench that was in no better shape than the lattice. Finn got down on one knee and rested his forearms on the upraised one.

"I'm not leaving Cori up there to do all the work herself, so you'll be telling me now what I want to know. No fits, Beverly. No hysterics."

"I don't have to —"

"You do because I am a cop, and I will take you to jail," Finn said. "Now what was going on in there?"

"It was an Asylum party." Bev rolled her eyes when the look on Finn's face said that explanation wasn't enough. "Asylum is a club for adventurous adults. It's very exclusive. The men pay more than you make a year just to join."

"And the women?"

"Women have to apply to be part of the scene, but we don't pay. Asylum looks for beautiful women. Intelligent women. And they chose me, Finn. I'm not twenty-five, and they still chose me."

"I can see how much they value your intelligence," Finn said, and Bev had the decency to be embarrassed. "Go on."

"The rules are the same for each party, but the venue changes," Bev said. "You never know where or when one will be until the last minute. If you miss two parties, you're out. That's only for the women. Because the men pay for a membership they can't get kicked out unless they mur—." Bev stopped talking. Finn cocked his head and raised a brow. Her pique returned. "You know what I mean. Believe me, none of those guys in there killed anyone."

Both of them knew that little slip of hers would stay in Finn's head until he was satisfied that was all it had been.

"So what are these rules?"

"Men have to wear tuxedos. Everyone has to wear a mask. The women can come as they please, but they have to look sexy. That's what Asylum is all about. Sexual fantasies, power fantasies."

"Sure, it sounds like a whorehouse," Finn said.

"It isn't. There is no touching or sex without consent. The men may have the money, but the women are in control. One word from any of us, and even the gold members can be disciplined for harassment." Bev's lips tipped. "It's nice to be in control for once."

"And the doll that man ripped to shreds? That was fantasy? A real woman dead upstairs was someone's fantasy?"

"I didn't know anything about that doll thing," Bev said. "We've never had a party here before. I've never been to one this exclusive. Usually there are fifty people in some house in Hollywood or Beverly Hills. All I know is that the man who owns the place —the guy who went bonkers — he makes companions."

"Sex dolls?" Finn said.

"Yes, if you want to be crude," she said. "But that's no different than any other sex toy."

"They look like women. They feel like women. You don't find that odd, Beverly?"

"That guy is an incredible artist. I've never seen anything like it. He's a master." Her defense was so genuine it almost amused Finn. But it wasn't a destroyed doll or Beverly's opinion of it that he cared about.

"He might have killed a young woman," Finn said.

"Oh listen to you, Mr. Rule of Law," Bev drawled. "You always told me not to trust the first information. What happened to innocent 'till proven guilty? Well, nobody in this place is innocent, but that doesn't mean anyone is guilty of murder. That includes the guy who makes the companions, and I don't even know him."

She paused. For an instant Finn thought he saw the woman he married. Then he realized he was seeing the woman she had become in their marriage, one who felt sad and trapped by circumstance. It would seem the big world had not made her less so. But the expression was gone as fast as it crossed her face. Beverly was a proud woman, and would never admit she made a mistake even if she had.

"Did you keep track of everyone through the night?" Finn asked.

"No," she said. "Look, I just want to go home, so here's what I know. This party was a special invitation thing. I mean it was still fantasy night, but we were waiting for something."

Finn pushed himself off the ground. The cracked asphalt was none too comfortable. He put his hands together to wipe away the small rocks embedded in his finger tips.

"What was it you were waiting for?" he asked.

"Nobody knew. The men who were invited are very important, and I heard one of them say tonight would change the world. That's what he said. Change the world."

"And the dead woman? Who was she?"

"She was a bitch," Bev said.

"I'll be needing something more specific, like her name."

"Cami."

Finn raised a brow; Bev raised her bare shoulders.

"That's all I know. We use aliases at Asylum parties. I don't know anyone's real name. No matter what you threaten me with, I can't tell you anymore than that."

"And why were you so angry with this woman if you don't know her?"

"I told you, she was a bitch." Bev's arms crossed again.

"Last I heard that's no reason to kill someone."

"Oh, please, Finn."

Bev leaned forward. She put her elbows on her knees and cradled her chin in her upturned hands as she collected her thoughts. When she looked at him again she seemed exhausted. This came as no surprise to Finn. She had been up all night, and even fantasies show their wear with the passage of time.

"You think I could kill that little horror, leave, come back, and pretend I didn't? Sorry, I'm not that cool."

"I'm not thinking you killed her. There would be blood on you, and I can see that's not the case. I'm still wanting to know why the fury? There was no mistaking that."

Bev sat back, feigning boredom when in fact the truth was she didn't want to look into her ex's eye when she answered.

"She was going to out one of the Asylum men. It's someone I care about, and he couldn't afford for people to know about his involvement in this club."

"His name?" Finn asked.

"I just told you—"

"Aliases. So you said," Finn answered. "What's his then?"

Bev opened her mouth. The man's name hovered on her lips, and Finn could see the pink of her tongue as she put it against her small, white teeth. Then her body shook as she tried to subdue a laugh. Her lashes lowered. Her voice twinkled when she said:

"Pinocchio."

Bev laughed in earnest and Finn joined her. Their moment didn't last long.

"Stop it," Bev said. "It's not what you think? It has nothing to do with his physical appearance."

"Is it only his nose that grows with a lie then?" Finn teased.

"It's about what he does. The man is an icon in a sensitive industry."

"And is he here?" Finn asked.

"He wasn't invited," Bev said. "And I didn't know Cami would be here either, or I wouldn't have come. Rumor had it that Asylum was going to kick her out. She was messing around threatening people's outside lives. It was like a game with her. I thought she was all talk, but this man —Pinocchio—he took her seriously."

"'Tis difficult to take down a regular person much less someone with money," Finn said. "What was she peddling?"

"I don't know." Her eyes widened when Finn seemed skeptical. "I honestly don't know, Finn. She was a bitch to me. She called me grandma, and she was going to ruin someone who didn't deserve it. Thank God somebody else got to her and saved me the trouble."

"I'd be advising you to keep that thought to yourself." Finn took a deep breath. He muttered her name once. "And all this for a man whose name you don't even know."

"At least I know who's worth fighting for. Not like you, putting everything on the line for some homeless guy."

"If I could arrest you for that, I would," Finn said. Bev laughed and the sound was cruel.

"I'm amazed your bleeding heart hasn't killed you." She slapped her knees. "Are we done?"

Finn looked down at her for a moment, and then stepped back to give her room.

"We are finished, Beverly," Finn said, and meant it. Never again would he long for this woman or what they once had. She got up. She raised her chin.

"FYI, Finn. I didn't say I didn't know his name, but he isn't here. Plus I would be breaking the rules if I told you."

Before Finn could pressure his ex for the information he wanted, Cori found them. She took a look at them both, and raised an eyebrow at Finn.

"Beverly and I are done." Finn lifted a shoulder as if to say all was as well as could be expected. He turned to his ex-wife. "Get your things. You'll be taken to the station so you can make a formal statement. "

Beverly smoothed her corset and tossed the long sweep of hair out of her eyes. She smiled at Cori.

"Nice to see you two are still partners."

"He's worth sticking with," Cori said.

"You always were a bitch," Bev said, and walked away.

Cori called out before the woman went into the building. She was smiling when she walked up to Finn's ex and lowered her voice.

"You know. Just between us girls, you may need to tighten up that corset."

Bev's pretty brow furrowed. She put her hands over her stomach as she turned and tilted her head to check out her behind.

"It's fine," Bev snapped.

"I don't think so, honey," Cori said. "You can still talk."

CHAPTER 7

His name was Enver and hers was Emi. Their surname was Cuca. Five years earlier they won a lottery in their home country of Albania. The prize was America. Enver and Emi believed with a fervor that was close to religious that anything was possible in the United States. They were not religious people, just hopeful, hardworking, and determined to succeed. Enver was an artist and Emi was an engineer. They shared a passion for their respective work, and an admiration for each other's.

Soon after they arrived in Los Angeles — Enver speaking little English —they found The Brewery and leased a small space in the corner building near the park. Enver painted pictures, but sold few; Emi looked for work as an engineer but found none. To pass the time, to entertain herself, Emi built things. One day she found metal pieces in a pile of discarded things outside their neighbor's door and fashioned a woman's head and shoulders. Enver thought the bust was beautiful and believed her sculptures would sell well. She made another and this time — after one too many *raki* — Emi and Enver went scrounging to see what else they could find to make her work more interesting.

They came home with a piece of silicone that had been discarded by the person who created prosthetics for the movies. This material was as soft as a baby's bottom, and when Emi made a second bust, they covered it with 'skin'.

This time they didn't just think Emi's sculpture was exceptional, they knew it. During one of the open loft events, a man came to Enver and Emi Cuca's place. He could not stop touching the 'skin' on the second bust. Eventually he wandered around looking at the paintings in the studio. He asked if Enver could paint the bust to look like a real woman and offered more money than the Cucas had ever seen. America was a wonderful place, indeed.

Enver painted the bust and the man asked them to make him a statue of a woman - crafted just so. Emi built the statue's structure, working with soft materials because the man wanted his statue to bend. Enver painted her, and she was beautiful. The man paid for the silicone woman. When he came back again, the man asked for something very different. He wanted a statue with soft skin. He wanted Enver to paint her so that she seemed real, and he wanted to be able to make love to her. A doll. This man was not embarrassed to tell Enver and Emi of his desire.

The artist and his wife were shocked.

They were angry.

At first Enver refused.

The man offered a sum for this doll.

Enver wavered.

The man offered more money.

Eventually Emi convinced her husband that there was no harm. She was sure she could build the woman, but it would take some doing. The 'skin' and the 'skeleton' would have to give and retract, be soft, warm, and receptive, but she could do it.

Emi urged her husband to do what the man asked. So Enver did and the doll they made was more beautiful than either of them could ever have imagined. Though he didn't tell Emi, Enver touched the doll once. He was curious about what his wife had devised to make the doll feel like a real woman. For many nights after that he lay awake berating himself for doing such a thing; for many nights he dreamed of doing it again. This both shamed and excited the artist, but soon all was well. The man took the doll away.

He was so pleased that he sent many more people to see Enver and Emi. Soon they only created dolls. They moved from the small, windowless space to another and another until they came to live in the grandest house at The Brewery. When one of their neighbors came to see the new studio, she was amazed at the dolls lined up in the workroom. She called them companions, and there came a moment when Enver and Emi also thought of them in that way. The husband and wife, though, had very different feelings about the companions. Emi thought of them as her children, Enver did not. They didn't share their thoughts with anyone, not even each other. Instead, they made each companion better than the last, creating them with great care.

Now here they were. Wealthy. Living in a concrete castle. They created their companions one at a time to each client's needs and desires. Always they kept a few completed companions for those who weren't sure what they wanted or didn't care what they got. But always Enver painted them with such love that they far exceeded expectations. When each was complete, Emi dressed the companion in a simple shift of fine linen. Enver put the companion in a large box with a pillow under her head.

Together they shipped each one to a new home.

Enver's companions had gone to every corner of the world, and still the orders came. It didn't surprise Emi that men wanted these beautiful dolls for sex. Men were strange creatures, never satisfied with what they had, always searching for perfection. Since real women weren't perfect —nor would real women desire these men who were imperfect each in their own way—the companions made sense. Emi was practical about that. Enver secretly tried not to think of what happened to his beautiful dolls after they left his studio.

It wasn't the desire that surprised Enver and Emi, it was the money that was spent on such things that made them shake their heads. They could have asked for the moon, and the men would find a way to pluck it from the sky. And why not? In the dark of night, when a man reached for his companion and his hands met warm skin and he kissed full lips that were soft and giving, the companion would be real to him and that would be all that mattered.

But now America was not a wonderful place, and there was no escaping reality. They were under suspicion of a terrible crime. The police believed Enver had killed that woman upstairs. Enver could get angry, yes, but he would not kill a woman. Especially not that one.

Still, Emi knew from her country that once the police decided a person was guilty they made it their business to find evidence to prove it. Sometimes that was easier than finding out the truth. In this instance they would find neither proof nor truth, but they would be back and Emi resolved to be ready.

Enver, though, had no resolve for anything. Exhausted by the interrogation, he had not spoken since they had returned home. He looked like a common criminal in the orange pants and shirt they gave him. The police had taken Enver's clothes and his shoes. It seemed that they had taken his voice, too. Now they stood staring at the front door. They had been doing it for a long while, but no one knocked. Finally, Emi said:

"I'll make coffee."

She turned and walked the length of the big room, ignoring the mess. She opened the cabinets and took out the cups, but Enver barely heard a clatter. Left alone, he shuffled into the part of the room where the beautiful sofas and chairs were now all mixed up, moved as the party guests cowered while he raged, moved again when the police separated them to ask their questions. The beautiful glass table was cracked. Glasses from which their guests drank were littered about, some were broken on the floor. One had spilled wine on the silk upholstery and it looked like a blood stain. A feather from a woman's headdress was stuck on the painting hung on the great wall. Sequins from the dresses the other women wore had fallen willy-nilly on the floor. They sparkled like silver and gold bird seed. But all the pretty birds were gone.

Enver picked one up. Holding it on the tip of his finger, he looked at it closely. He thought of the people who had come into his home, played with his dolls, done ridiculous things to one another, dressed in their costumes, and hid their faces. He was disgusted from the moment he laid eyes on them. One man put a collar and leash on a woman and made her get on her hands and knees like a dog. That was wrong. Another man hit a woman's bottom with a leather strap. That's when Enver knew the truth. If real women were nothing more than things to these people, how would they treat the companions in their care?

And then, out of nowhere, the man who started it all

appeared. That man who was like a thing.

And then...

"Sit down."

Emi raised her voice because the room was so big. Enver didn't move. It was getting very hard for Emi to speak as if nothing was wrong. It was difficult to be the one who was calm, when all was chaos. Emi came toward him. She slammed the mugs down on the cracked table and fairly ran across the room to her husband. Emi slapped his hand, and the little glittery thing flew away. He started and blinked, but said nothing.

She took his arm and pressed her fingers into his skin. That skin was crepe-like and his muscles were long, not bulky as they had once been. He was an old man and she didn't know when that had happened. It struck her that she might be an old woman, and that was why he so loved the companions.

Then Emi thought again. He wasn't old. Inside there was still fire and desire, and that was the problem. He was soft because he was an artist, that was all. He thought only of beauty. She was the one who was forged like steel because she worked with metal. It was opposite of what it should have been for a man and a woman, but she loved him and always would.

"Husband," Emi whispered.

Enver looked through her. He walked away, out of the room, disappearing up the stairs like a ghost. Emi started after him, but changed her mind. Her anger was too hot, so she returned to the kitchen and started to wash the kettle. But even that— the mundane thing, the rote thing — could not calm her. She grasped the granite and hung her head.

Hot tears welled behind her eyes. Her skin was on fire, her heart was beating against her chest. She was so afraid, and Enver did not care. She took the glass kettle and smashed it against the wall. It broke into big, thick pieces and tiny shattered ones. Her husband did not come to see what had happened, her husband did not come to see if she was hurt. He had not asked her if she was afraid, or if she knew what happened. He did not ask her if she believed that he didn't hurt that woman. Enver did not turn to her for comfort and that made her the most angry.

Emi stalked across the room once more, flung herself onto the stairs, and stormed up them. Her hard shoes clumped on the metal. She was not a fat village woman, but she was not like the dolls: long-legged, large breasted, delicate of face. She was a woman who had worked hard to make a success of their lives, and Enver had ruined it all whether he admitted it or not.

"Enver! Enver!"

She called out as she pounded up the second flight of stairs where the walls narrowed and the ceiling was low. Her voice echoed back at her, and she knew she sounded crazy like Enver had all those hours ago.

Emi paused briefly in the doorway of the workroom and then plowed through it. She batted at the legs and the arms hanging from the ceiling. She tore feet out of a box and threw them as far as she could. She shoved a companion, the one Mr. Smith had ordered - weren't they all Mr. Smith - red haired, broad hipped thing with especially prominent nipples on her low slung breasts. Enver named the doll as he always did, but Mr. Smith would give it another. Mr. Smith would pretend the companion loved him. Or he would believe it. Or...

With a great cry, Emi took a broom and swiped at the faces lining the wall above the worktable. Some of them bounced off the table, and clattered as they fell to the floor. Others went askew so that their parted lips and sultry eyes now stared, not at their own body parts across the room, but up at the grey ceiling. With a great cry, Emi raised a heavy boot and brought it down on the face at her feet. It had been the pretty little face, like that of a farm girl. Emi crushed it.

Still Enver did not come.

"Enver." She cried for her husband and her voice caught.

Taking a deep breath, Emi trembled with disgust, and then she was calm and strangely at peace. There was nothing to be done, and so this horrible energy was wasted. It was for others to do things, and for them to wait. The police would run themselves ragged, but they would find nothing. They would never find the man who arranged for the party and paid them for their services. He was only a contract. He was a money transfer. Let them play cat and mouse, the police and this man. Let them try to solve a mystery that really could not be solved.

Convincing herself that all would be well Emi went through the workroom, casting her eye on the things she had destroyed. Emi would have her work cut out for her when she put them back together. She found Enver standing where the bed had been. The frame was still there and the box springs, but the curtains and bedding were gone. The headboard had been dismantled and some of the carpet on the platform had been cut away. Emi wished the police had taken everything. This place meant nothing to her; it never had. This felt like standing by the grave of a stranger. Finally, Emi breathed deep. Her nostrils flared, her lips compressed.

"What did you tell the police?" she asked.

"I told them I held her, and that's how I had blood on me," he said. "I told them the truth, that I didn't know her.

I told them I cut the doll to show those people she was not real. I destroyed my art because it is bad. I know that now."

He turned his head away.

"You didn't tell about him, did you?" Emi asked. "They could send us back if you did that."

Enver shook his head. "I can't tell what I don't know."

Emi stopped asking questions. Her husband was right. They knew nothing about the Asian man and his business. As for the woman, they had been truthful. They had no idea she was in the house. In retrospect it made sense that the man asked her to come, but it had been a mistake. It had been a mistake from the first.

"Shall I help you get out of those clothes?"

Emi didn't look at him. She hated to see him in the clothes of a criminal. His own, she knew, would be tested to find evidence that Enver was a murderer. In their country a small person had no chance against the police. In America it was different. The police must be positive. Judges did not take bribes. Lawyers told stories and the best story won. She, Emi, would find a good storyteller, but now she would make things better the only way she could.

"Enver. Come."

The artist lifted his eyes and blinked. He shook his big head; he had used up his words talking to the police. Emi was questioned, too, but for the most part she sat alone in a room. The blonde detective accepted that Emi did not know the people at the party. She believed Emi when she said she did not know the name of the dead woman. She was the wife, after all. Only the wife.

"Enver, I need all the truth. I don't care if the truth and what you told them are not the same thing. Please. Please. I need to know."

She moved her hand so her fingers touched his. For

a long while he didn't move and then his own fingers twitched. A moment later he held his wife's hand, but it was clear there was no intent to comfort her. When he took a deep breath, his torso tilted one way and his head went the other.

"Why would I hurt that woman?" he said.

"I know you did not hurt her," Emi said. "But..."

His eyes moved to his wife, his head barely moved.

"I called her Cami like he did. I watched her like he did, that's all. I didn't speak with her, but he did. You know that."

"Yes, I believe you." Emi moved her hand so that their fingers laced. "But the other thing..."

"No. I did not tell them. There was no need," Enver said.

For the first time in a long while, Enver looked at his wife. He smiled like a child wanting reassurance that the needle would not hurt.

"I didn't hurt her," he said. "I didn't."

"I know. Shhh. All right," Emi cooed. "And the man? Where did he..."

"He was gone like always. How would I know?" There was the spark of his rage again, but it was short lived. "If he comes back, I will kill him. Him I would kill."

Enver let go of her hand and walked away. Emi knew where he was going. Her anger flared and then fell away. How could she deny him? It was all he had left now, and soon even that would be gone if she had her way.

Emi took a last look at the tape across the room, she let her eyes linger where the bed had been. That woman dying wasn't the worst thing that had gone on in here. She would have it cleaned out; she would have all of it taken away.

Emi left the room without giving the door on the second landing a look. She knew it was closed. She knew it was locked again. She went down to the kitchen. There she cleaned up the broken glass on the floor, and poured herself a drink. When she had many drinks, she went to the shower. She took the scarf from her head and the smock from her body. For a long while, she stood looking at herself in the mirror. Finally, she got into the shower. She washed her hair twice. She scrubbed her body. And Emi Cuca cried.

CHAPTER 8

"You be gettin' me up too early in de mornin', O'Brien."

Geoffrey Baptist's admonition was accompanied by the clatter of plates as he served Cori and Finn. Bacon and eggs for Finn, salted cod and steamed cabbage for Geoffrey, coffee and a smile for Cori. Napkins were put on laps. Silverware was picked up. Cori reached for the sweetener, and Geoffrey sat his skinny self on a chair in between the two detectives.

"You're always here early on Wednesday, Geoffrey. That's when the beer is put in, so I don't think we've kept you from your beauty sleep," Finn said. "But we appreciate you making us breakfast. We've been up since two, and we were needing something to fill our stomachs."

"So it be bad business or good keepin' you awake all dis night?" Geoffrey's impressive dreads swung across his shoulders and swayed down his back as he looked between them.

"It wasn't good business, that's for darn sure." Cori raised her cup and blew on the hot coffee.

"Good business be a woman in da bed, a drink in de

hand. Now dat be good business no matter if you be in Trinidad, no matter in L.A., no matter where."

Geoffrey threw back his head and laughed large, the sound of it filling Mick's Irish Pub. It would have spilled out onto the street had the door not been closed to everyone but Finn and Cori. Originally from Trinidad, Geoffrey had bought the pub a few years back, brightening up the place without changing a thing but the proprietorship. The heavy, rough-hewn beams were original. The neon O'Doul's sign in the window still fritzed when the weather turned wet. The Guinness neon never did. An impressive collection of liquor and beers stocked the bar. Corned beef and cabbage was still served on St. Patrick's Day. The dartboard still hung where it had been placed onopening day in the fifties. It was Geoffrey who was new and bright as a freshly minted penny.

Because Geoffrey had too many wives in Trinidad — and an equal number of unruly children —he took himself off to Los Angeles to start anew. The move was as much to get away from the havoc he created among the women he loved as to find a way to provide for them all. Geoffrey, after all, was an honorable man.

His skin was dark, his smile bright, and his dreads long. He had so many knit beanies that Finn never saw the same one twice. Today's was orange and green with a bit of blue thrown in for good measure. Geoffrey Baptiste, friend to Finn, had the best people radar in the city. The minute Finn and Cori walked in he saw things were off. A quick heads up from Cori on her way to the ladies room, and he was up to date on what went down at The Brewery. Now he had his two cents, and he was going to put it on the table whether Finn wanted to hear it or not.

"O'Brien. O'Brien. I know'd you bein' sad about your

lady, but you listen here to Geoffrey now. I got me many ladies. They all be wantin' sometin'. Sometime Geoffrey give dem what dey want; sometime Geoffrey try hard, but don' give what dey want. Here's de trick, O'Brien. O'Brien," Geoffrey said. "You be listenin', O'Brien?"

Geoffrey's long finger tapped the table and Finn gave him a quick look. He didn't crack a smile knowing it would ruin Geoffrey's fun to do so. The man loved nothing more than an audience hanging on his every word. Finn went back to his eggs; Geoffrey to his counsel.

"So, what it be my beauties need?" Geoffrey threw out one finger after another as he made his list. "Money. De love. De space. Oh, yeah, I give 'dem space so dey can be happy, too. And sometimes de ladies want sometin' Geoffrey know he cannot give, so he don' be tryin'. See what I'm sayin', O'Brien? Do ya see, mon? You only do what you can do, O'Brien. We all be happy wit dat."

Finn's lips twitched. He raised a brow. Cori's giggle was drowned out as she drank her coffee.

"And did Cori leave anything out when she told you about the ex-missus, Geoffrey?"

"I don' be tinking so, O'Brien."Geoffrey's brows pulled together and Finn almost lost it. The man was so sweet of soul that he never knew when his leg was being pulled.

Cori's elbows were on the table, and she held her cup in both hands. Her blue eyes twinkled as she pursed her lips and blew a waft of steam into the space between the men. Finn thought her lipstick was fetching. It was a tangerine color that would leave a kiss for Geoffrey to wash off her cup after they were long gone.

"Come on, O'Brien. If your friends can't try to cheer you up, whose going to do it?" Cori put her cup back on the saucer and Finn smiled.

"I'm not in bits you two," Finn said. "I've been in this country since I was seventeen. Now and again my language is a throwback, but I gave up wandering the moors and drinking myself into a stupor over a lost love long ago."

"Liar." Cori snagged a piece of bacon from Finn's plate.

"He be lookin' sad to me." A piece of salted fish was the period at the end of that statement. Cori shivered as she watched him go in for another forkful.

"I'm not sad. I'm not angry. 'Tis confused I am, as my mother would say."

"And you'll cop to the fact that your jaw dropped when you saw Bev's party clothes," Cori said. "And this Asylum thing? A sex party? That would have knocked my knickers off."

"Perhaps I was lacking in the bedroom and drove the poor woman to Asylum," Finn said.

Geoffrey howled and slapped Finn on the back.

"You be doin' fine in der, O'Brien. I know'd. You be like Geoffrey. We quiet, but we be good men in de bed."

Cori and Finn accepted his pronouncements about the bedroom, but not that the two men were alike or that Geoffrey was quiet. Geoffrey waved his fork at his friends. A piece of fish flaked off, and he swiped it up without missing a beat.

"It be dress up, dat's all. Puttin' de masks on de faces? Crawlin' on the floor wit no clothes on? It weren't Carnivale. It weren't bein' all sexy, dat I know. Seems your old woman be mad 'bout sometin', O'Brien. Dat's not what you be doin' when de lovin' be good."

"Agreed." Cori polished off the hijacked bacon.

"Agreed here, too. And both of you can forget one minute's worry about my feelings," Finn said. "The matchmaker in my Irish village once told me that people who are quick to walk away are the ones that never intended to stay. She was right, and my heart is mended. I count myself lucky. Sure, I couldn't afford that woman now."

Cori leaned back in her chair. She put her hands together, applauding and smiling. She was convinced that her partner, her friend, wasn't protesting too much. Finn took a slight bow. Geoffrey beamed and then became serious.

"So what do you 'tink was goin' on in dat place wit de sex and de dead lady?"

"Same old, same old in L.A. It was all about power. Those who have it, and those who want it." Cori sighed and raised a brow.

"I'm thinking you're off base, Cori." Finn pushed his plate away and sat back. "The men in that room weren't as interested in the ladies as they were in whatever business brought them there. I'm betting it was about the power of money. The women were window dressing."

"And do you think Bev is protecting one of those people because she wanted in on the payday?" Cori said. "Or maybe she was just protecting her territory. Nobody but the criminally insane kill without a reason."

"True," Finn said. "Those people were put out and angry when we detained them."

"But they were more than that," Cori argued. "They were aggressively arrogant. Someone knew who that woman was—maybe they all did—but Bev was the only one other than the man with the knife who was angry."

"Bev may have gone astray," Finn said. "But she murdered no one. I swear that on my life."

"I didn't say she did," Cori said. "I'm saying that she's taking a calculated risk keeping that pretty mouth of hers shut."

"I would have known if she was lying to me." Finn

defended her again.

"And can you tell if she's lying by omission?"

Cori knew she had Finn on a spot. His ex moved out and served him with papers as soon as he was released from the hospital. He never saw it coming. That woman had lived her lie until the very last minute.

"Dis girl who be dead? Did she go to dis party wit'out her bag?" Geoffrey pushed his plate back, turning his long narrow face from one detective to the other.

"We didn't find a purse," Finn said.

"And they use made up names partly to promote the fantasy and partly to protect themselves," Cori said. "But this group was an Asylum subset, hand picked. They are so rich, so much masters of their own fate, that I doubt belonging to this club would have major consequences if the public knew of their extracurricular activities."

"No man likes to be put upon, but a rich man most of all." Finn tossed his napkin on the table and pushed his chair back."If what Bev said was true, there was at least one man who was worried."

"Den it be dat man who killed her." Geoffrey said.

"He wasn't there," Cori reminded him.

"Could be nobody see him, " Geoffrey persisted.

"Maybe there are other ways in and out," Cori said. "We could have missed something."

"I don't see how that could be, but we'll look again," Finn said, but his mind was still on the motive. "Perhaps it's shame we're looking at. Money doesn't mean someone can't be ashamed of what they are doing."

Cori laughed, "God I love you, Finn. You are such a—"

"Fine heart," Geoffrey said.

"Thank you, Geoffrey," Finn said. "And 'tis a possibility. Perhaps there was a Catholic among them. Aren't we the masters of shame and guilt?"

"That dog ain't gonna hunt, O'Brien." Cori crossed her arms on the table. "It's all about having fun and controlling their destinies. Two of those guys are major players. They lunch with presidents, and I can think of one or two presidents who might have a mask and tuxedo in their closet."

Cori's finger tapped the table, outlined a circle, and kept tapping the middle of it as she spoke.

"Brand is everything, and those people know it. The last thing they want are the *Me Too* broads digging their teeth into the jugular, or evangelicals up their asses, or BLM on their doorstep. That kind of crap would bleed out their money so fast. For all the Asylum nonsense, they are practical people. There is a lot to protect, and brand is to be protected at all costs."

"And dis dead girl? If she be as mean as de ex-wife say, O'Brien, maybe she be mean to more den one of dees guys."

"Hearsay, speculation, wishful thinking," Finn concluded. "Until we know who she was and how she was going to make trouble, we don't have a path to walk down. There is a huge difference between tattling to a wife and bringing someone of great power to his knees."

"And that's my cue. I'm headed off to the morgue."

Cori dabbed at her lips with her napkin and then tossed it atop Finn's. He smiled, liking it better when her lips weren't the color of the sunset. "

"Thanks for seeing to it, Cori" Finn said.

"Not a problem. I have to be there anyway to wrap up the report on that last file we had for Fowler," she said.

"He'll be appreciating that." Finn pushed back his chair. "I'm back to The Brewery. Not that I don't trust Officers Hunter and Douglas's canvass. It's just that they didn't seem all that invested in their work."

"And I be waitin' on da delivery, then I be goin' back to da bed. Good luck findin' out who did dat mean girl."

Geoffrey gathered up an armload of dishes. He called out once more as the detectives were going through the door.

"You be forgettin' the old missus, O'Brien. She good as dead to you, O'Brien. Dat be de ting makin' you happy."

Finn gave him a wave. His heart was fine, but it would take a lot to convince Geoffrey that he had been comfortable with his divorce for a good long while. Still, Bev was on his mind: her anger, her transformation, her hatred of the victim. Everyone in that place was suspect, and Bev could be no exception.

Finn wished Cori luck and turned left, going for his car that was a block down. Cori's was in front of Mick's. She got in, and watched her partner in her rearview mirror. Satisfied Finn was walking tall and happy, Cori put on her seat belt. She adjusted her mirror, gave her lips another shellacking, and put on her sunglasses. As she gave her teased hair a little pick up and thought about what Geoffrey had said about the mean girl.

He meant the girl on the slab, but Bev had outed herself as a mean girl too. Though Cori didn't let on in front of Finn, this hard-edged turn in Bev was no mystery to Cori. There was a nagging thought that the ex missus Finn O'Brien might be mean enough to bash a woman's face in. She had, after all, left a bloody trail when she ripped Finn's heart out. The next logical step for Bev if she was threatened might be to take out the competition for real.

Cori dropped her gloss into her purse and pulled into traffic knowing that there was a silver lining. The blow Bev had dealt Finn wasn't fatal. He had recovered nicely unlike the woman in the morgue.

Now that was a blow.

CHAPTER 9

"Detective Anderson, it's been way too long. I think last time you were here Dr. Bronson had the pleasure. Or was it Doctor Kalihi? No matter. I'm the lucky one today. Come in. Come in."

Paul Craig, Los Angeles' coroner, gave Cori's hand a shake as he drew her through the door. His smile was as bright as ever, but his eyes were red-rimmed. Not that Cori would have expected anything less. In the early hours of the morning, Paul had agreed to Finn's request for an immediate autopsy. The identity of their victim was the only thing her partner could think about, and Paul was willing to help.

"Don't you make a girl feel like a queen, doc," Cori said.

"And don't you let anyone hear you say that. I don't fancy being brought up on charges of some sort or another. That's why I prefer the dead. I can say anything I want, and mum's the word."

He waved Cori into his office. It was a homey space with books on the desk, in cubbyholes, and on shelves. Framed caricatures of doctors and corpses, news clippings about Paul's cases, and family pictures hung on the walls. His desk was piled high with work, but there was an order to it. Cori took a chair. Paul sat in his own, put his hands flat on his desk, and grinned.

"So how are you liking it in East L.A.? A little different than working with Captain Fowler, I imagine. Captain Smith is a good woman, don't get me wrong. Good cop. My mother was like her. She played things close to the vest. Guess that's why I married the woman I did. I like a little chatter now and again."

Cori tried not to laugh. She had no doubt that he provided most of the talk in his house.

"It's different, I'll grant you that. She's got Finn and me running in ten different directions. Assaults, burglaries, homicides, you name it."

"These budget cuts are eating everyone alive." Paul commiserated. "I can't remember the last time things were this bad. Harbor UCLA has a forty percent increase in gunshot wounds and our stacks are full here. We can house four hundred and fifty bodies, and we're at four-seventy-five. Piled on top of each other. Such a pity."

Paul shook his head at the sad state of affairs, and Cori knew this wasn't an affectation. He believed death demanded dignity. Scum of the earth who took a life or the corpse of a life taken, Paul gave each one his due.

"I'm sorry to be making extra work for you, doc," Cori said.

"We'll get to everyone eventually. I didn't mind letting your lady cut in line. Since you were going to be here anyway, it seemed to me that this would be rather efficient use of my time."

He talked as he rifled through the files on his desk. When he found the one he was looking for he passed it over the desk.

"We'll get this out of the way first," he said. "Seems your victim was pumped full of insulin."

"No surprise there. He was diabetic." Cori opened the file and looked at the fact sheets. "And he was old. Old people get their medications mixed up all the time. Maybe he got the dosage wrong."

"Three down and then take a look at number eight." Paul waggled a finger toward the paperwork. Cori followed directions, and whistled when she saw what he was referring to.

"Well, look at you," she said. "You're a regular Sherlock Holmes."

"Took me a while to find it, I admit." Paul sat back, beaming. "I checked between the fingers and toes, scalp, behind the ears. I was ready to call it an accidental overdose, and then I found a prick at the groin. Lots of flaps and folds in someone that age, but I got it. He was injected twice."

"This is good. Now I'm hoping they can lift some prints off the bottle. I doubt it, though. The syringe only had the victim's fingerprints. Whoever did this was probably smart enough to wear gloves when handling the vial." She put the file down and gave it a pat. "But this is all good stuff. I was beginning to doubt my own gut."

"Never do that. Best barometer ever. Now, what say we take a look at your young lady. This is definitely a record for me. But with the wife gone I couldn't sleep, so happy to come down in the dead of night and get a jump on things. Not that a murder can have a good outcome, but if I help you along in grabbing whoever did this one I'll be a happy man."

He got up and ushered Cori into the hall, stopping to

push aside a gurney upon which a naked man rested. He was very young, very thin, and very dead. His head was turned so that Cori had a good view of the bullet holes in his body. Mortal wounds could seem so insignificant. Nothing more than little red dots on his temple, neck, and chest.

"That's the boy from the slow chase on the freeway two days ago. I was just about to take a look when I got Finn's call about your girl."

"I thought it was a stolen car call," Cori said.

"As far as I know it was, but he came out with guns ablazin'." Paul paused, his hands clasped in front of him, his head inclined as he considered the body. "They look so different when they're cleaned up, don't they? When we got him he was wearing jeans two sizes too big, a jacket with a death's head decal, and a couple of T-shirts. I stripped him down and look what we got: a skinny kid with a teddy bear tattoo on his hip. Maybe some girl told him it would be the cutest thing and it would turn her on, so he got inked. Or maybe he's got a kid somewhere, and that's how he remembered the baby. Nobody will remember him, and that's the pity."

"What a waste." Cori noted the tattoo. Her eyes flicked back to the mosquito bite dots where the bullets had entered his body. It would be a different story when Paul started poking around inside. He would find a mess: a brain imploded, heart with a hole, lungs punctured.

"Indeed," Paul answered and then again. "Indeed."

He patted the man's head as he was known to do when he paused too long beside one of the dead.

"So, we're off."

The spring was back in the ME's step. He led the way to one of the glass-fronted exam rooms. The stark white room was cold and adorned only with the tools of Paul's trade. On the long metal table was the naked body of the faceless woman.

* * *

Finn took his jacket off, slung it over his arm, and made notes in his book. He had spoken to an angry middle-aged man whose paintings reflected his attitude. It was no wonder he sold few, nor was it a surprise that he didn't want to talk to Finn. The detective spoke to a teenager whose parents were out of town and who was late for the school bus. He had a nice chat with a lady who ran a cooking school out of her unit. She had seen nothing, was unaware of who the Cucas were, and crossed herself when Finn told her about the murder. Then there was this last interview, unit 5B. Serina. Mutilated baby dolls and plastic window coverings were her thing.

Finn ran the back of his hand over his nose, trying to clear the dust away. The artist, Serina, worked with a laser that cut fancy designs into huge sheets of colored plastic. Those sheets in turn were hinged and used to cover windows big and small.

Like indoor shutters.

The machine churned while they talked. It had kicked up microscopic particles of plastic, irritating every inch of Finn. He was thankful he had no hair on his head in which it could embed itself. Serina's side business —her real passion— was creating nightmare baby dolls. The price of the dolls was extraordinarily low she told Finn. She assured him business was brisk, her art could only go up in price, so whatever he bought would be an investment. He passed on the sales pitch. She gave up trying to change his mind and told Finn she didn't know the Cucas well. She had also not seen anything weird the night before.

Finn spoke to Serina at 11:45 a.m. At 12:15 p.m., he talked to the gentleman whose business it was to turn cannabis into edibles. Finn found the pineapple shaped cookies very appealing, but he declined a sample. He assured the man that he could not imbibe on duty. When it was established that Finn was as chill as he would ever be, they talked about the murder.

"I slept good last night, so I didn't even know what went down 'till you showed up. I had me a hit of Banana Master, and then decided to test Blackwater. If you ever can't sleep, I'm telling you that's the key. It takes an old hand to handle both of them. I'd recommend Banana Master if you're looking to leave it all behind. You'll sleep like the dead."

Finn responded with a 'good to know', and steered him back to business. The edible artist took off running. The Cucas, he told Finn, weren't unfriendly but neither were they friendly. They used to open their place for The Artist's Walk, but now it was appointment only for the Cucas. This was understandable given that Enver's art was R rated. They got kids coming to The Walk after all. Finn inquired after The Walk. Twice a year studio doors were thrown open to the general public. People roamed in and out as they pleased. It was like a festival, the man said. Thousands came, and most artists made big bucks during the event.

Question: Is your studio open? Did children enter your establishment?

Answer: Trying to trip me up on the kid thing? *Giggle.* No can do, brother. *giggle-giggle.* No kids in here unless accompanied by an adult. No samples. *Snort.*

Question: Is there security at this event? Is there security in the compound?

Answer: Yeah, at The Walk. I've seen 'em. Otherwise we kind of do our own law. Shame is where it's at. You do something bad, and we all shame you, man.

Question: Then why the fence and barbed wire?

Answer: It ain't the compound, it's what's outside. We aren't stupid.

Question: Do you have to make reservations to come to The Walk?

Answer: What?

Question: *Repeated*

Answer: No. No. Come. Look. Walk around. Buy stuff.

Finn let that information sit in his brain: public access, thousands of people roaming around the place in one weekend. Limited security. That meant someone could have come in with the purpose of scoping out a specific unit. This made no sense in context of what went down the night before. The Walk had been a month earlier, and the Cucas' place wasn't open. Still, a person with training, someone who knew what they were doing, could find a way into the Cucas' building. The man went back to molding —and sampling— his wares. He would forget the detective had even been there. Before he left, Finn had one more question.

"Did Enver Cuca always close off his studio during the festival?" Finn asked.

"Only the last two times. August and October. I'm pretty sure Enver's appointment only now, so he doesn't need The Walk."

Finn thanked him, stepped back into the California sunshine, and took a minute to look around. The Brewery was a small city, seemingly filled with mostly happy and bright citizens. People went about their work with a passion. Then again, why not? Art was fantasy and fantasy was fun until it turned in to a nightmare. What struck Finn as odd about the people he spoke with was the lack of curiosity about the murder. No, that wasn't it. It was the lack of horror or sorrow. So far, the news of what happened was taken in stride. Perhaps it was because they didn't know the artist well and the victim not at all. Or maybe these people lived on a fringe where everything was art, even death.

Taking a deep breath, Finn swung his head toward the gated entrance. He looked the other way toward the interior of the compound, and that's when he saw the unmistakable green of grass. It was a jarring sight in this sea of concrete. He made his way around the building to a small park that separated two of the living areas. In the center of the park was a man-made mountain of chicken wire baskets, doors, sheets of plywood, paintings, clothing hanging off any number of structures, a child's tricycle, and a toilet.

"Taking or leaving?"

Finn swung his head. Standing beside him was a mere mite of a woman. Her face was wizened by wrinkles and crevices, but there was a sparkle in her eyes and a whimsy in her blue-tipped short hair that spoke of a young spirit.

"Beg your pardon?"

"Oh, love the accent. Very subtle, but so nice," she said. "Are you visiting Gunther? He's the only Irish we got around here."

Finn shook his head.

"No, and I'm afraid it's been a while since I was in my home village. Hard to lose the accent when you get off the boat already a young man."

"Don't try. Very sexy." She looked back at the pile of stuff, and put her fists to her tiny hips. "You haven't got anything to leave, so I suppose you're taking. Can I help you look?"

"I was doing neither," Finn said. "I was contemplating whether this is art or not?"

"You can't tell?" When she saw Finn flush, she put a hand on his arm. "Don't worry about it. Half of all art is crap, but don't tell the people who make it. You never want to hurt an artist's feelings. They crumble, poor things."

She gave a nod toward the mountain.

"This is our shopping mall. If someone moves out of their place, or doesn't want something, or they don't like one of their paintings it all ends up here. Free to take something, free to leave something."

"Recycling at its finest," Finn said.

"Pretty much." She put out her hand. "My name is Mitzie. Not many of the folks around here make enough to buy new things. Even if they did, it's a lot more fun to shop this way. Want to see what I got?"

"Lead the way," Finn said.

Mitzie took him to her loft, a fine unit with a window of its own. The furniture was new. The place was spotlessly clean, and something wonderful was cooking in the oven. Finn looked upward toward an open loft.

"My loom is up there. I make some good pin money doing fabric art. I enjoy the heck out of myself, but I'm not dependent on it. Want coffee?"

"I won't turn it down."

"Excellent." She talked as she took down the cups and poured the brew. "I'm a little unique around here. I've got money, so I don't have to hustle. I'm also Grandma Moses. I don't find that a particularly attractive handle, but a lot of these kids don't have family. It makes me feel all warm and fuzzy to think I serve a purpose."

"Do tell."

Finn took the steaming mug, and sat on the sofa. Mitzie crossed her legs, sank onto a large floor pillow, and wrapped both her tiny hands around her mug.

"My husband died two years ago. He was a big time lawyer. Good guy. Indulged my artsy-fartsy ways for forty years. When he was gone, the big house, the charity lunches..." She pulled up her shoulder. "I don't know. It wasn't the same anymore, so I came here. I didn't really leave it all behind, though.I brought Frank with me. Sometimes I can hear him telling me that I'm doing beautiful work. He was that kind of guy."

"Sure, a good man is hard to find. Having one for forty-years is lovely."

"It was." Mitzie fell silent for a moment, but her reflection didn't last long. "So, that's what I picked up in the heap."

She pointed to a painting of a nude woman with a screw through her stomach. It filled the wall on which it hung.

"And what is it that spoke to you exactly?" Finn asked. Mitzie rewarded him with a full throated laugh.

"I needed something big for that wall, and that was the only thing available. I'd love to know which of my neighbors painted it."

Finn smiled, grateful that they were not going to be in for a discussion of women's rights, art, or philosophy.

"So, have you found out anything about what happened last night?" Mitzie said.

"Missus?"

"Oh, come on, this is a small place. By now everyone knows you're a cop, and we all know about the murder. Very exciting."

"You wouldn't know it from those I've spoken with.

They seem to take it all in stride," Finn said.

"That's their way. If they aren't the one dead, then a murder is only a matter of interest and not concern," she said. "I, on the other hand, love nothing more than a good mystery. Are there any beans you can spill?"

"I'm afraid not," Finn set his mug aside and rested his arms on his knees. "We've just begun to look into the matter. Do you know the artist in the tall building. The one—"

"Who makes the sex dolls." Mitzie finished for him. "Of course I know the Cucas. Enver does beautiful work, but the credit should go to Emi. She's the one who builds them. Their structure is so delicate, so realistic. Enver's art wouldn't be half as impressive without the foundation."

"Then you know them well?"

"I know Emi better than Enver, and that isn't saying much. They're very old country. If I had to guess, I'd say I was a little over enthusiastic for them," Mitzie said. "I also think they were a little embarrassed by the turn their work has taken. It was hard to tell with them. Then again, maybe they just got too busy. They were already making good money, but six months ago they got a huge commission. Emi told me they signed a nondisclosure."

"That's interesting. Do you know the specifics?" Finn asked.

"I love to know everything about everything, but I couldn't drag it out of her. She wasn't happy that I tried. It must have come with a nice payday because Emi got a high-end 3-D printer. Those things aren't cheap. And the furniture..." Mitzie rolled her eyes in mock envy. "Boco do Lobo and Fendi. My man made good money, but he would have had to work another lifetime to afford things like that. Emi let me in to see it, but it was obvious Enver wasn't happy. That was very unusual. Could be they were having some personal problems. Personally, I think he didn't want anyone around here to know how well he was doing. God knows. Relationships are weird, aren't they?"

Mitzie took a drink of her coffee and considered the question.

"You're preaching to the choir, Mitzie," Finn said. "Do you think there is a reason to fear someone here might rob him? Perhaps that's why he didn't want anyone inside."

"Well he sure isn't afraid of me, and he wasn't happy I was there."

Mitzie's tiny body rocked backwards and forwards again when she laughed. That smile of hers faded fast when she saw Finn's expression.

"You're serious? Well, that's an easy one. Nobody wanted his money or his things. Artists want recognition, they dream of fame. If Enver hit the mother lode either the people around here would want to know how he did it..."

"Or?"

"Or they would want an intro to his patron or the gallery that picked him up. Enver was pretty open before all this, but he withdrew of late. Even when I saw him out walking he looked edgy. Distracted."

"Did you ever see him angry or violent?" Finn asked.

Mitzie shook her head.

"Emi wasn't bruised, if that's what you mean. Then again, how would any of us know what goes on in these places? The walls are so thick you can't hear anything much less someone getting beat up."

Finn knew that to be true and sadly had no time for gossip. The day was getting on.

"Well thank you, Mitzie. I best be on my way."

Finn got up and started to take his mug into the kitchen,

but Mitzie popped up and took it from him.

"Don't you dare," Mitzie said. "Artist though I may be, my generation didn't let men do the dishes."

"You're a treasure, missus," Finn said.

"Yeah, that's what my guy used to tell me. It's nice to hear it again." She saw him to the door, pausing before he left. "I am sorry about that crack. I feel for the person who died, I'm sorry for whoever killed her, but I don't think it could be Enver. I'm praying it's someone outside this community. These are good people despite the fact that some of them are kind of wacky."

"I hope you're right." Finn handed her a card. "But if you hear anything, even if it seems of no consequence, you call me."

"Sure will," Mitzie said. "And you remember where I live. Coffee is always on."

Before Mitzie closed the door, Finn took a step back to ask:

"Do either of them have any good friends here? Or did you see people from the outside going in and out on a regular basis?"

"I saw a young woman visitor over that way once or twice, but she could have been going to the places near the back fence. I remember it being in my consciousness that she was going into the Cucas'. You know how that can be?" She pulled a face. "I'd make a terrible witness."

"You're doing fine," Finn said. "Did you ever see her with anyone else?"

"No," Mitzie said.

"And her car?" Finn asked.

"If she came by car she would park in the lot. No cars allowed in the quads unless you're loading or unloading something," Mitzie said. "Now and again I saw men go into the Cucas' unit. Clients I suppose. I didn't really see those guys more than once."

"Can you describe the girl?"

"She was young and white. Petite. Long hair. That's about it."

"Can you take a guess how often you saw her?"

"Really, I can't say." Mitzie shrugged her apology. "Regular around here is seeing somebody from the outside more than once. She could have been modeling for Enver. You know Enver and Emi take commissions right?"

"So if a gentleman wanted a doll to look like his girl-friend or his wife—"

"Which would be redundant, wouldn't it?" Mitzie laughed. "More likely he would have commissioned the woman of his dreams. If he traveled he could keep her at his apartment in Paris, away from the respectable ladies in his life. If you've got enough money you can hire a super model to pose, have Enver do his thing, and take her home forever and ever. She'd never get old. Imagine that."

"'Tis a thought," Finn said. "Though none I would ever have."

"Even if you had that kind of money, I doubt you'd throw it away on one of those things. I bet you'd have better things to do with your hard earned dollars."

"I doubt I'll ever have that problem," Finn said.

Mitzie smiled, and Finn did too. Both knew money was not the root of all evil; it was the root of dissatisfaction, arrogance, and boredom. Once anything could be bought, nothing had value. With one of Enver's dolls a man could have the perfect woman, but never have to wonder if she loved him for his money or himself. There was no real intimacy in that, only an odd sort of insanity.

Finn took his leave, walking only as far as the end of

Mitzie's building. The morning had turned to afternoon, and he could feel the fatigue of the long night. Mitzie had gone back to her loom. The compound was quiet as people attended to their work. He leaned against the cool concrete wall, and it felt good against his back. Finn flipped a page in his notebook and wrote: *how would we know? Commission? NDA??*

The latter he underlined twice. He flipped the book closed and let his eyes wander from one block of buildings to another. Finn thought of what Mitzie had said. No one could know what went on in any of these units and especially in the Cucas'. The building was huge, sound proof, and constructed like a fortress. It was difficult to see through the high windows from ground level. The man who had called 911 had only seen something strange up there. What he saw was indistinct. He seemed surprised that a crime had actually been committed. Upon questioning, he admitted that he didn't like the people going into the Cucas' place. He didn't like any outsiders on the premises at night. What he saw in the window was excuse enough to call the police. He figured they would get rid of everyone inside.

Finn pushed off the wall. He checked his phone, saw no text from Cori, and decided to soldier on. The sun was high in the cloudless sky. While it was a pretty to look at, Finn often grew tired of the endless sunshine. His memories of his village's gentle rains and green fields intruded on days like this. He could only imagine how his parents missed their homeland. Now his father was gone. One day he and his brothers and sisters would send his mother back for a visit and Finn would go with her.

Setting aside his plans, he started for the next building only to turn and look at something that gave him pause. It was a small thing that would have gone unnoticed had his mind not wandered. Finn took a step and then two into the common area. He shaded his eyes with both hands to make sure he was not mistaken, and then he smiled.

"Thank you Mother Mary," Finn mumbled.

He dropped his hands, pocketed his notebook, and went on with a spring in his step.

CHAPTER 10

"Can I help you?

Finn turned at the sound of the voice. He turned again, and once more as the question was repeated. The voice seemed to come from different parts of the warehouse. He looked up, down, over, and under as he tried to identify a human being amongst the 'things' that crammed the space. He found none. There were boxes that stood higher than three men, and plasma screens wider than ten more. A Foosball table the size of a living room was pushed up against one wall. It would take giants to turn the handles and make the wooden teams move. This place gave Enver Cuca's workroom a run for its money in terms of oddities. Finn couldn't identify the person speaking, so he assumed he was being tracked by a camera and spoke to the ceiling.

"I'm trying to get to the roof of this building," Finn said. "Can you direct me to the stairs?"

"No can do, bucko. It's private up there," the voice answered.

"I'm thinking, you'll make an exception." Finn lifted his credential. "LAPD. Detective O'Brien. 'Tis been a long morning. I'd be obliged if you would show yourself, and keep me from having to hunt you down."

When the voice didn't talk back, Finn waited. Then he heard:

"Here I am."

Finn looked over his shoulder as the door to a glass booth opened only a few feet from him. He turned and faced the curious thing that emerged. Finn assumed there was a man inside the silver jumpsuit. He hoped there was a human face behind the darkened glass faceplate of the head gear. He imagined normal hands and feet under the heavy gloves and big, sturdy shoes but he could be wrong.

"Have we been invaded, then?" Finn asked.

The face mask flipped up. Beneath the dark glass and the glittering silver was a mischievous young man, no older than twenty or so.

"Wouldn't that be cool?" He had the huge grin and the wide-eyed wonder of an eight year-old. And, like an eight year old, he was as easily dismayed as he was delighted. "Who called the cops on us this time? I swear, this is all above board. Everything's got a permit."

"Do your neighbors complain often?" Finn asked.

"Not too often. It's annoying when they do," the man said. "You wouldn't think people here would freak out at what we do. Some of them make way weirder stuff."

"And what is it you do?" Finn twirled his finger as he talked. The man did a three-sixty, happy to show off his outfit.

"Today I'm burning myself up," he said.

"And why would you want to do that?" Finn asked.

"Fun and games," he said. "We make bigger, better, awesome, over-the-top games and stuff. Want to see? We're in the last testing stages on this one."

"I admit, I'm curious," Finn said.

"Great. I'd love to get an outsider's reaction. Come on. Over here. How are you with a baseball?"

"Better with a soccer ball, but I can manage," Finn said.

"Good enough."

The man's arms were akimbo as he walked back to the glass booth. The puffy suit crinkled and skritched with each step. He flung out a gloved hand.

"So we make big fantasy games for anybody with enough money to buy one. Mostly we sell these things to corporate events or theme parks. Sometimes people buy games for themselves, but those people have big bucks. We are talking no-holds-barred, sky's-the-limit. You imagine it, and we figure out how to make it. If you can't imagine it, we do that for you too."

He handed Finn a softball.

"But I'm kind of a sucker for tradition. This one's my baby. So this is like an updated dunk tank. Ever seen a dunk tank?"

"I've fond memories of dunking the principal at our school's festival when I was in fifth grade," Finn said.

"Then we're on the same page," he said. "So I get in here..."

He pointed to the glass booth from which he had recently emerged. It didn't look much like a dunk tank to Finn. There was no water, but there were metal grommets running up and down the two solid walls that faced one another. The grommets anchored hollow copper tubes. There was no plank for the man to sit upon, but before Finn could ask about any of this, he was being given directions.

"You stand here." he pointed to a mark on the floor. Finn obliged. "As soon as the door closes and I put my arms above my head you throw the ball at the target, okay?"

"Got it."

Finn palmed the ball with both hands as the young man waddled inside and closed the door behind him. He turned laboriously. When he was finished, he pulled his mask down, secured it, and then held his arms up.

"Okay, boyo," Finn muttered. "Prepare yourself."

Finn wound up, threw the ball, and hit the pin. The minute it made contact Finn fell back, cursing. Fire shot out of the grommets. It burned so hot it was blue at the heart of it; it was propelled so furiously it sounded like the roar of a jet engine. The flames engulfed the man inside. Finn froze, but the blast only lasted seconds before the flamethrowers embedded in the wall clicked off. Finn lunged for the door thinking to rescue the man, but there was no need. He opened the door, waddled out of the booth, and when he snapped up his face mask he was laughing.

"It's okay. It's okay," he said. "Awesome, isn't it? I mean, did your heart stop or what?"

"'Tis a heart attack you'll be giving everyone if you don't warn them what's coming," Finn said.

"It takes a lot to get people excited this days," he said. "Anyone who sees this at a Comicom or something is never going to forget it. And this suit is incredible. I could get burned up all day, and not feel a thing. You don't even get hot."

"I'm going to be having nightmares." Finn ran a hand over his head and tugged at his jacket to compose himself.

"I didn't even scream. I've got resonators, so when I scream it makes everything super horrifying. Do you want to do it again and I'll scream?"

"I've enough horror, thanks," Finn said.

"Yeah, you're right. I've been playing around with this all morning." He peeled off his suit and tossed it on top of something that looked like a helicopter with hair. He rotated his shoulders under a T-shirt that had a cat with a knife through its head on the front. He held out his hand. "Peter. O'Brien, right?"

"That's it," Finn said, noting the man's skin was cool to the touch.

"So what can I do you for?" Peter said.

"I need to get to your roof. It's about what happened last night, " Finn said.

"What happened last night?" By his reaction, Finn chalked the young Peter off the list of those who had a personal interest in the woman in the loft.

"A woman was killed here early this morning." Finn said. "I understood that news didn't take long to be shared at The Brewery."

"Depends on the news," Peter said, only to be distracted by a hat with big goggles attached. He offered it to Finn. "Total virtual reality. Want to try?"

"Not unless it's a time machine and will take me back to the wee hours of the morning," Finn said, all the while thinking how difficult it would be to deal with children if he could not keep this man's attention. "How is it you didn't hear about the murder?"

"Because I don't live here, which means I'm not a part of the whole artist community thing. There's kind of a weird split at The Brewery."

He walked through the warehouse. Finn followed, feeling like he was on the back lot of a carny. His eyes were everywhere, even though he concentrated on Peter's steady stream of conversation.

"You've got the real artists in the low rent buildings. Those guys are literally hand-to-mouth. They live and work in the studios, and spend more on raw materials than they do on food. They are the true believers. Most will never be successful, but when they are they move out."

Peter raised his arms and waved them over his head. A garage-size door opened. He never stopped talking.

"Biggest artist colony in the country, subsidized by the city. It's fantastic concept. Great PR for L.A." Peter said. "Take a load off."

They were in an office. The door closed automatically, rolling down from the ceiling, andlanding on the floor like a vapor lock. Air conditioning kicked in. Lights shined softly at the end of the room. Finn sat down on a plastic chair shaped like a large hand. The upturned palm was surprisingly comfortable.

"Want some water?"

Peter didn't wait for an answer. The bottle he handed Finn looked like it should hold wine.

"So you've got the starving artists," Finn said as he pulled out the glass stopper. "What else?"

"Past the park, you've got the nice lofts with windows and separate work areas. Lots of furniture makers, interior designers, jewelry artists. That group has a market; they make a living from their art because they make useful things. And then there are a few like me and my brothers."

Peter grabbed a bottle for himself, and perched on the edge of a long table.

"Me and my brothers get paid to play. Best job in the world." He chuckled, thinking fondly of his oversized toys, only to sober a minute later. "We work long hours, but we don't live here. Sometimes we stay over if we're on a tight deadline, but this isn't home."

"From the look of things you're successful," Finn said.

"We are because we're businessmen first and creative second. We make a lot of money catering to a specific high-end market. One of my brothers is a special effects expert, my other brother is an engineer, and I'm the *imagineer*. My sister-in-law does the marketing."

"Sure, you're like Disneyland," Finn said.

"Pretty much. I think it up, my brothers figure out how to make it, and we sell our games to whoever can afford them. We used to have a huge business with conventions and corporate events. The market's down a little, but it will come back. Still, we're better off than most."

"Are you here every day?" Finn asked.

"I come in every day. We have other spaces where we test small models. We do the final construction and real time testing here," Peter said, tiring of his tutorial. He was curious about Finn. "So, what exactly are you looking for?"

"I'm talking to people in the complex to see if they remember anything unusual last night. This went down in the three story building on the other side of the park—"

"Oh, Enver and Emi. It wasn't Emi that got taken out was it? I'd feel awful if it was Emi," Peter said. His response wasn't personal, it was sympathetic.

"No. She's fine," Finn said. "We are trying to identify the victim."

"Doesn't Enver know who was in his own place?" Peter asked.

"It would seem not," Finn said, not wanting to go into the particulars of the party.

"You sure it was a human?" Peter laughed and then held up a hand. "Sorry, I'm not joking about a dead person. It's just that Enver and Emi, well, you know what I'm talking about. Companion doll is a nice name for making a hunk of plastic a person can screw. It is totally weird."

"So you know the Cucas well?" Finn said.

"Nobody around here knows anybody well. I think Emi is super cool. She's a visionary; a real construction whiz. Honest to God, what we could do if we teamed up," Peter said. "Which we almost did"

"She was going to work for you?"

"No, not for us. We were talking to them about collaborating on a haunted house deal. We were going to build some movable units. That's what we call them. Enver calls them companions. Enver was going to paint them. He's got a fine hand. That man can paint a movable unit like nobody's business. It would have been awesome to work with them."

"Why didn't your deal work out?" Finn asked.

"Emi and Enver just dropped off the map." Peter's expression changed to one of sincere confusion. "I was surprised. We were paying top dollar. Emi seemed so excited to take it to the next level."

"Did you have them sign an NDA?" Finn asked.

"No, it never went that far. We each brought something to the table," Peter said.

"Did you find someone else to collaborate with?"

"We did and they're fine, but the project won't be all that it could be. Enver is a genius with a paintbrush, but Emi has a super cool way to create smooth moving limbs. I tried to get the secret out of her, but she wouldn't tell. She showed us a prototype and whatever she did with those joints was brilliant." He smiled in a nod to his professional admiration. "I think she has a patent pending on the joint bearings mechanism she was using. I wouldn't have told me either because she's going to make a fortune if she can get it into production. Just imagine how something like that could impact prosthetics." Peter waved his hand knowing this was neither here nor there. "Whatever happened, the partnership never materialized. We moved on. It was just business."

"When was this?" Finn asked.

"Six months ago; maybe eight. I'd have to check. My brother was the point man. I have heard that Enver told one of his neighbors he was working on something that was amazing. Far reaching. World changing."

"Want to guess what it might be?" Finn asked.

"That's artist talk, my friend," Peter scoffed. "I mean, give me a break. No matter how good he is, those dolls are nothing more than an American pie for a bunch of rich old dudes. If they hit big money, I'm guessing it has something to do with Emi's joint bearings."

Finn nodded, adding to his notes as he did so: *joint bearings/ patent/ money/check Asylum men - investors?*

This time Finn drew a box around the notes because big money was always important. Possible outside investment. Mitzie's mention of an NDA. Peter's talk of a patent pending. Bev's assessment of the victim as a bitch wanting to bring down a successful man. Moneyed guests waiting to see something revolutionary. All were nice little bits of string that might weave themselves into a ribbon that would eventually tie up a motive for murder.

"You have a telescope on the roof. I'd like to take a look," Finn said.

"Do I have a choice, you being a cop and all?" Peter said.

"Of course." Finn smiled. "But with you being a good citizen, I know your choice will be the right one."

Peter grinned, set aside his drink, and popped off the table.

"You know, I bet if you worked here for a week you would be a lot of fun."

Feeling he was quite fun as it was, Finn didn't bother

to comment. He followed Peter to a freight elevator. He was grateful to reach the roof where Peter's voice didn't fill every inch of space.

"'Tisn't this prime." Finn walked toward the edge of the roof and put his hands atop the retaining wall. "I'm surprised some developer hasn't put up a shiny new high rise."

"It will happen as soon as this part of town is considered cool," Peter said.

Finn knew he was right. The immediate surrounding area was nothing but small industrial buildings. Beyond that, the City of Angels rose in a skyline that had become as identifiable as New York's. It glittered in sunlight, but Finn knew it was only the clement weather and distance that made the place look like Oz. Wilshire Division was proof of that. It was part Emerald City, part crumbling dark Gotham. He missed it.

Beyond the city were the hills of Hollywood. The sprawl of everything in between laid itself out neatly from this perch. But the city was not as orderly as all that. It was full to bursting with people who insisted on wedging themselves onto every inch of available land. Freeways wound through it all, spreading tentacles far and wide. They went into Pasadena and Flintridge on one hand, and the valley on the other. A major artery flowed to the coast. The road to the ocean was clogged on any given weekend as city dwellers flocked to the shore. Behind Finn the mountains, still tipped with snow, rose up. The air was so clear it seemed he could reach out and touch them.

"You've a nice set up here," Finn said as he looked around the roof top.

The three brothers had made the space their home. There were three couches, five chairs, and two barbeques.

It all made the roof feel rather cozy. A refrigerator was rigged to hijacked electricity, and there was a telescope.

Finn walked over, and looked through the lens without adjusting it. There was a direct shot to the third floor window of the Cucas' place. He could clearly see where the bed had been; where the girl had died.

"Do you and your brothers ever tire of watching the stars and watch your neighbors instead?" Finn asked.

"I cannot tell a lie. We take a peek now and again. I don't know what we thought would go on in there. Orgies with all those plastic chicks, I guess." Peter put his hands on the top of the wall and bounced on the balls of his feet. "But there was nothing that would get a guy all hot and bothered. To tell you the truth, spying on them gets kind of boring."

"But you've seen through the window."

Peter flipped around and put his back against the wall. "Sure. The last couple of months there's been a girl up there. I think they sublet the top floor 'cause she doesn't do much. She sits there, or walks around, or lies on the bed. I'm not sure she lives there fulltime, and she sure doesn't work. She's got to be bored out of her mind."

"Have you seen her take a bath?"

Finn asked the question even though he knew this was impossible. Even artists couldn't make water flow if the pipes weren't hooked up.

"I've seen her drop her drawers," Peter said. "We all have. She's pretty enough, but not really my type."

"Would you know her if you saw a picture of her?"

Peter thought for a minute and then said, "Yeah, I might. You know, sometimes I think she was drunk or high. Come to think of it, maybe she didn't live there. Maybe she goes there to get wasted."

"What made you think that?" Finn asked, resting his arm on the telescope having seen what he needed to see.

"I don't know. She would sit for a long time. Then she would get up and weave around like she was kind of drunk. That's the only way I can describe it. Plus, I only saw her now and again. I'm not here all the time, and I have better things to do then check on the neighbors."

The little boy was gone, and Finn saw a different man in Peter. This *imagineer* was also an analyst. He had to figure out how something worked, before he could imagine how it could work better.

"Was she alone?" Finn prodded him when the silence stretched too long. "Did you see Enver Cuca with her?"

"Not Enver. But twice I saw a man," Peter said. "Now that was super cool."

"And why was that?" Finn asked.

"Well the guy in that window was pretty amazing," Peter said, reenergized to a point of giddiness. "My brother's didn't believe me, but I swear it was him. The first time I wasn't sure. The girl was sitting on the floor and he was sitting in a chair. He was stroking her hair. The second time I saw him sitting on the bed with her. I got a pretty good look that time, but then I stopped looking. You don't spy on this guy."

"And who is it we're talking about?" Finn asked.

"Ding Xiang."

Peter grinned as if he expected Finn to be hearing a brass band given what he had just told him. When Finn didn't react, Peter's arms dropped and his head bobbed.

"Come on, man. Ding Xiang? He's only like the God of tech: immortal, the ultimate mind, inhumanely brilliant. Some people even say he's Satoshi Nakamoto.

"And that would be?"

"Boy, you need to get out," Peter said. "Satoshi Nakamoto is the guy who invented Bitcoin. Digital currency?
Big, big bucks. Topple governments and financial institu-
tions. New world order?"

"Do tell."

Finn pulled his bottom lip up, took out his notebook,
and sat on the couch under the L.A. sun. He asked Peter
to spell those names nice and slow.

CHAPTER 11

Cori found it hard to look at the body of a young person, because it could be her daughter dead, never coming back, a life taken too soon. She hated seeing a little victim of crime, too. A dead child reminded her of her grandson, Tucker. Anyone who snuffed out a life not yet begun, or a life half lived, was pure evil in Cori's book.

At the moment, she was looking at a murder victim without a face; the woman found in the artist's residence. Cori could tell she was young and that she came from means. That was evidenced by the cut of her hair and the care of her body. It would be sad when they figured out who she was because then Cori would have to notify the next of kin. It was her least favorite chore. Right now, though, she was in full cop mode and damn curious about the dead woman.

This girl had been beautiful, of that there was no question. She was not tall, but she was perfectly proportioned. Her breasts were high and large for her delicate frame. They were also real. It was clear she did no hard labor. Her hands were small and unmarred. Her fingers were long, the nails manicured. Her feet were smooth. Her pedicure was the same as her manicure. It was hard to see her tan lines because her skin had taken on the ice-milked chalk of death. The girl's pubic area was shaved, and the swimsuit she wore to cover her nether regions would have barely saved her from an indecent exposure rap.Another few square inches of fabric had covered her nipples. There were narrow tan lines running over her neck and back where the straps would have tied.

Not even those tiny tan lines could distract from the new markings on her body. Between the wee hours of the morning and the early hours of the afternoon, the girl had been butchered. This was done in the nicest way possible given that Paul was doing the butchering. The M.E. had cut her from pelvis to breast. He pushed open her rib cage, sectioned her organs, and emptied her stomach. When all was said and done, Paul packaged up the leftovers and packed them back into the cavity and closed her up with coarse, even stitches.

Her arms were graceful, and her neck long. The head that sat upon it was elegantly shaped, but it too was disfigured. While her long dark hair hadn't been cut, her skull had been opened and her brain removed. What was left of her face had been pulled down over the skull so that Paul could see first hand the damage done by whatever hit her. All of this was recorded and photographed before her mutilated face was stitched back in place.

"You should join a quilting bee, doc," Cori said. "Nice work."

"I like to send them on as close to one piece as possible. That way the angels won't stare when my patients stroll through the pearly gates."

"You're lucky you're taken, doc, or I'd have to make a

play," Cori said as she leaned over the corpse. "Did she bite the big one right away?"

"Her heart was beating for a few minutes after the attack was over. The bruises around the temple area are light so there wasn't a lot of blood pumping, but she was alive."

Cori's eyes swept over the woman's face —across, up, and down and then back again. When she and Finn had found her it looked like her face wasn't there at all. Now that she had been cleaned up, Cori saw that it was still there, pressed into the depression where her cheek and temporal lobe had collapsed.

"She took more than one hit?" Cori asked.

"Yes. Still, if you're asking if that is the cause of death, I can't say yet. I'm thinking suffocation."

"You're pulling my leg." Cori straightened and rested her hip against the table.

"There were bone fragments impacting her nasal passages. Given the damage she sustained to her nose and the maxilla..." he pointed to the spot where her upper lip would have been. "She probably couldn't breath through her nose or open her mouth. I found teeth in the pharynx. Between that and the bone fragments, she would have had a very hard time breathing. There's some petechial hemorrhaging, so suffocation isn't out of the realm of possibilities. She wasn't conscious, thank goodness."

"Would she have survived if we got to her sooner?" Cori asked, thinking of Officers Hunter and Douglas and their hesitation. If they were responsible for this girl's death, the whole department was going to suffer. It would be worse for all of them if she was some rich Asylum guy's woman.

"Don't worry about it. Between the traumatic brain injury and disfiguration, it was a blessing she didn't make it. Her quality of life would have been nonexistent. No one could have saved her."

Cori nodded. Her bottom lip disappeared between her upper teeth. She gave it a nice little bite to remind herself that this was all business.

"Look here." Paul pointed to the eye that was open— the one that was still fairly intact. Cori pushed away from the table.

"I don't know what you're looking at. The eye is flooded with blood. The other one is mush. I can't even see what color her eyes were," Cori said.

"Brown. Actually, more hazel. Very pretty," Paul said.

"If you say."

"Take my word for it. Lovely eyes. She was a beautiful young woman based on my measurements. It must have been quite a party if they were all like her."

"It was unique," Cori said. "Four men and a bevy of lovely ladies. All in various stages of undress."

"The men too?"

"No," Cori laughed. "The women."

"Thank goodness for that. Nothing worse than a naked man parading about. Usually, we don't have anything to show off that's too impressive," Paul said, and Cori chuckled. "A party like that reminds me of when I was in medical school and just married. My wife kept a tight hand on the finances. I worked so hard, such long hours, and I didn't understand why she didn't want me to have any fun.

"One evening we had a particularly heated discussion, and I stormed out of the house. I went to the North Beach. That's in San Francisco, you know. This was well before the city became unlivable. Anyway, I found myself in front of The Condor."

"Let me guess. That's an aviary where all the birds fly around a metal pole shaking their tail feathers," Cori said.

"Correct. But The Condor was a world famous strip joint," he said. "Carol Doda was the star. She had a forty-five inch bust, if you can you imagine. Well, I put my weekly lunch allowance down, bought entry and two watered down drinks just to show my wife who was boss."

"What did she say when you told her?" Cori asked.

"I never did. I was so mad at myself that I went a week bumming morsels off my fellow residents so she wouldn't know what I'd done."

"I didn't know a guy could be embarrassed about something like that," Cori said.

"It wasn't the money, or the fact that I ended up in a strip joint that shamed me. I never told her about that evening because the whole gesture was a bust."

Cori rolled her eyes and asked, "Pun intended?"

"Oh, no. No, no, but that would have been very funny," Paul said. "The truth is, as I sat with my horrible drink watching a naked woman stare into the distance and pretend to dance, I realized how sad it all was. Carol Doda was a freak of nature and she traded on that, but I don't think she was happy. The man at the table on my right snored as he slept. The guy closest to the stage fidgeted with whatever was under the napkin in his lap. I realized that was the saddest hour of my life. I was in that dark room with lonely people when I could have been home with a wife who loved me."

Paul sighed and stuck his hands deep into the pockets of his white coat. His eyes were on the dead girl. His mind was back in time; he was a young and stupid man again.

"I expected excitement and some sort of acknowledgement that I was a man in control of my destiny."

"Women do the same thing only we end up sleeping with someone we hate or hanging off that pole," Cori said.

"Everybody's got their saddest hour, doc."

"Well, one good thing came out of it. I learned that I was more turned on by the human anatomy when it wasn't moving —except for my wife mind you. Those are the two places I find the closest relationships: with my wife and with my patients. My wife never stares into the distance when she's with me, and the patients don't expect anything from me at all." He turned to look at Cori. "Maybe the people at that party of yours last night feel the same way this morning."

"You think too well of your fellow man," Cori said. "The people at that party included the president of a major bank, a CEO of a tech company, and a magazine publisher. I've never heard of the magazine, but it's supposed to be a big deal in international business. We never got one guy's name. His lawyer was at the station before we were, and had him headed home in five minutes. She was good. I have to give her credit."

"Women rule the world," Paul said.

"Women make it a more interesting place, and especially at this party," Cori answered. "Finn's ex was a guest."

"Oh, my," Paul said.

"I must say, she fills out a corset real well," Cori said.

"How did Finn take it?" Paul asked.

"He says he's good. Still, it's got to bother him. She made it real clear that she hated this little lady." Cori pointed to the body. "That puts her right in the middle of this mish-mash. Everyone in that place swears they don't know who she is. They all used aliases. Rules of the club."

"Well, that's a fun little game," Paul said. "Did Bev have one?"

"Aurora." Cori's cheek bulged where she had parked her tongue so as not to say anything more.

"Very Disneyesque." Paul said, neither intrigued nor amused. "But back to work. Our lady needs an identity. A real one."

Cori hung on every word that fell from the doctor's lips; her gaze followed each gesture. What this girl was now would lead her and Finn to who she had been in life. That was the key to solving her murder.

The doctor ran through the basics. Blood had been sent to the lab, but Paul didn't expect any surprises. Given the shape of the organs he doubted they would find drugs or excessive alcohol. The liver was pink and healthy, the heart free of obstruction, lungs were clear. She was missing her appendix and her thyroid. The thyroid was unusual for a person her age — which he put between eighteen and twenty-five.

Musculature was in good shape, but she was no athlete. He speculated that she belonged to a gym because her muscles were long and lean. Her abs were taut, but that had more to do with her age than a strenuous workout. Bottom line, had she not been dead she would be the picture of health.

The lower jaw was surprisingly intact considering the damage to the upper face. Pictures had been taken. The teeth she had left were well cared for. Braces had been applied. Paul found no evidence of fillings, root canals orother invasive dental procedures. If there was any it might have been done in the upper jaw but there the destruction was massive. He collected all shatters and shards of teeth and bone, and sent them along to the lab. He asked for an expedited report, but with such perfect teeth matching dental records was a dead end.

"Now, let's move up a bit," Paul said.

Both hands cupped the girl's face at cheek level without

touching her, a gentle expression of care.

"Right here is where it gets interesting. You see how the nasal, temporal and zygomatic bones are literally pulverized?" Cori nodded, knowing she would have to look up the word zygomatic, but she didn't want to stop him when he was on a roll. "The frontal bone here remains intact."

Cori tiptoed up to peer to the other side of the girl's face.

"But that only happens on one side. So did the perp come at her with a flat object and maybe she turned her head just when he swung whatever he used, and that's why the damage wasn't uniform?"

Paul mimed the attack, clutching something in both his hands as he swung an imagined blow. He stopped as his hand hovered over the girl's destroyed face. Dissatisfied with whatever he was doing, he took two steps back. He swung his imaginary object again.

"No, no, I don't think so." He did the motion again, and this time he smiled. "Cori, I believe whoever did this used something rounded and thick on one end, but tapered on the other." He held up one finger. His smile turned to a grin. Then that finger dived to the other side of her face. "This part of her face was also damaged, but not to the extent of the other side. So if you are standing where I am standing now—at the side of her head, and about this distance — and you raise..."

He pulled his arms up again.

"...And you strike."

He brought down the invisible thing he was holding.

"And you were my height give or take three inches. And this was the angle. The head of the murder weapon would demolish three-quarters of her face. The other quarter would show only trauma like you see here. That would be because the end furthest away from me has the most density and weight; the closer end is narrower. Even at a ninety degree angle, the heavier head of the thing would crush the bone with the blow. But because of the taper, the other end would give a glancing blow. To make the impact uniform, the heavier thicker end of the object would have to come down straight on the face. To do that I would have to take say two more steps back. This object had to be at least twenty four inches long."

He stood up straight again.

"You didn't find a baseball bat lying around, did you?"

"Is that what we're looking for?" Cori said

"Something along those lines." Paul nodded and dropped his arms.

Cori held up her index finger. "Are you saying the person who did this was as tall as you?"

"If the bed were as high as this table. Was it this high?"

"No," Cori answered. "But it wasn't low to the ground. There was a platform, the bedframe, box springs and a very deep-pocketed mattress. It was all top of the line."

"It also must have been quite firm. If it wasn't, it would have provided a cushion when the blow was administered. The damage would have still been horrific but not this bad."

"I didn't lie down on it," she said. "Itlooked brand new. I doubt that anyone slept in it on a regular basis."

"Was she in the middle of the bed or to the side?"

"Middle," Cori said.

"Okay. Let's assume a fifteen inch box spring, eighteen inch pocket, another two inches with a pillow top. That brings her down by, what, four inches from the table? Even if you took precise aim, you wouldn't hit her straight on if you were standing within a foot. If the perp was standing say two feet back for the reach of such a weapon to land squarely on the face. But that distance would also affect the strength of the blow. Your perpetrator was close to the victim when it happened, as close as I am now. I'd also venture to guess they stood between five foot six and six feet tall. Only a guess, Cori. You'll need to look at the blood spatter. Was there anyone walking around with flecks of blood all over them? Crushing the skull would spurt the blood."

Cori shook her head.

"The guy we tagged was soaked in blood, but no spatter. He said he leaned over the bed and put his hands on her shoulders to wake her. He pulled her up and didn't realize she was hurt."

"A little hard to miss."

"The room was dark. Finn and I turned the lights on. The blood on his shirt was consistent with someone doing what he described. We've already got his clothes to the lab including his shoes. If there's spatter, they'll find it." Cori said. "What about his weight?"

"I can't speculate on that, nor did I say it was a man. It could have been a woman. Any woman would be strong enough to do this if she had the right weapon and was angry enough. I know the weapon had to be heavy and shaped like a bat, but I've ruled out a bat," Paul said. "There aren't any splinters, shavings, or dust in the hair mouth or throat. Whatever hit her wasn't wood. Metal bats are strong, but they are also light. Aluminum wouldn't do this kind of damage."

"What about a composite bat?" Cori asked.

"Baseball fan?" Paul said.

"I've been known to dig into a box of Cracker Jacks." Cori smiled.

"Sorry to disappoint. Those things have a trampoline effect. They're tough, but there would be a bounce. This woman's face was pulverized."

"Was there any sign of sexual assault?" Cori asked.

"It didn't appear that she had sex recently, but she wasn't a virgin. I did a kit as a matter of course. Also sent along scrapings." Paul picked up one of her hands. "The other thing you should know is that there was no preceding struggle. Her legs were not askew as if she were trying to get away. There was no bruising to indicate that she was thrashing. No defensive wounds. It's as if she lay there and let it happen."

"Could she have been asleep?" Cori asked.

"Sure," Paul said. "If she were a deep sleeper someone could have come into the room, and that would be that."

"Or she could have pretended she was asleep. The whole party thing was a game so she could have been waiting for a lover," Cori said. "Maybe more than one. Bev said that consensual sex was part of the entertainment. This girl might have given her consent to who knows how many of the men that night."

"Did you ask the men?"

"They admitted to having seen her before, but they say she wasn't a guest that night," Cori said.

"A party crasher." Paul's head did a little wiggle.

"In more ways than one," Cori said.

"Be that as it may, I think you're looking for one person and I am almost positive that person had second thoughts. Or they were horrified by what they'd done," Paul said. "It's no easy thing to do this kind of damage and not have some visceral reaction. Think about it, even if our friend here didn't cry out there would be the sound of bones breaking. That alone might give a normal human being a shiver," Paul said. "And the first blow did most of the damage. I would guess there were no more than two after that."

"A jealous lover in a fit of passion who retreated when he realized what he had done." Cori mulled that theory over.

"Very possible," Paul agreed.

"The man who owned the studio was distraught," she said.

"That's a place to start," Paul said.

"And Bev," Cori said. "She was angrier than a nest of hornets. She's tall enough, and strong enough to do this."

"I wouldn't want to be the one to go there," Paul said. "But I fear you must."

"First things first," Cori said. "We need a name for our lady from The Brewery."

"I wish I could oblige." Paul reached under the table and brought up a plastic bag. "Here are her things. A dress. No shoes—"

"We've got the shoes, and let me tell you she was shittin' in high cotton" Cori said. Paul looked at her as if she were speaking another language. "She had money, Paul. Geeze, you Northerners."

He sighed, and turned the bag a quarter turn.

"No underthings. No jewelry. The little lady was very comfortable in her own skin. The dress is very well made. Custom I suppose since there was no label." Paul pulled up his lips, his shoulders rose too. "So there you have it, Cori."

"Guess it's back to work for me."

"For both of us," Paul said. "I hope that ten more haven't come in while we've been shooting the breeze."

Cori and Paul turned their back on the girl, leaving her naked and alone in the cold room. They walked to the front office and waited for the elevator together.

"You know, Cori," Paul said. "I keep thinking about

the differing force of the blows. That speaks volumes to remorse."

"So does picking her up and holding her tight," Cori said, thinking of Enver Cuca and his blood soaked shirt.

"Or grief," Paul said. "Maybe you're not looking at a *real* murderer. A crime of passion is different from intent to kill."

"Oh, lordy, doc. Murder is murder if you've got one person alive and one person dead. That's the law. We can't afford to have soft souls."

"Then may I make one suggestion if you need to question Beverly O'Brien again?" Paul said

"What would that be?"

"Keep Finn out of that conversation if you can."

"You're preachin' to the choir," Cori said. The elevator door opened. She got in, put her finger on the down button, and said, "Thanks again, doc. Get some sleep."

And Cori was gone.

CHAPTER 12

There were quite a few things Finn O'Brien missed about Wilshire Division, and his office was at the top of the list. Modest as it had been, it had a door that he could close. The solitude let him focus on his work. That door also shut out the anger that flared when someone remembered the officer who had died by Finn's hand.

The fact was, Finn missed Hollywood in all its iterations. Families, freaks, runaways, rising starlets rushing off to their auditions. He missed seeing Batman and Superman battle it out for prime space in front of Grauman's Chinese Theater even as theyshamed tourists into paying for the privilege of taking their photograph. Finn missed the hills where the rich folk hid behind the walls of their homes and businesses and did unspeakable things to one another in their off hours. He missed the lowlands of Fairfax and Little Ethiopia, and the food booths at Farmers Market. He loved The Grove, the synagogues, and television studios. Finn O'Brien missed the crazy quilt of real estate. He missed the rainbow population that bubbled with dreams and disappointments.

Most of all, Finn missed Captain Fowler. He had a deep and abiding respect for the man who had reluctantly taken in the tarnished detective. Fowler had given Finn a fair shot, and that was all he ever wanted. The captain was intelligent and unflappable. He was loyal to those he commanded until they betrayed that loyalty. Finn couldn't have asked for more in a captain.

Now he and Cori were lent to a different division because money was tight after the riots. Ranks were diminished as disillusioned officers took their retirements. Where Wilshire Division had been a kaleidoscope, East L.A. was daguerreotype. It was a richly shaded, but it was a monotone of a place. Finn's office was a desk that faced Cori's. They could talk to one another across the expanse, but they could say nothing that wasn't meant for other ears. Until she got in, Finn was the lad on the school yard eating lunch alone. The cool kids kept their distance, but never let him forget they were there.

Finn had made no friends by questioning Officers Hunter and Douglas's decision not to engage at The Brewery. But the two cops told a story of intimidation and high-handedness by the on-loan detective. It was passed on in whispers loud enough for Finn to hear. His colleagues cast sidelong glances, hoping to make him uncomfortable in their midst. Such an inflation of the events was not unexpected, Finn just found it wearying. He longed for a door he could close. It was mid-morning. He and Cori had slept well, grabbed breakfast when they woke and gone their separate way. Cori to a hearing; Finn to the office. Now Carol Smith, Captain of East Los Angeles Division, was at the door of the bullpen calling him away.

Her name left no particular taste on the tongue. The woman herself left no particular impression on Finn and

Cori. She had welcomed them by laying out their work load, addressing Finn's possible problems, and telling Cori she was the only female detective onboard. They had been assigned cars and desks and neither detective had seen hide nor hair of the woman until now.

Finn didn't bother to cover the report he was working on. If anyone in the room wanted to see it, all they had to do was look. He walked by one empty desk, but at the next a detective glanced his way. The man looked as if he'd been with the force for a hundred years. He snapped a rubber band. O'Brien smiled at him. He snapped it again, and this time the darn thing flew across the room. If he had meant to hit Finn, the man was a poor shot. The captain had not waited, so Finn walked the long hall alone and went into the office where the assistant was nowhere to be seen. He leaned his head through her door and knocked on the jamb. Captain Smith gave him permission to enter with a crook of two fingers. She pushed a few measured inches away from her desk. Finn sat in a straight-backed wooden chair opposite her. On her desk he counted four stacks of papers, two pens, a coffee cup imprinted with the division logo, and one picture. The picture faced her so he could not see if it was husband, family, or dog she cared to remember during the working day.

The woman's chin length hair was brown as were her eyes. Parentheses created by deep lines framed her small mouth. They seemed to be proof of age, not humor. She wore no make-up, but her skin was burnished brown as if she spent all her free time under the sun. It was difficult to tell if Captain Smith ever laughed or frowned. She was doing neither at the moment.

"Let's talk about The Brewery, Detective O'Brien."

Finn brought her up to speed. His report was to the

point in regards to the first responders. He told it without judgment or asides. If Finn's assessment of his new captain was correct, she would read nothing into his words. He told her where Cori was, what she was doing, and that the autopsy had been completed. He went through his visit to The Brewery that day, and told her that they were hoping to identify the victim soon.

"The other people in the building? What about them?" she asked.

"All but one gave us their names and contact information. The women are accounted for. The four male guests are well-connected. I'll have my initial report to you by end of day."

"Very good," Smith said. "Anything else?"

"I have the name of a person seen visiting the location that is intriguing. I'll let you know if it pans out." Finn said. "We questioned the residents of the unit at length. The gentleman who owns it discovered the body and was in a state. He had blood on his person. Given the nature of the attack, his appearance was not consistent with the commission of the crime. Everyone knew the victim by an alias. We believe some knew her real identity, but they did not share this information."

"That seems a bit odd, doesn't it?" she said.

"Not considering that these people were guests of Asylum. The venue was rented, the owners stated they were unaware of what type of gathering it would be, and the building was a destination only. The rental was arranged through a third party."

Captain Smith allowed herself a small smile.

"Asylum is interesting. Not my idea of a good time, but to each his own."

"As you say, captain," Finn said.

"Did you talk to the host?" she asked.

"If he was there he didn't identify himself. The attend-ees were handpicked, and there was business to be done. It appears to be something outside of Asylum business, but I am seeing Ali Keyes, the owner, in another hour. I hope he'll be able to shed some light.

"I'm further hoping Mr. Keyes can help us ID the victim. It appears there are strict rules about sharing personal information. I believe Mr. Keyes can break them under the circumstances."

"Okay," Captain Smith said. "Hopefully we'll have a hit on the fingerprints soon, so don't push Mr. Keyes quite yet."

"I've got all data bases looking including Homeland Security and Global Entry. She was very well turned out, I'm assuming she had money. That might mean travel."

"Well and good, O'Brien," Captain Smith said. "I know we've had you running since you got here, and I appreciate the hard work. I have full faith in you, but this one is delicate."

"It certainly encompasses a different class of folks if that's what you mean," Finn said.

"That is exactly what I mean."

Captain Smith picked up a pen and ran it through her fingers. Her nails were bitten to the quick and that sur-prised Finn. Somewhere inside, past the perfect calm, the woman was roiling. It was no easy task being a captain in any city, but this division must be particularly challenging.

"This 'class of folks', as you say, have been busy trying to minimize last night's fallout."

She raised the pen and put it to her lips before tossing it on the desk. The captain rested her arms on top, leaned into it, and laced her fingers together.

"I got a call from the mayor's chief of staff. He informed me that he would like us to treat this incident with kid gloves. It seems that the mayor's very reliable intel indicates that none of the people at the party knew the girl. Nor did they have anything to do with the murder."

"Truly," Finn said.

Captain Smith's wide plain eyes blinked. Her expression never changed, but Finn saw an itch of amusement at the corner of her lips.

"Sometime before end of day, I will receive notarized statementsattesting to that fact. Each of these sworn statements will include the individual's precise movements during the party."

Now it was Finn who tipped his lips, but the gesture did not even come close to a smile.

"'Tis kind of the mayor and his staff to do our work for us. I'll be able to take an early lunch and have my hair cut."

This time she chuckled, and in doing so transformed. Her eyes sparked, and she smiled. It was tight and fleeting, but Finn counted that a victory.

"You can do without the haircut, and you'll have to wait for lunch," she said. "To be clear. I don't care if God himself took videos of those folks and angels are vouching for them. You will not stand down in any quarter. We have our job; the mayor has his delusions. I'm simply telling you to watch your butt because it's a hard time for cops."

"Sure, that's an understatement, captain."

"And you're doing double hard time. I have no prejudice one way or the other on the matter. Nor am I unaware that my guys from last night are feeling a little raw." She held up a hand when she heard Finn's intake of breath, and saw him poised for a rebuttal. "I'm not saying you were wrong. They should have gone in. There might have been a chance to save the victim."

"There wasn't," Finn assured her. "But..."

"All I'm saying is that for every person who is happy to see us there are ten that would like to take us down. Don't blame those officers for their caution, and make sure you and your partner aren't the ones in line for friendly fire. Don't forget the mayor can play hardball too. Do you understand me?"

"I do, captain," Finn said.

"Good, because I would like there to come a day when I send you and Detective Anderson back to Captain Fowler in one piece as much for your sake as mine."

"Detective Anderson and I would like nothing more," Finn said. "Not that we haven't enjoyed our time here, Captain Smith."

The woman was not charmed, only satisfied by his assurances.

"Pass along our conversation to Detective Anderson," she said. "I want to know all there is to know, every step of the way. I'm not fond of being called on a politician's carpet or finding my division on the front page of the newspaper."

"I'll speak to Detective Anderson when she gets in. She's swinging by The Brewery again, wanting to check one more thing."

"Good work. Both of you."

Captain Smith picked up her pen again, simultaneously reaching for a thick folder. Finn stood up, but didn't leave the office. Captain Smith raised her eyes, butshe kept the posture of someone already on to the next task.

"Something else, O'Brien?"

Finn looked at the woman a moment longer. There was something else. There was his ex-wife. He should tell

Captain Smith about Beverly. He should, but he didn't.

"No. Thank you, Captain."

"You're welcome, O'Brien."

Finn walked away, convinced that he would tell her when and if there was a need to know. By the time he got back to the bullpen, he was convinced that the connection didn't matter any longer. He was wrong on one count. The connection did matter to everyone but him.

CHAPTER 13

"Anderson, you are dumber than a brick."

Cori threw her head back, shook out her hair, and put her hands on her hips. She took a long deep breath both out of frustration and an attempt to inhale the clean air above her, not the stench beneath her. Actually, Cori wished she didn't need to breathe at all.

She stood knee deep in trash in a huge dumpster. Her brilliant idea to run through the garbage at The Brewery had been half-baked. Much as she hated a pun, this one seemed apropos. She had found any number of half-eaten, half-cooked, half-digested meals in this stinky metal box. She had also found paper, glue, a huge wad of gum, and a bag of sand. She had rifled through banana peels, apple cores, dog poop bags, and empty shampoo bottles.

She was reaching for a paint can, chuckling at the folly of thinking she would find a smoking gun in the trash, when she was attacked from above. Cori threw her arms over her head, yelped, and fell forward as she tried to duck out of the way of the stuff that was raining down on her head. Whatever it was, it felt as hard as rocks. She must have cursed pretty loud because the next thing she knew she had company. A young woman was hanging over the side of the dumpster. She smiled and asked:

"Are you throwing yourself away?"

Cori righted herself, swiping at her hair as she glowered at the pretty girl who was watching her. The girl's face was pierced with hoops and studs: ears, nose, lips, and temple. Whatever hit Cori wasn't just hard, it was sticky. It clung to her teased hair like burrs on a hunting dog.

"Am I what?" Cori said.

"Throwing yourself away?"

The girl's head rotated. She looked over her shoulder and then turned her face up. She swiveled her head side to side before looking at Cori again. Finally, she pulled herself further over the rim of the dumpster to look inside.

"Is there a camera in there? That would be such a cool piece. I mean, wow. Making a video about how it would feel to throw yourself away. I am totally down with the concept."

The girl, tired of holding herself up and slid down an inch or two. Cori swiped at her shirt though she doubted it would ever come clean.

"No, I'm not throwing myself away," Cori said. "But at this point I might as well. I stink like a pig."

Cori swung her purse to the front of her body, wiped away something on the clasp that looked like raw meat, and took out her ID. She showed it to the girl.

"LAPD," Cori said.

"Oh." The girl raised her chin as if she understood everything now. She did not.

"Well, if you're not taping, can I? It would be awesome. Cop in Garbage. What a title. Or Garbage Cop. Pig in a Bin. Would you say you stunk like a pig on camera? That would be even better."

"Not gonna happen, honey," Cori said.

"Okay."

The girl crossed her arms in such a way that Cori thought she might be swinging on the edge of the dumpster. She wasn't, of course. Cori had piled up some boxes to give herself a step up, and that's what the girl was standing on.

"I'm sorry I tossed my crap on you. I couldn't see you in here."

"No problem," Cori said. "I'm almost done."

"What are you looking for?" The girl shifted her weight, seemingly happy to hang there all day.

"There was a problem in that building last night, the big unit," Cori said.

"That doesn't surprise me," she said.

"Yeah? Why's that?"

"I'm pretty sure Enver and Emi keep sex slaves. I've seen a woman up there." The girl pointed to the third floor. "She doesn't ever sleep. She's always moving around like she's trying to find a way out. Once she walked right up to the window. I thought she was going to punch it out and jump. I made a sign and held it up. I shined a flashlight on it. It said DO YOU NEED HELP? She stood at that window still as could be, but I guess she didn't see my sign. Then a guy came and took her away. You know, it could be she didn't speak English. Do you think she couldn't read the sign? Emi and Enver are foreign. They could be sex traffickers."

"I don't think so on the sex trafficking thing." Cori flipped her shoulder bag behind her again and leaned against the side of the container. She couldn't get any dirtier if she tried so she might as well be comfortable. "How did the man take her away? Did he drag her away? Did he hit her so she fell away?"

"Oh, no, nothing like that. It looked like he touched her on the shoulder, and she turned and went with him. I guess she didn't need help." The girl seemed disappointed.

"Was it just one girl or were there others?"

"I think only one."

"What did she look like?" Cori asked.

"It was always kind of dark. I didn't see her super well. Well, not dark, but there are a lot of shadows, and it's high up. She looked small. Not like a little girl, just small."

"What did this man look like?" Cori asked.

"I don't know. I mean, it was a while back. It couldn't have been Enver. He's tall. The girl was alone a lot," she said.

"And you don't know anything about the other person?" Cori asked.

She shook her head.

"No. I'd say he was a customer. They go in and out making sure everything is just perfect because Enver's companions cost so much. I've run into some of them. They are weirder than weird." She made a face and Cori wondered if she had taken a good look around The Brewery. Weird was in the eye of the beholder.

"So you know Enver and Emi pretty well?"

"I used to," she said. "Enver gave me a super good hint about technique on skin tone because I'm a painter. Once Emi made me some meat pies that were awesome, but I can't remember what she called them. Then they got busy, and I didn't see them anymore. I was kind of hoping they might take me on. You know, I could paint the dolls with Enver. I don't think he ever gave it a thought." She became wistful, only to perk up a second later. "So what are you really doing?"

"I'm looking for clues. Something might have been thrown out in the trash after that party last night. Something that would help me find out who killed that girl," Cori said.

"Some chick got offed at a party? Was it a sex party? See, I was right, wasn't I? She was a slave."

"I don't know," Cori said. "Cross my heart, I'd tell you if I knew."

"Did you find anything worth keeping in there?" She lifted herself up and took another look.

"Nope. "

Cori went to the side of the dumpster and waved the girl away. As soon as she was off the boxes Cori hoisted herself up, swung her legs over, and climbed down. She swiped her hands together again. Cleaning them was hopeless until she found some soap and water or a blow torch.

"Did you look at Enver's dumpster?" the girl said.

"He has his own dumpster?" Cori said.

"Yeah. I mean, look at where he and Emi live. Perks come with that place." She pointed to the one Cori had been rutting around in. "This one is for my block." She pointed behind her to the low rent district, and then waved her hand the other way. "Enver's is over there."

"Show me," Cori said.

The girl bounded away, disappearing around the corner of the building. Cori picked up her jacket, slung it over her shoulder, and followed. A minute later, Cori stood beside the girl checking out the Cucas' private trash bin.

"How come it's so small?" Cori asked.

"Because it's only for this unit. Sometimes when the other one is full I'll dump here, but mostly we respect each other's spaces," she said.

"Good neighbor policy, huh." Cori found a couple of

slats of wood, piled them in a basket pattern, tested the platform, stepped up, and climbed in.

"I love your accent. Where are you from?" the girl said.

"Texas. Long time ago," Cori said.

"I guess it hangs on, huh?"

"You should hear my partner. We're a regular United Nations," Cori said.

That was it for their *kafe klatch*. Cori was now truly in hog heaven. Enver and Emi had found time to clean up after all that happened. The remnants of that fateful evening were all there. Bottles, fancy plastic plates, discarded food, napkins, and a few of the condoms Cori had seen in the bowl. Thankfully, they were still in the wrappers. She sidestepped those just in case.She moved the top refusea-side before dividing the interior into quadrants.

In the first quadrant she latched onto a hank of hair. Fearing it was another body, she pulled on it carefully only to find it was one of Enver's discarded dolls, torso and head only. Enver had been right to toss it. The eyes had molded so that one was higher than the other. The full lips were not bee-stung. Instead they bore a strange resemblance to a catfish Cori had hooked in the river near her house as a kid. She set it aside all the while wondering if there wasn't a market for discounted companions. Say a guy couldn't afford a perfect one. He got a discard, put a bag over its head, and he was good to go.

It was in the third quadrant that she found a plastic grocery bag, the handles tightly knotted. It was light when she picked it up, and soft to the touch. It didn't smell like garbage. It didn't feel like garbage. Cori started to work the knot.

All the while her young friend talked about painting, videos, pigs and cops, more painting, and the weather. Just as the pierced girl predicted a wet winter, Cori opened the bag. She reached inside, and with two fingers pulled out a piece of fabric. It was damp as if it had been washed. Cori held it up, noting the dark spots on the garment. If those dark spots were the victim's blood, that would be so fine. Tying the bag handles again, Cori was satisfied that there was nothing else to find. She climbed out of the dumpster, happy to be back on the ground.

"Found something, huh?" The girl seemed excited.

"You never know."

Cori looked up into the sky. The day was getting on. She was dirty, tired, and satisfied. She was also grateful to the girl who had led her here.

"What's your name?" Cori asked.

"Pedal," the girl said.

"Like a flower?" Cori asked.

No." She laughed. "Like to the metal. My mom says I popped out ready to run. Want a drink?"

"Thanks a bunch, but I need to get back to the office."

"Okay. I'm in 601 if you change your mind." She started away only to turn around and walk backwards. "Not just today. I mean whenever. We're always in and out of each other's places. We love each other. That's the way around here."

Cori watched Pedal skip away, and then started for her car. She could do without the friends around here since it seemed there might be one who could just love you to death.

Giving her hair a shake, hoping she didn't smell too bad but knowing she did, Cori had a revelation. Dumpster diving was an art in this place. Video was a way of life. Sharing was a matter of course. Put all that together and there might be something more to find. Whatever the 'something' was, it could have migrated from the crime scene. Someone might have picked it out of the dumpster. They could have passed it on to someone else who turned 'it' into an art project. In this place anything was possible. Cori paused. She started to walk, pondering, wondering what she might have missed and what someone else might have seen.

A couple of yards away from where she stood was a cluster of small units. She wouldn't have noticed them had Pedal not shown her the private dumpster. Outside one of those units, lined up like bowling pins, were small statues. Cori ambled over, put her hands on her knees, and took a closer look. They were modern and not particularly well formed. Some had been glazed and others just fired. One caught her notice. It was a sweep of clay that looked like a lady wearing a mantel. Kind of like a madonna if you used your imagination. Cori thought it was beautiful. She also decided she would come back with Amber and Tucker when this was all over. She might even invite Lapinski. They'd make a day of it. Just as she was about to leave, the door of the unit opened.

"You can take one. They're free."

Cori squinted. The person who was talking to her was standing in the shadows and she was in the bright sun. When she focused, the first thing she saw was a young man. He was both beautiful and handsome. His hair was black and curly, his skin pale as parchment. His dark eyes were friendly behind wire-rim glasses. His clothes had seen better days, but he wore them well. He could have been middle eastern or Spanish; Indian or all American. He was also young enough to be her kid.

"Thanks for the offer. I might come back and check out your stuff when I'm not working."

"No problem," he said and gave her the once over. "You look like you've had a hard day."

Cori couldn't argue with that. She was a mess. She raised her hands.

"Would you mind if I washed up. I'm going to stick to the steering wheel if I drive with all this gunk on my hands."

"Sure, come on in."

The young man held the door wide. Cori took a step up only to hesitate. Before she went through the door, she took notice of the second thing.

"Does that work?" She pointed at the Ring doorbell.

"Sometimes. Mostly it plays this little song whenever anyone passes by. It drives me nuts."

"Do tell," Cori said as she swept into his living room. Before he closed the door, she said. "LAPD, and I'd like to take a look at your phone."

* * *

Finn was twelve minutes early to his appointment with Ali Keyes so he grabbed a cup of coffee and waited it out. When ten minutes had come and gone, he walked the block and a half to a very fancy high rise on the Wilshire Corridor. He announced himself to the doorman, who announced his arrival to someone in the penthouse.

The elevator that took Finn up to the fifteenth floor was mirrored. He found it difficult to look at so many of himself, so he looked at his boots instead. When the door opened, he had taken the first step to exit the elevator only to stop and press the button that would keep the door from closing until he understood the situation.

Standing in front of him were two children. A boy and a girl. Both dark haired and of Indian extraction. They looked at him with huge eyes, and said not a word. The little girl, no more than six, appeared especially peeved at his arrival. The boy had a truck. The girl a crayon. Finn was just about to speak, to ask if he had come to the wrong floor when an extraordinarily beautiful woman swept down the hall and gathered the children to her, pulling them back.

"I'm so sorry. Please, please. Come. Come," she said to Finn.

When she tipped her head toward the children, her black hair cascaded over her shoulder. When she spoke to them, her voice was warm, her words lilting despite her crisp British accent.

"I have told you, wait until a visitor comes to the door before you greet them."

The woman stood up. One hand remained on the little girl's shoulder, the other she extended to Finn.

"Vida Keyes," she said. "And these are my children. Our welcoming committee."

"Detective O'Brien," Finn said.

Ali Keyes' wife was movie star beautiful with her deep dark eyes, her full lips and perfect skin. Her clothes were casual and expensive. Her figure was voluptuous and, while other men might admire her, the woman would have no eyes for them. It was clear from her open smile, the way she spoke to her children, the welcome she gave Finn, that she could find no greener pastures.

"Come, come. Ali is expecting you."

Vida Keyes shooed the children ahead, and Finn heard them squeal as they went back to their play. Vida stood back and let him go into the apartment before her, all the while keeping up a pleasant conversation.

"I'm afraid our children have learned how to read the lights on our security system. They know when the elevator is coming and rush out before I can stop them."

"Then I hope 'tis only friends coming to your door," Finn said.

"I believe so," she answered. "Won't you have something to drink?"

"Thank you, no," he said.

"I hope you don't mind if I leave you, but I am busy with the children. It was lovely to meet you."

With that she was gone to do what rich, happy mothers do with their children. Finn looked after her for a moment, and then checked out his surroundings. Everything in the living room was expensive, but the errant toy under the sofa, the candid family pictures, the way the furniture was set close enough to have a real conversation made it homey. Finn walked to the sliding glass doors. There was a balcony outside that was as large as a patio, and the view was spectacular. Finn was not one to lust after person or thing, but he would be happy to have a view such as this.

"It's awesome, isn't it?" Finn turned to find Ali Keyes behind him. "Hope I didn't scare you. Sometimes I get so lost in that view I'm startled when someone talks to me."

"I'm not easily surprised, but thank you for asking."

"I suppose in your line of work that could be detrimental." Ali swept his hand toward the furniture, inviting Finn to sit where he pleased. "Did Vida offer you something to drink?"

"She did," Finn said. "I'm good. I've only a few questions for you about the event you held at The Brewery."

Ali's head went up and down. Both men turned their backs on the view. Ali Keyes sat in an overstuffed chair, Finn on the edge of the couch. The man was as comfortable in his skin as his wife was in hers. He was narrow, his body lithe, his face long, but his good nature was full blown.

There was no artifice in Ali Keyes, he seemed to be an open book. He was thirty-five, perhaps. Young and rich. A father. A happy husband. Yet his business led Finn to believe there was some flaw in this perfect picture.

"I've been advised of the problem the other night," Ali said. "I was sorry to hear about what happened. Asylum gatherings are carefully curated as are our members. But this was not a true Asylum event. We were only asked to coordinate the venue and extend invitations to a limited guest list."

"So I understand," Finn said. "But the party was exclusively Asylum members and I'd like to confirm my understanding. You vet the women, but the men are welcome as long as they pay a fee. Is that correct?"

"Yes."

"So do you vet the gentleman?" Finn asked.

"Our membership paperwork requests full disclosure, yes," Ali said. There was no guile here for which Finn was grateful. "Many of our members lead very public lives so this is a formality because we are already aware of who they are. But there is a lot of private money, old money, in the hands of people who do not leave a public footprint. Sometimes our members are foreigners. Those people we look at a little more closely. If there is a hint of anything untoward in their background, they are refused membership."

"And Cami?"

"Cami." Ali sat back. He smiled and shook his head. "She came highly recommended."

"By whom?"

"By one of our members who has not been active for sometime. Sadly, she really wasn't appropriate for our group. I assure you, she was not invited to the event at

The Brewery. I further assure you that none of the invited guests had anything to do with harming her."

"I appreciate that, but I am in charge of a murder investigation and I must ask."

"And I'm afraid I can be of little help," Ali said.

The man's teeth were brilliantly white when he smiled. His black hair fell over his brow making him look almost boyish. Finn was not fooled. No boy came to live as Ali Keyes did without risk taking and experience.

"I am only asking for two things. The information you have on the woman, Cami, and the name of the person who hosted the party."

This time Ali Keyes's smile was not wide and bright. It faded a bit as if he felt bad knowing he was going to disappoint Finn. Before he could, Vida Keyes appeared.

"Is there anything I can get you?" she asked. When her husband said no, she disappeared again.

"Your wife is very gracious," Finn said.

"She is. She is also beautiful, educated, and wise," Ali said. "Ours was an arranged marriage, detective. Old fashioned, I know, but I count myself a lucky man."

"With good reason," Finn said.

"Thank you." Ali sat back in his chair. He crossed one foot on his knee, rested his elbows on the arms of the chair and laced his fingers together in front of him. "The beauty of an arranged marriage is twofold. First, those arranging the union have both parties best interests at heart. Vida's family and mine wanted us to be happy. Our families knew us best, and so we were married. Both of us are very respectful of family and tradition.

"And the second beauty of such an arrangement is the thrill of discovery. I learn something new about my wife every day. Hopefully, she is delighted with what she learns about me too."

"I've a feeling this is leading somewhere, Mr. Keyes," Finn said.

"It is." He uncrossed his legs, he dropped his hands. "I do not wish to interfere with a murder investigation. I am sorry about what happened to Cami, but I also have a responsibility to my members and the women who come to Asylum gatherings. Like my family arranging the perfect marriage, I have the best interests of my clients at heart. I want them to be safe, happy, and anonymous. Therefore, I cannot give you these names. I will if I am compelled by law, but at this moment I am not.

"You see, detective, Asylum is not my only business. I have many thriving concerns. Asylum is one that is a bit more unusual, but I take it no less seriously than my other businesses. Asylum is meant to give people the thrill of discovery, to bring fantasy into lives that are so successful they also become predictable. Please forgive me, but if you wish to depose me, call my lawyers."

"Then I suppose there is nothing more to be said, sir." Finn rose. Ali Keyes did the same.

"I am sorry, detective. I do wish you the best of luck. I am not sorry that Cami will no longer be a problem. I am only sorry the way in which the problem was taken care of," Ali said. "I will call my lawyers and ask if I might divulge the name of the company that acted on behalf of the man who arranged the party. That is the best I can do."

"I appreciate it," Finn said.

The men walked slowly out of the penthouse and toward the elevator. Before they got there, Finn paused.

"Why were you not at The Brewery if it was an important event."

"Because I am not important enough, I suppose. I was

not invited," Ali said. "Also, Asylum is not something I find interesting. I'm delighted others do, but I would rather be home with my family."

"And is that where you were when Cami was killed?"

"Yes. My wife and children can vouch for that. We have a live-in maid. Feel free to ask her anything you like She will be truthful. There is also a doorman twenty-four hours. The night man is Richard. He will be happy to assist. There are also cameras throughout the building."

"I had to ask."

"Of course. I would do the same." Ali was about to push the button to call the elevator when he took a moment. "If I might ask, detective, how did Cami die? Haven't you a weapon to get fingerprints or some such thing? Something that points to the person who did this? There were only four of our members there that night."

"She was bludgeoned. Her face," Finn said. "And, no, we have no leads but we've only just begun our investigation."

"That's a bit of poetic justice," Ali said. "Cami did love her face—both of them."

"I beg your pardon?"

"Nothing, really. Only that like many people she had a public face and a private one."

"Are you speaking from personal experience?" Finn asked.

"Detective, please."

With that, Ali Keyes laughed and pressed the elevator button. The doors had not yet closed when he turned around and went back to his perfect home, his perfect family, and his perfectly clear conscience. Finn doubted he would give one more minute's thought to Cami or her death. This was not malicious. It was simply business.

CHAPTER 14

"...So, I say to him. No, your honor, Lapinski with an 'i'. And the judge says, 'oh, well and good'. I mean that judge was going to hold me in contempt for mouthing off the last time I was in front of him, but when he brings it up I tell him it wasn't me. I say 'it was another Lapinsky with a 'y', and, with all due respect, your honor, you can't hold me in contempt for something another Lapinski did'. That was that. No contempt."

"So all's well that ends well, Thomas," Finn said.

"Except it wasn't another Lapinski," Thomas laughed. "It was this case. It was a quick pleading, but it was me and I did get a little unruly. But, Finn, if it's that easy to confuse that judge then he shouldn't be on the bench. I'm telling you, we are not looking at the best and the brightest these days when it comes to the guys who wear the robes. Besides, he couldn't rule on anything except the matter at hand even if it was the same case. He was in a snit about old news."

"And how was this matter at hand resolved then?" Finn asked.

Lapinski raised his shoulders. He inclined his head,

and his expression left no doubt that he had triumphed mightily. Thomas Lapinski, though, could not resist adding editorial.

"It wasn't even a contest," he said. "I did a little bit of black magic, and a lot of digging. Guess what? The air-bag manufacturer didn't send out the software update when they said they did. That meant the car's warning system wasn't updated. It was completely flawed at the time of the accident. My client will be well taken care of for the rest of her life."

"And you're going to be so rich that you'll be buying a new boat when you get the other one wet," Cori said as she joined them.

Lapinski stood. Cori waved him down. She was not unaware of his affection for her, but she wasn't about to cut him any slack until she was sure a relationship would be good for both of them. Still, she felt something for Thomas Lapinski. He was the unlikely third leg in Finn and Cori's friendship stool, and their secret weapon. A while back Lapinski burst into Finn's office at Wilshire Division and tried to convince both detectives to sue the department for injuries suffered in a freeway pile up. They had declined the offer, but Lapinski's knowledge of tech, his unflagging optimism, and his curiosity about everything made him the kind of genius whose help they welcomed now and again. Not to mention, Cori found his admiration kind of nice. Lapinski was funny and kind and it had been a long time since she had an ardent suitor.

"You look like you'll be needing a drink, Cori," Finn said.

"Good grief. I thought a hot shower would put me in order." She looked at Thomas. "What do you say? do we have time for a drink, or are we headed to dinner?"

"At your disposal," he said. "And now that you know I'm a man of means after that settlement, you get to choose where we eat."

Finn went to the kitchen for the drinks. Cori settled on the couch next to Thomas.

"I'll take Maria's," she said. "After the day I've had I need a wagon load of carbs."

Finn came out of the kitchen, handed them each a beer, and took the chair opposite the couch. Finn rested ankle over his knee, enjoying the company, knowing it would soon be quiet in his apartment when Cori moved home the next day.

"Great, we'll save The Four Seasons for another time," Lapinski said. "So what have you two been doing that's got you running?"

Finn and Cori took turns filling him in on The Brewery mess. In the process, they shared information with one another since they had seen little of one another. As usual, Lapinski found it all beyond fascinating.

"So you're thinking a crime of passion?" The lawyer said.

"I haven't the faintest idea." Finn took a long drink of his beer. "The economic structure of The Brewery is something that's niggling at my brain. The bloody man and his wife are a mystery. If it were me, and there was a dead body in my upstairs, I'd be working overtime to help the police just so they would leave me alone. Those two are clamshells, and we can't pry them open."

"They're smart," Lapinski said. "Most people blow it by talking too much. I predict the next time you see them, they'll be lawyered up."

"They're Albanian," Cori said.

The men looked at her, waiting for more. Cori shook her

head as if to say her comment should be self-explanatory.

"Didn't you ever see that movie *Taken*? Albanians are always the bad guys," she said. "I say we assume they did it."

"Now that's what I call excellent police work." Lapinski chuckled.

"Well thank you, honey pie." Cori pulled on her Texas drawl, teasing Thomas before she became serious."The Cucas have permanent residency, but that doesn't mean much if you get on the wrong side of the law. Think about it. We talked for hours and the only thing we know for sure is that they want to stay in the U.S., the husband is talented, and the wife is the brains behind the business."

"And," Finn cut in, "if, as Bev says, our victim was a troublemaker, and she was messing with any of that, there is your motive. But we saw the man. The only thing out of place was the blood on his shirt. His explanation for it was plausible."

"It's not like there would be much else to see," Cori said. "Paul said this was a straight out, wham, bam, thank you ma'am, you're dead."

"There's even something more worrisome in my head," Finn said. "The woman in the window. We've statements from the neighbors. There was a woman in their upstairs, more than once, staying long enough to draw attention, and yet they deny knowing her."

"But we don't know if it was our victim," Cori said.

"When we have an I.D. we'll revisit and show our witnesses. Mitzie and Peter only need a picture, even Ali Keyes will be able to confirm without spilling any secrets. Until then, we'll let the Cucas rest for a day." Finn took a drink of his beer, his brow furrowing. "I still go back to the man, though. He is at the center of this. I feel it in my bones. He had a knife as big as a machete and a huge rage."

"Then why not use the knife to take the victim out?" Cori said.

"And why was he ticked to begin with?" Lapinski asked. "If he didn't kill the girl then why draw attention to himself?"

"Don't you have any nuts, O'Brien?" Cori got up and went to rifle through the cabinets. She called out from the kitchen. "Tell Lapinski what Cuca told us."

The men listened to Cori wreak havoc on Finn's kitchen for a minute before Finn began again.

"He said he was distraught when he saw the dead girl and it worsened when he saw one of the Asylum men doing something untoward with the companion downstairs. Whatever happened upstairs, was blamed on downstairs. A woman, a doll," Finn shrugged. "I don't think the man knows the difference between a real woman and one of those things."

Cori came back in and settled herself on the arm of the sofa. She offered Lapinski the can of nuts. He shook his head.

"It does bring up an interesting moral question," Thomas said. "If they look as real as you say, if they feel real, then is there some line crossed if you don't treat them like humans? I mean, is it possible to rape a doll? If so, and he hurt a human being in defense of the doll, is that on the same legal footing as defending a real woman?"

"'Tis above my pay grade, to answer a question like that." Finn took a drink. "As an officer of the law, I cannot make a judgment since he was doing nothing illegal if he owned that thing. I can hold him on drunkenness perhaps. But as a man, I don't understand any of it. It seems to me there must be some sickness in these people."

"I have a feeling Mr. Cuca felt the same way. The neighbors say he became progressively reclusive as his business grew. Maybe he was ashamed of how he makes his living. He admired the art, but the first time he got an eyeful of what people do with it he freaked out," Cori said.

"There is a difference, you know. Perception, reality, fantasy."

Thomas scooted up on the couch, energized by the discussion. He swiped a hand through his hair. He talked so fast Finn and Cori had to hang on his every word for fear of missing one.

"I've seen it all in my practice. It's amazing how people can work themselves up. When a person is hurt—especially if they were near death— they lie in bed reliving whatever went down. They decide the driver of the car that hit them meant to do it. If an operation doesn't cure them, then the doctor was incompetent or he actually wants them dead for some reason. When they sue and don't get the settlement they think they deserve, then I'm a shyster or criminal. They think I consciously want to ruin their lives. Perception. Fantasy. Reality. All of it is wrapped up into one experience, and all of it gets warped as it tumbles around in a brain."

Thomas shook his head. He put a hand on Cori's knee, but it was only a gesture of inclusion.

"Very few people can control their emotions. They can't be objective when their life takes a bad turn. Worse, they can't look at their own failings. I think your Mr. Cuca loved his art but hated what happened once it was out of his hands. All those people abusing something he lovingly created must have pushed him to the brink. It's a low blow."

"Lapinski, you're one smart shyster," Cori said. She gave his hand a pat, moved it off her leg, and dove in for a handful of nuts.

Thomas Lapinski beamed at Cori's compliment, and Finn smiled. Pity the man didn't see that his brilliance was only a small inroad to Cori's affection. It would take a patient man to win her over. One mistake in love had turned her into a single mother and a wary woman. Still, Cori's love life was none of his business. Cami's murder was.

"But, Thomas, this party wasn't all about pleasure. Whoever put it together had business to do. It was so important these very fancy men couldn't say no to the invitation."

"Except the host wasn't a person." Cori put the can of nuts on the coffee table and dusted her hands. "The invite went through the Asylum offices at the request of a corporation. The guests were directed to download an app, the invite went through, and it disappeared from their phones once it was accepted. I can't imagine there isn't some way to retrieve that invitation. I'd like to have a look at it."

"Don't bother wishing. Self-destructing message apps are amazing. You won't find a history," Lapinski said. "It's like Snapchat, but whatever Asylum was using was probably more sophisticated."

"Amber used Snapchat before she went back to school," Cori said. "It always looked like trouble to me. I'm glad she got rid of it."

"I'm not a fan, but that's the attorney in me," Thomas said. "I would also assume the invitation was sent to private numbers or emails. Even if you confiscated their phones, you might not have the phone it came in on."

"So what would you suggest, Thomas?" Finn asked.

"Try to find out if there was someone who didn't accept the invite. It might still be on their phone," Lapinski said.

"Do you know how the women were invited?"

"I assume the same way," Cori said. "I'll find out"

"Do you have the name of the corporation? I can do a deep dive and try to figure out who is behind it. At the very least I can look at what they produce and get some idea of what might constitute an 'earth shattering' announcement."

Before Finn could speak, Cori had her jacket, purse, and Lapinski in hand.

"Oh, no you don't. Dinner time. We've done more in the last forty-eight hours than we usually do in a week," she said. "When you get on that damn computer you never quit." Lapinski got up and buttoned his coat, but his smile faltered when Cori asked: "You want to come, O'Brien?"

Finn shook his head.

"Thank you. I'll be fending for myself tonight."

"Okay, I won't be late. If you're asleep, I promise to tiptoe past the couch," Cori said. "Leave the key under the mat if you decide to take off."

"I will," Finn said. "But before you go, I have one more question. Thomas do you know the name of the person who invented Bitcoin?"

"I do. Satoshi Nakamoto," he said. "Why do you ask?"

"Does he have another name?"

"Not that I know of." Thomas helped Cori on with her jacket "Again, why?"

"One of the neighbors saw a man in the Cucas' unit. I've written down the other name he gave me, but I can't remember. All I do remember is that he said it might be the man who invented the Bitcoin."

"Nobody has ever seen him, so I doubt your guy would have a clue what Satoshi Nakamoto looks like," Thomas said.

"The man didn't say it was him. He said whoever he saw was 'said' to be him."

"Call me when you have the name, and I'll run it down. If it turns out to be Satoshi Nakamoto I want to shake his hand when you find him ."

With that, Finn walked them out. He watched until Cori and Thomas were at the bottom of the stairs, and then took a minute to enjoy the soft night air. It was a quiet evening. Lights glowed golden in his neighbor's windows. The stars were bright, and there was a sliver of a moon. He looked at the *Sento,* his landlady's Japanese bathhouse, and thought he might ask her for an hour in the big tub.

As a war bride, her husband had built it to keep her homesickness at bay. When she was widowed and left with a blind daughter to provide for, she had opened the bathhouse to a select group of clients. Since Finn had lived in his apartment, she had welcomed him into the *Sento* to soothe his troubles

Tonight a soak in that bath was an enticing idea, but Finn had no problems to wash away only mysteries to solve. One day he hoped to find the person who took his brother's life. Sooner than that, Finn was determined to put a name to the dead girl from The Brewery, and another to the girl who haunted the top floor of the Cucas' apartment unless they were one and the same—

"O'Brien?"

Finn looked away from the sky where Venus had been winking at him. Cori was at the bottom of the stairs looking up at him.

"Have you sent Lapinski on his way, Cori?" Finn asked.

"He's waiting in the car." She took a step up. Then another. "Look, I wasn't going to say anything 'till it was done, but if I don't say it I won't get a wink of sleep. I'm dog tired and I need my rest, so I'm not going to take any guff from you about this. I'm just going to tell you the way it's going to be."

"Then time to get whatever it is off your chest." Finn turned toward her. He rested his hip against the stairwell wall that ran the length of the walkway, crossed his arms and gave her his full attention. "Sure, I wouldn't want to be responsible for you losing your beauty sleep."

"Stop smirking and cut the deep-dive into the Irish," Cori said. Finn settled his expression into one appropriate to his partner's mood. Cori took a deep breath. "Okay, here it is. I'm going to be late tomorrow 'cause I'm headed out to talk to Bev."

Cori held up a hand, anticipating his objection.

"Look, she's involved in this thing no matter how you look at it. You didn't tell Captain Smith about her, and that tells me you're none too sure how you're feeling about things."

"But—"Finn got no further. Had Cori been a cat she would have arched her back and hissed at the interruption.

"I mean it, O'Brien. I'm sympathetic, mind you. I near lost my mind when Amber got involved in our business and almost got herself killed." Cori shook her head, trying to banish the horrible memory. "Family should never even come close to what we do. I was going to fib and tell you I was going to church, but you wouldn't believe that. And God would damn me to hell if I lied about His house, so this is the truth. I have some questions for Bev, I'm going to ask them, and I'm going to do it alone. Got it?"

"I do, Cori," Finn said, but Cori kept on.

"I mean, I know you can pull rank here. If you want to stop me you can, but it's for your own good." She tossed her hair. She pushed her hands into the pockets of her jacket and stared him down. "So, you can talk now, but it won't change anything."

"'Tis kind of you to let me know how it will be."

Cori opened her mouth. She was still leaning into the next step, ready to take it if she had to get in his face. When it dawned on her that there was not going to be a fight, she buried her disappointment behind a flare of her nostrils, a lick of her lips. She pulled her shoulders back. She looked majestic.

"Well, you're welcome." Her head snapped down. Her eyes cut away from his. Finn tried not to laugh as he waited to see what would come next.

"Yeah, well, that's it."Cori turned away, went down the stairs, and started toward Thomas's car.

"Cori." Finn called to her before she was halfway across the lawn.

"What?" she snapped as she turned back around.

"I remembered the man's name. Ding Xiang. Tell Thomas."

"Sure. Whatever."

With that Cori was gone, and Finn knew she hadn't heard him. That was fine. She deserved to enjoy her victory. Thomas opened the door for her, waving back at Finn after she was safely in the car. Finn waved too.

There was no question that Cori was a friend for life. She was wrong about Beverly and her impact on him, but she was right that it would be better if he did not do the follow up. Woman to woman might get further than ex to ex. It wasinformation Finn wanted, and he didn't care how it came to them.

Leaving the night to itself, Finn went back inside, cleared away the empty beer cans and nuts. He put the folded sheets on the couch. Everything was in order but he wasn't tired enough to turn in, so he got his jacket and left the apartment. He paused after he closed the door, and then put the key under the mat. You never knew what might drag you away in the dead of night, and he never wanted to leave Cori out in the cold.

* * *

"So what happened?" Lapinski asked as he drove toward Maria's.

"Nothing," Cori said.

"Well, that's good."

"Yeah." The light from the street lamp shined softly on Cori's hair. Lapinski thought she looked beautiful; Cori was only thinking about Finn. "He turned a corner, Lapinski. All that talk about being over Bev wasn't bull."

"Now you don't have to worry about him," Lapinski said. "You can concentrate on us."

"What?" she said, clearly not thinking about Lapinski and an 'us' as she squinted into the oncoming headlights.

"Just wondering what you were thinking about," he said.

"Sorry, nothing really. Finn asked me to ask you about someone, and I can't remember the name."

"Brain dead," he said as he took her hand. "You need food."

"You're a gem, Lapinski." Cori gave his hand a squeeze and then let it go. "Drive on."

"My pleasure, Anderson," he said.

Her stomach grumbled. Lapinski smiled; Cori didn't. They were thinking the same thing, that all felt right with the world. The difference between them was that Thomas Lapinski was looking forward to things getting better still while Cori Anderson was wondering how long it would all last.

CHAPTER 15

According to Finn's mother, the middle of the week was the time to be prudent. When he was small, there was no television, no staying up late, and no midnight snacks on a school night. When homework was done, Finn and his brothers and sisters would go to their prayers and beds.

He could not argue that this was not a 'school night'. It was Wednesday, middle of the week, but his ma was nowhere near Mick's Irish Pub and he was old enough not to have any homework. So Finn O'Brien was wearing out his welcome at the dartboard. He had a Guinness in one hand and the last dart in the other. He bent his knees, held his right hand near his brow, and teased those watching.

"'Tis headed for the *Little Audrey*," he called as he feigned his throw.

"In your dreams, O'Brien," hooted a deep baritone voice.

"Throw already." A woman said, but her chiding was all in fun.

"Here it comes." Finn rocked. He let the shaft fly straight and sure until, at the last moment, it deviated a millimeter to the ring and bounced off. There was a collective groan, a spattering of applause, and a lot of laughter.

"Sure, I was robbed." Finn threw up his arms. "'Tis a London's 5 board. Geoffrey, what happened to the Irish Black that used to be here. Geoffrey!"

Finn pushed through the weeknight crowd. He was still chuckling when he slid onto a barstool next to Gretchen. Beautiful, tall, dark haired and eyed, she was a firefighter and a regular at Mick's. Gretchen was a woman used to pressure, and one who believed that all the boredom of the job was worth the one moment she saved a life, a home, or a business. Her work was a calling, and she never considered another path. Her father and his father before her had done the same.

"O'Brien, don' you be blamin' de new board," Geoffrey said. "You be givin' Mick's a bad rap if you sayin' de board be bad. Everybody be losin' now and again."

"I guess you wouldn't believe me if I told you I threw the game would you, Gretchen?" Finn gave her his best smile.

"Not on your life," she said. "But I'll buy you another round as a consolation prize."

"That is kind, but if I have one more I'll be asleep on this stool."

Finn took another drink, and saw he had two more good swallows before he would call it a night. He put it aside to make it last a bit longer.

"O'Brien, he be havin' a big case." Geoffrey put all his weight behind the word 'big'. When Finn saw the twinkle in his eye, he knew what was coming next. "He be seein' de ex-wife, and it weren't no picnic."

"Ah." Gretchen gave Geoffrey a knowing look and offered Finn a sympathetic smile. "Still nursing that broken heart, Finn?"

"As much as Geoffrey would like you to think so, no," Finn said. "And I'd like barman to keep his opinions to himself."

"No opinion." Geoffrey shook his head and those dreads swayed on his shoulders. He had changed his beanie to an elegant black knit. "Love be love. It don' go away easy. I say dat don' matter. Not how many you love, just dat' you be true to the one you wit. You not wit her, you don' be true."

"Love the one you're with, Geoffrey, that's how the song goes. I'll have another." Gretchen slid her glass across the bar, leaned into Finn, and whispered. "It's Coke. I've had a long day too."

Geoffrey went to fill her glass. She rested her chin on her upturned hand and with the other pulled her long hair over her shoulder. A small scar ran through her right eyebrow. Her nails were short, her hands were strong but delicate looking. Finn had seen her dressed for work. He preferred her this way, in her jeans and a flowery shirt of some billowy material.

"Do you believe that? Love the one you're with?" Gretchen asked.

"I fear I am a romantic. I'm wanting a woman to watch my back for all eternity." Finn drained his glass. "But my ex was not the one. Still, my heart longs for the happy ending and holds out hope it will come."

Gretchen chuckled. "After all this time, how could I have missed that you believed in rainbows and unicorns?"

Finn swiveled on his stool. The woman deserved a man's full attention, especially for a conversation like this.

"And what about you, miss?" he said. "Rainbows or fireworks?"

"They both fade away before you want them to, so that's

a false choice. But let me think," Gretchen said. "Okay, here goes. I love a good burst of fireworks now and again, but they need to be few and far between to be appreciated. The rainbow? Every girl wants the rainbow."

She raised her chin to indicate her naked ring finger.

"I had it once. Didn't work out. I wouldn't turn down the chance to try again."

"But..."

Finn urged her on but before Gretchen could answer, a roar erupted from the back of the pub. Someone called to Finn to check out the bulls eye the woman with the cheeky laugh had tossed. Finn smiled and waved, but he did not want to end the conversation with Gretchen. He always had an appreciation for her beauty and an admiration for her calling, but now he saw her character. He knew she was smart, but now he understood that she was thoughtful. She was quiet, but she could speak her mind.

"The topic was rainbows, I believe." Finn let his hand drop to the bar. His finger tapped the top of her hand.

"Well, if you really want to know the truth, I am somewhere between you and Geoffrey. I'm a practical kind of girl. If I'm going to have a man home with me, I want him to be the kind who will linger in the morning and kiss me before he leaves. If he says he will call, I want him to follow through. If he won't then he doesn't have to say anything, and I appreciate the time we had together," Gretchen said. "So I will settle for a little bit of the rainbow and hope there are a few Screaming Mimi's thrown in for good measure. In the end, it's the choice that matters. I hope I choose well."

"I'm thinking you deserve more, Gretchen."

She picked up his hand and laced her fingers through his. She looked at the coupling, smiled, and then raised her lovely dark eyes to him and said:

"That's exactly what I'm talking about, Finn. You just gave me a little of that rainbow."

"You're an easy one to please."

"You might change your mind if you gave me a whirl," she teased. "I may surprise you."

"I may surprise myself."

Ten minutes later Finn paid the tab. Geoffrey saw them off. As Finn walked with Gretchen to her apartment, he was very happy that he had left the key under the mat.

* * *

Emi kept her eyes down, but slid them toward her husband now and again as if expecting something to happen. Anger? Fear? Sadness? Frustration? She saw nothing out of the ordinary. He worked as he always had: diligently, lovingly, brilliantly.

It was a day and a night again. They were in the workshop, side by side, creating the things that made them rich and now caused them grief. It seemed a lifetime ago that the police had come, and yet an instant; it seemed a dream, and yet all too real. But Enver acted as if their problems had nothing to do with him. It was as if the police had not questioned him like they would a common criminal. It was if a girl had not died in this very house. As if those horrid people with their sick play acting had not soiled their home. It was as if that man—the jellyfish—had not gone upstairs to finish what he started, and take what belonged to him.

Enver had slept for the night and most of the day; Emi could not. When he wakened, he ate and went to the workroom, reminding Emi that they had orders to fill. Two companions had to be finished by the end of the week. The first was near completion. She was one of their best. Her long blonde hair was fashioned into loose braids. She had smaller breasts than were usually requested. Emi took great care with the companion's femur to make sure it attached to the hip properly. It was imperative that the hips moved smoothly. When they did Emi felt a surge of pride. She had, indeed, done something no one else ever had; she had created a joint that moved better than a human's. She had made a 'skin' that contracted and stretched like that of a young girl. All this would have brought them millions of dollars; it would have kept them secure their entire lives. Now Emi wasn't sure what she could do with these things she had made. She wasn't even sure she could continue working with Enver. Emi sealed the companion's skin permanently, so that the seam could not be seen with the naked eye. She had not even shown this technique to the jellyfish man.

Enver was working on the second one now. He painted the eyes—his masterful signature. His face was so close to his work that it almost seemed he might kiss the thing. Emi turned her head away because if he did she would be sick. What he was working on wasn't a woman. It wasn't even a companion. It was silicone stretched over a face and skull made of plastic and metal. It rested on a satin pillow, the back of the skull exposed, the head hairless.

Emi sighed and pulled a metal foot, ankle, fibula and tibia in front of her. She arranged them just so, fiddling with her unique joint. It was a puzzle to figure out how to integrate the leg joint to meet the client's specifications. The man wanted his doll to stand pigeon-toed, her pretty little feet turned inward like a child's. It was not for her to tell the client that it wouldn't be possible. It was for Emi to figure out how to make it so that the companion could stand in the way he wished.

The bright lights of the workroom shined on the table. Behind them the finished companions hung on their metal rods. The boxes of limbs were back where they had been before the police searched the workroom. She could hear the 3D printer laboring to build a breastbone. The police had found nothing to interest them, as Emi knew they wouldn't. They made Enver open the locked closet on the second landing. They closed it when all they saw was a companion sitting in the corner on a chair. Emi heard one officer say he was going to have nightmares after seeing her in the shadows. The other one said he wouldn't mind getting locked in the closet with her. The first one said the other man was sick. The second laughed as if there was something funny about all this.

Emi was happy that Enver had not heard this exchange. Even she, for whom the companions had long ceased to hold any allure, was angered by the men's attitudes. There was no recognition of the art only of the prurient thing the art represented. The officers closed and locked the door. They returned the key. They had no idea what they were looking for much less what they were looking at.

All these things were in Emi's brain, but she would not speak of them. Instead, she opened her mouth to chatter as she normally would, but Enver spoke first.

"You should go to bed now. Finish in the morning."

"I'm fine," Emi said. "I'll wait for you."

Emi tightened a screw, and lay a skin over it. She ran her finger down the appendage to see if the new screw could be felt through the skin. It was as smooth as silk. Her hands were steady. That was a good thing.

"Go downstairs," Enver said.

His wife straightened, no longer hunched over her work, and looked at him. He had not raised his voice, but she had heard something different. His rage had shaken him more than the meeting with the police. His anger frightened him more than the blood on his shirt, more than the dead woman. All of it had come as no surprise to Emi. His emotion was a long time coming, and now she wasn't sure what ground she stood upon. She started to object, but thought better of it.

"Alright."

She put aside her tools, and left the leg on the table, careful not to change the angle of the ankle. She could pick up the work in the morning without having to readjust it. Emi slid off her stool and unbuttoned her smock. She put it on the hook where it had hung since the moment they had moved into this space.

"Shall I leave you coffee downstairs?"

He shook his head. She hesitated, casting about for something she could comment on to engage her husband. Before she could find it, he stood to his full height, and put his paint brush down. To Emi's surprise, he took her in his arms. His embrace was not warm. He was not in need of her comfort or her counsel. This was a gesture of partnership, of understanding, of resignation, and solidarity. It implied a promise not a conspiracy.

"We'll see the lawyer and find out what we must expect. We have rights," he said.

Emi nodded. Her cheek moved against a chest that felt hollow. Emi knew she should accept what he had to give; she knew better than to push her husband. And yet she couldn't help herself. The words came out .

"We need to talk about her."

"No, no need. It's done. I am sorry, but it's done."

"No," Emi said. "But...she..."

Enver let her go, and returned to his work. His big hands picked up the small brush, the bristles of which were no thicker than an eyelash.

"Enver." Emi put her hands on his back.

He shook his head. Emi patted his back. He shook his head again, but harder than the first time. She made fists and pounded on his back.

"What about when he comes back," Emi said.

"He won't." Enver shook her off.

"He will." Emi heard her voice rise and felt her fists pound harder. She could never hurt Enver, and yet she was striking him. "You would. He will. They will find out what she did, what you did."

Enver turned on her, and grabbed her wrists. He said nothing. Her words hung between them. It was too soon for him to think clearly, but at least he had made a plan. They would talk to a lawyer. It didn't matter what they felt, only what they could do.

"Enver?" Emi said, the question a plea for his attention.

Enver let her go, turned away, and continued his work. Emi stood behind him, watching for a moment as he added a touch of pale blue to the brown eye just near the iris. Enver knew when his wife left the room, but he gave no notice. Instead, he considered the face he was creating. It was, indeed, beautiful, but the companion would never be all it could. Not this one, not any other one from this time on, and that was sad.

Enver put down the paintbrush, picked up a rag, and wiped his hands until they were very clean. Then he washed his hands and dried them. He was tired, but he couldn't bring himself to go to Emi. Before he went to sleep, though, before he turned out the light, he would check on her. He would reassure her that everything would be all right. He walked through the workroom and down the first flight of stairs. The last thing he wanted was her to be afraid, because he was afraid enough for them both.

CHAPTER 16

The last time Cori drove to Newport Beach was when she and Amber had a girls day out. The plan was to treat themselves to a fancy lunch and buy the cheapest thing at an expensive store. After that, they would head home to giggle about how the other half lived. Things didn't turn out quite as planned. The clothes and food were way overpriced, and the women overly thin, blonde, rich, and arrogant. Cori got tired of their side-eyes that marked Cori and her daughter as interlopers, but for Amber's sake Cori ignored the slights. Eager to make a commission, the sales ladies didn't care if Cori's wallet was overly stretched. She bought Amber a T-shirt. It cost a half days wages; the fancy burger lunch cost her the other half.

Still, the experience was not lost on Cori's daughter. Amber came away with a new appreciation for the hard earned dollar. That lesson was underscored after her boyfriend took a powder when she got pregnant. Amber even apologized for pressing her mother into buying her the shirt. The good news was that Amber was still wearing that T-shirt all these years later.

Now Cori was heading to Newport for another girl's

day out. Today her time would be spent with Beverly O'Brien. She slung one arm over the steering wheel, yawning as she inched along in traffic. Last night between the burrito/taco/enchilada combo, Cori told Lapinski about her task. While they waited for the flan, Thomas looked up the address Bev had provided, and his whistle said it all. He turned his phone her way, and Cori was impressed. When he dropped her back at Finn's, her partner was nowhere to be found. She wouldn't be sharing the news that Bev had made a very soft landing. When it was clear he wasn't coming home, Cori stayed awake a little while longer. At first she wondered if he'd gotten himself into some kind of trouble. Then she concluded the trouble he had found was probably not nefarious, but it was definitely needed.Cori spent another few minutes trying to figure out how she felt about that. Before she could find the honest answer, she fell asleep. For the next five hours she slept like the dead. When she got up, she left a note giving Finn her itinerary ending with an ETA at the office. Now here she was, cooling her jets as a security guard examined her credentials.

"LAPD?" he said.

"That is correct," Cori answered. "I have an appointment with Beverly O'Brien. This is the address she gave me."

The guard, clean-cut and young, held up one finger, and stepped back into whatever shelter he had emerged from. The gate remained closed. Cori ran her fingers across the steering wheel to the beat of *Jailhouse Rock*. She hadn't made it past the jail birds singing before the gate opened. Cori drove onto a half-moon driveway that could park thirty cars on a good night. Since she seemed to be the only visitor, Cori parked smack-dab in front of the huge white house. It looked just as good as it had in Lapinski's picture.

The main structure was two stories. Long, low appendages winged off either side. The building on the right she pegged as a four car garage despite the expert way the doors were camouflaged so as to not break the aesthetic of the architecture. She would love to see what was behind those doors, but the only way that would ever happen would be if she had a warrant. Even then, entry wouldn't be a slam dunk. Whoever owned this place might honor a warrant, but only after an army of lawyers tried to stop its execution.

Cori took her jacket out of the back of the car and put it on, noting the almost surreal quiet. She looked behind her. The gate guard had disappeared again, but Cori had no doubt that she was being watched. Not that it was necessary. First, she was a cop and trustworthy by default. Second, there were cameras everywhere. Third, she was too tired to do anything untoward nor did she have reason to—yet. Cori reached into the car for her purse and headed for the front door, admiring the landscaping as she went.

Giant palms softened the corners of the modern structure. Their leaves were as big as elephant ears. Ferns trailed delicate tendrils along rock walls. Their tips touched a patch of grass here and artfully mounded moss there. Cori appreciated the artistry. It would have been easy to go all fake rocks, a few plants, and a requisite waterfall. Or the designer could have taken a cue from the house and kept everything clean, giving the place no more personality than an operating room. All in all, it looked perfect from the outside. Then again a lot of rotten things kept their shiny skin far past the discard date, so Cori reserved her final opinion.

All the foliage worked to a higher purpose, making it seem that Cori was standing on a whole lot of land.

Houses that fronted the water in Newport commanded stratospheric dollars, but those dollars didn't necessarily buy much terra firma. She couldn't wait to see how much sand sixty-three million bucks bought.

Cori walked out of the sun and into the shade of the entrance. It was as big as Amber's bedroom. The front door was a stunning one-of-a-kind piece of art, breathtaking if you were into that sort of thing. Cori was a tchotchke kind of girl herself. She preferred things that made her smile at a memory or fancy frames to hold pictures of the people she loved. She liked a little glitter, but she sure didn't want to spend every last cent on it. Although, given what she'd seen of this place, a six figure front door probably didn't mean much to the person who owned it.

Cori rang the bell and heard nothing. That was not unexpected given the size of the house. She passed the time checking out the door. Cast of copper, it had aged to a stunning blue/green patina. The relief sculpture was of vines and outcroppings that reminded Cori of a fancy climbing wall. It stood ten feet tall, but up close she saw there was a break at the seven foot mark. Those seven feet made up the working door, and the break above was a keystone. Cori leaned closer. Under the vines, sitting on the outcroppings, were tiny people. Children...

Before she could determine if those children were fully clothed, the door swung open, and the sight of the brilliantly blue Pacific Ocean smacked her in the face. Hollywood couldn't have done it better. The sky was robin's egg blue and cloudless. It melted into a deep, deep navy at the horizon point. In the middle of the sea, the water turned cobalt blue before it frothed white and ran onto the sand. The sight of it was dazzling, mesmerizing...

"Miss?"

Cori smiled, when she came to her senses.

"Makes you believe in God, doesn't it?"

The maid didn't smile back. The woman was good, but she wasn't that good. She knew what Cori was talking about, but it wasn't her job to be impressed by, covetous of, or in any way seduced by her surroundings. It was also a hanging offense to engage with anyone who came through the door.

"Detective Anderson." Cori did the wallet flip for her and showed her badge. "I'm here to see Ms. O'Brien."

"She's expecting you."

The woman fell back. Cori stepped inside and moved to her right as the maid shut the door. That thing was even more impressive from the back side. The vines seemed to have grown through the copper. The outcroppings on the front were matched by indentations on the back. From this angle, the castings of the children were all spindly legs and little butts. It was as if they were crawling through the door, playing instead of trying to escape.

The maid walked on with Cori trailing behind. While the front of the house was stucco, the back of the house was glass. The interior was a minimalist's dream. Cool and inviting, the great room was furnished with couches and chairs upholstered in ice blue and pale yellow. The floor was marble, warmed by white throw carpets. Those rugs were so big it would have taken ten men to 'throw' them. There were no family pictures on the walls or tables, nothing to give Cori a clue about the inhabitants. There were no paintings which didn't surprise her. Why bother with a Picasso or Renoir when Mother Nature put on such a spectacular display?

"This way, miss."

The maid was standing on a patio. Cori chuckled as

she joined her. *Don't let the rabble linger.* But the detective couldn't resist pausing to look at the structure. The huge glass doors retracted into the walls so that outside was in and inside out. Cori walked inside and out again.

"Nice," she said.

"Yes, miss."

They crossed the terrace and walked down a wide, curving staircase. The mansions on either side of the property were evident, but not intrusive. Cori was being led to the lower patio. There an infinity pool and a Jacuzzi. An outdoor kitchen shared space with couches, a cabana, chairs, lounges, tables and umbrellas. Everything was tasteful, peaceful, and pricey. Below that was the beach where there were more lounges, umbrellas, and kayaks.

Cori heard the maid say 'miss' once more, and knew it was a command to get a move on. No one lingered here without permission. That was one way to keep a house clean. Don't let anyone use it. Cori went on her way, rotating her shoulders under her polyester blazer. It was getting hot. She would give anything to have a beer and a dip in that pool.

She caught up with the maid who had stopped and was raising her hand at waist level. The woman was a master of understatement. Cori hoped that she let loose once she got off because working in this place had to be soul crushing. As if on cue, an offshore breeze lifted one of the white linen panels that surrounded the cabana. There was Beverly O'Brien, naked as a jaybird, resting on a round day bed.

"Ms. O'Brien," the maid said.

"I'd recognize her anywhere," Cori answered. "Thanks."

The maid smiled—genuinely this time. Thank you wasn't something she often heard. Cori waited until the woman was well out of earshot before crossing the pool deck. She stopped in front of the cabana.

"Knock, knock," she said.

Bev rolled over and pulled back the curtain. The good news was that she wasn't stark naked. She wore the bottom of a swimsuit so small that Cori wouldn't insult a postage stamp by comparison. The bad news was pretty much the same as the good news.

"Well, well." Bev raised one arm above her head, showing off her beautiful breasts.

"Nice," Cori said.

"Thanks. All natural."

"I know. I've got two of my own, they just take up a little more space than the ones you've got," Cori said. "Not that anyone seems to mind. Do you want to scoot over so we can girl talk here, or shall we find someplace less comfortable."

"You are so quick with that tongue, Cori. I can see why Finn appreciates you."

Cori, bit her lip. If they were on even ground, she would have knocked Bev's pretty teeth clear down her throat for the innuendo. But they weren't on the same footing. Cori had the upper hand. Bev just didn't know it yet.

Bev swung her legs over the edge of the day bed, pushed through the curtains, walked past Cori, and dove into the pool. She came up for air half way down, and went under again. When she finished showing off, Bev got out of the pool and grabbed a fluffy white towel. She draped it over her shoulders and then sat at a table under an umbrella. There was a tall glass filled with something cold waiting for her. It was fresh. The ice hadn't even begun to melt, unlike the maid who had evaporated.

Cori would have laughed if Bev's little show wasn't so pathetic. Keeping a pleasant look on her face, she walked the length of the pool.

"I'd have Katrina bring you something to drink, but you probably want to get right down to business. Sit."

"Don't mind if I do." Cori pulled out a chair, looking around as she took a load off. She could get used to living like this if selling her soul was an option.

"Nice Digs. How'd you get the loan?"

"The owner is a very good friend," Bev said.

"With benefits?"

"Is that an official question?" Bev picked up her drink and took a sip. Then she waved away her own question. "Oh, forget it. Of course with benefits, as if it matters. Or did Finn send you here to find that out."

"No," Cori said. "And he didn't send me."

"I'm surprised he didn't have the guts to come himself."

"Bev." Cori put one arm on the table and leaned in just enough to get the other woman's full attention. "I'm going to say something to you off the record. Finn has more guts in his pinky than you or I will ever possess. Not only that, he's a nice guy. When you are old and grey, when you've had your third face lift, and your all-natural boobs are hanging to your knees, and whoever owns this shanty has kicked you to the curb, you'll be sorry you didn't hang on to him."

Cori sat back, took the purse from her shoulder, and put it on the table. Bev hadn't moved, but Cori saw a flicker of fear in her eyes as her future came into focus. She covered up fast with a pair of fancy sunglasses. Cori took off her jacket. Now they were just two women ready for battle.

"I am curious about something," Cori said. "If this is what you wanted, why marry a cop in the first place? I mean, what did you expect?"

"I didn't expect him to be Don Quixote and tilt at windmills," Bev sniffed. "He could have walked away after he was cleared and had a cush job with a private security firm. He had offers after all that, and he blew it."

"Well," Cori said. "That clears things up. I guess you both landed on your feet then."

"I guess we did," Bev said. "Can we get to it?"

Cori smiled, she took out her notebook and opened it. She also took out her phone and put it on the table. When she looked up again she could see there were water droplets on Bev's lashes. She looked very pretty if you discounted the wrinkles starting around the eyes. Bev's expression was one of resignation, perhaps sadness. Cori hoped hers was unreadable. She was looking forward to surprising Beverly O'Brien.

"I'm glad he's got his head on straight," Bev said. Cori nodded. There might be some hope for Bev yet.

"I'm glad, too," Cori said, and in the next minute hope was gone.

"So what do you want?" Bev stretched out her legs and took a sip of her drink. "I told you everything I know about Cami."

She used the edge of the towel to pat her lashes dry, and then let it fall back to cover her breasts.

"I want to talk about what happened before the party," Cori said.

She picked up her phone and tapped the screen, waited, tapped again and handed it to Bev as a video started to play. The other woman watched all the way through. She sat for another thirty seconds before she put the phone on the table, and pushed it toward Cori.

"Do you want to see again?" Cori asked.

Bev shook her head.

"This was recorded on a Ring doorbell in a unit that

faces the back of the Cucas' unit," Cori said. "I admit it isn't the clearest video, but it works for me. So, do you want to tell me what I'm looking at?"

"I hit her. I pushed her. So what?" Bev shrugged.

"You're on this video assaulting a girl who was killed. You had to be pulled off her. You don't see a problem?"

Cori tapped the screen again and the video played. She held it up.

"You. An Asian man. The victim. I'm out of here as soon as you tell me what you were arguing about and who the dude is?"

Cori stopped the video at the point where Bev pushed the victim. The action froze on the girl falling. Her face was obscured by the man who lunged for her. Sadly, Cori still had no idea what the girl looked like. She had been wearing the same dress when they found her, so it was definitely the victim in the grainy video.

"Come on, Bev. Why waste my time and yours?"

"It's no big deal. I was going into the party, and I heard her laughing," Bev said giving in faster than Cori expected. "I couldn't believe it would be her after the trouble she caused, so I went to check it out. I saw her. I lost it."

Bev pulled her legs up and put her heels on the chair. Her toe nails were polished white. She tugged at the ends of the towel; agitated and unhappy to be talking about the victim. She was also smart enough to know that she didn't have a choice.

"Cami had been at a couple of Asylum parties. Some of the women are friendly with each other, but that's not my thing."

"Are they friendly enough that one of the women would have had an outside relationship with Cami?" Cori asked.

Bev shrugged. "Could be. The ones that come in to-gether are usually into threesomes, or watching if things goes that far. Sometimes they hang with one man in pairs because that's his thing. It wasn't mine. I was looking for someone who wanted a relationship, but open."

"Everyone should have a goal," Cori said.

Bev ignored her.

"You'd have to ask the other women if they knew she was there or if they brought her. If I had to guess, I'd say Cami found out about this party and showed up on her own," Bev said. Seeing that wasn't enough for Cori, Bev went on. "What I know is this: I saw her taking pictures of the men a while back. I must not have been the only one to report her because I heard she was black balled. When I heard that laugh of hers, I couldn't believe she was going to crash an Asylum party—especially this one. It ticked me off bad."

Bev leaned forward and tapped the screen on Cori's phone. The video played. She looked at it for a second and then tapped it again, stopping the action before turning it face down on the table.

"Was she taking pictures of you?" Cori asked. "Is that why you lost it?"

"Lord, no." Bev snorted a laugh and shook her head. "The men pay a lot of money for anonymity, and she didn't care. She was so brazen. So entitled." Bev rolled her eyes. "I thought I'd taken care of the problem, but that guy picked her up like she's something special. I don't know what happened after that. I went inside, and figured that was that."

"Then how did she get upstairs?" Cori said. "Nobody saw her go through the front door."

"How would I know?" Bev said. "I'd never been to that

place before."

"And..." Cori twirled a finger, urging her to pick it up.

"And the party was going the way those things go. The men were getting antsy because whatever was supposed to happen wasn't happening. It was late. I went to the bathroom. I came out. Another girl was waiting to go in, but that's when the crazy guy goes off. We're hanging back, and this girl says 'I hope Cami's okay'. She thought she saw her upstairs when she was looking for another bathroom. She told me not to say anything because we weren't supposed to be up there."

"And you didn't think to stay put considering there were cops all over the place?" Cori said.

"The uniforms were busy," Bev said. "I thought I'd see for myself what Ms. Cami was up to. If I'd known you were up there, I wouldn't have gone."

"Who was the woman in the back?"

"They call her The Madam." Cori gave Bev a look, but it wasn't enough to get her to change her tune. "I'm telling you what they call her. Try talking to Asylum. Maybe they give out the girls' real names. I don't know what the protocol is for the women."

"And the Asian guy who had helped Cami after you pushed her around?"

"He's not Asylum." Bev dismissed the question as if it were an insult. "You can spot a player a mile away, and he isn't even close."

"And you're sure you don't know him?" Cori pressed.

"I'm sure." Bev lifted her chin and her eyes narrowed. She was annoyed until she was enlightened. Her head went up and down slowly. "Oh, you think I'm trying to protect him. You don't think he owns this place, do you? Not likely. I do have some standards."

"So who does hold the deed to this place?" Cori asked.

"I figured you already knew since you're a hot shot investigator." Bev unfurled her legs. "It's Jeremiah Stotler."

"Why does that name ring a bell?"

"He is only the biggest name in PG films. The man makes billions. Did you see that front door?"

"Yes," Cori said, still not getting it.

"Didn't you ever take your kid to see *The Baby Jungle* movies? That front door is masterpiece; it's an *homage* to those movies."

"I hated those movies, and so did Amber," Cori said.

"But you bought a ticket like a billion other people," Bev said. "So I guess you could say you're paying my rent."

"Was Cami trying to move in on you?" Cori asked.

"Hardly a move on me. I saw one of the other girls try to make a move on her, and Cami made her cry. And if she put the moves on Jeremiah, he would have turned her down. He may make movies for kids, but he doesn't screw them. I don't know how old she really was, but Cami was a brat."

Bev took a minute. She drummed her fingers on the table.

"Look, she was a blackmailer. Her greatest joy in life was ruining people. I heard she tried to shake down a televangelist. I don't know if it's true, but rumor has it he paid her big bucks not to out him about Asylum."

"So Stotler is Asylum?"

"He is. That's where we met," Bev said. "We were already seeing each other when Cami set her sights on him. He took her threats seriously, so I did too. All those mommies and daddies would be upset if they found out how he was spending his free time. Not to mention the fact that this info would come on the heels of the scandal with that little girl who starred in *Girl Fun Two*. She was turning tricks on the side. Granted she was eighteen..."

"I thought she was twelve," Cori said.

"So did the guys she was doing." Bev rolled her eyes and smirked. "But that's not the point. The point is, Jeremiah is the final word in wholesome family films. All that politically correct outrage could bring him down like that."

Bev snapped her fingers, pushed aside her drink, and dropped her feet to the hot concrete. She worked her towel like a puppet pulling its own strings as she leaned forward.

"I'm exactly where I want to be, Cori. I wasn't going to let that stupid girl ruin it all just so she could get off."

"And the man who tried to intervene?"

"I told you, I don't know who he is and I don't care. He just kept whimpering like a girl and fretting. It was disgusting. What kind of man acts like that?"

"You got me," Cori said. "I wouldn't know how to whimper if you paid me."

"Are we done?" Tired of the interrogation, Bev sat up straight in her chair. She cocked an eyebrow at Cori.

"One more thing. I'd like to talk to the man of the house," Cori said.

"He's at work."

"Then I guess that's where I'll have to see him." Cori stood up and draped her jacket over her arm. Bev got up too, suddenly serious and surprisingly sweet.

"Cori, don't screw me if you get in to talk to Jeremiah. Okay? Say you heard about Cami from someone else. I mean, he's the one that filled me in on her. I don't know if he meant me to keep it to myself or not."

"The police don't volunteer information," Cori said. "But you made a good call telling me what you know.

After all, you're the only one that we can prove laid hands on a dead woman."

"You've got to be kidding," Bev threw her head back and laughed. "Did you see how I looked when I walked into that room? I looked like a star, not a hair out of place."

"You did," Cori said. "But then again you're a pretty good actress."

"Wow, a compliment," Bev said.

"Yeah. You should have got an academy award for acting like a wife."

Cori saw herself out.

CHAPTER 17

"She's got a name."

Finn snapped his fingers against the paper in his hand. It had been two days since he and Cori had a chance to catch up. Cori moved out of Finn's apartment, and Thomas helped her put her house back together. Finn had been in court and also managed a final interview with the Fernandez family who seemed to be missing a son. Finn suspected the young man of a drive-by killing under the colors of The Locos. Strangely, no one knew where he was now. Cori made a detour to Wilshire Division. She filled in Detective Porter who had taken two of her cases when she and Finn were lent out. Finn testified at a parole hearing of a serial rapist who he put away well before his own troubles. Had he been relieved of his duties, he still would have attended this man's parole hearing. Finn intended to see the man die in prison. But right now, The Brewery problem was top of mind and the news was good.

"We've got a name and picture."

He got up from his desk to stand behind Cori's chair. He spread the paperwork in front of her, the victim's picture front and center.

"Pretty."

Cori picked up the photo. The girl's face did justice to the body Cori had seen in the morgue. She was petite. Her hair was long and dark. Her face was delicate and there was a Slavic tilt to her eyes. Her cheekbones were razor sharp and her lips full. Sadly, for all her physical beauty, she wasn't a beautiful girl. There was an underlying cruelty in her that was evident to Cori. She shuffled through other pictures in the file.

"She was hanging with an impressive crowd. This is the Met Gala. " Cori pointed to a copy of an article from the New York Times. "How old is she?"

"Nineteen," Finn answered. "Her name is Roxana Masha Novika."

"That's a mouthful."

Cori looked up intending to have a full conversation with Finn. What she saw were two other detectives far too interested in their business.

"Let's get some coffee." Cori took her laptop while Finn took the file. Both preferred the break room to the bullpen.

There was a Naugahyde sofa in the room. One arm was silver where a rip had been fixed with electrical tape. There were threemismatched chairs, a round table, and a stool. Today there was nothing to eat, but the coffee was fresh. Finn got two mugs while Cori pulled Roxana's information up on the screen.

"Homeland Security came through. She had a global entry and with an asterisk to keep an eye on her," Finn said. "She holds dual Citizenship. Russian no less. From the looks of her passport she started traveling before she was out of diapers. What have you got?"

"If the mayor wasn't getting flack from the Asylum

people, he would get a call from the State Department. Her father's a big name in Russia. An oligarch, if you please. Oil guy," Cori said. "Her name should have been Evita."

"She's dead too," Finn said. He put two mugs of coffee on the table and pulled out a chair.

"She's no Evita anyway. She wasn't riding daddy's coattails." Cori took up her coffee and had a sip. She looked stone faced at her screen. "When I was nineteen I was knocked up, and wondering if I would be struck dead if I wore white at my shotgun wedding. This one's been profiled in W, Vanity Fair, Wired and a zillion more places. She gets her suntan in Italy, skis in the Alps, and the little miss is a top tier influencer."

"A what?"

"Like a movie star without the movie," Cori said. "Her job is to look beautiful, and make other people think that they will be beautiful and rich if they do as she does. She sets the standards, she sells the dream."

"And who pays her to do this?"

"I'll show you." Cori pulled up Instagram and found Roxana's page. Finn raised a brow at the pictures of the girl in her bed, in the bath, standing atop a skyscraper, posing with a bottle of pills. She smoked. She had a drink. Always there was a product or two somewhere about.

"She was taking drugs on social media?" Finn pointed to the latest picture.

"No. Look at the caption. *Daily Dose.* She's pitching a weight loss drug. Companies pay to have these kids tout their products. Then they get on YouTube, Instagram, Facebook all the social media sites and other people follow them. The more followers you have, the more money you get. It's huge business. This one could buy and sell us ten times over even without daddy's money."

"For doing nothing?"

"Pretty much. But Roxana was more than a pretty face hawking fashion if we can believe Bev." Cori scrolled down. "She's calling out some big names here. She's insinuating all sorts of things about the executives or their companies. Fraud, cheating. She does it so sweetly. I can see why Bev didn't like her. I can see why Stotler would be afraid of her."

"I would be," Finn said. "Even a lie is taken as God's truth on these sites."

«Lapinski has been picking up slander and liable cases because of this, but suing can make it worse. Bad press can't be buried anymore." Cori sat back and took a deep breath. "It's a brave, new, ugly world, my friend."

"But if she was making so much money advertising for companies, why bother with blackmail?"

"Because she could. Because it's an experience. Because she's a mean girl and high school is now the whole world." Cori crossed her arms. "It's hard enough being young, but kids have been brainwashed. They think that everything online is real. They're ashamed if they don't have what those people have. They look for guidance online, they look for relationships. They think this chick is showing them real life. Meanwhile, normal kids are losing their minds because they aren't rich or famous and influence no one."

"And the ones doing the influencing are bored, or so afraid to lose it all that they take risks?" Finn said."Are you thinking this one went too far?"

"I would say so," Cori answered. "Or maybe she was branching out. Trying to position herself as a social justice warrior. That would be a good little scam. If they don't pay she gets kudos and more followers for calling these men out; if they do pay she's richer and gets perverse kicks out of their fear."

"It probably never crossed her mind that adults can play dirty too," Finn said. "Now we need to find out which adult decided to take her out of the game."

"Cross Bev off the list," Cori said. "I'm serious. No worries there."

"I know. The video is damning, but it was a school yard rumble. She couldn't have wielded a weapon with that much force and not have a speck of blood on her."

Finn shuffled the papers. He handed Cori a copy of a crime scene photo. It showed the plastic, numbered tents that marked where the techs found blood spatter.

"On the window. The blood is seen at five and six feet. On the right it would have sprayed the same height, but there was a person standing on that side. The person with the weapon would have had blood on their torso, hands, and on their face unless they were covered in some manner. The spatter is here." He pointed to the right. "—and here." He pointed to the left. "But not here". This time he pointed to the space parallel to the victim's head where the perp would have stood blocking the curtain.

"Is there anything in that file on the blood analysis?" Cori asked.

"Only that it was all the victim's. Either she was sleeping and someone came quietly upon her, or it was someone she knew and she wasn't fearful." Finn said. "If she was as arrogant as Beverly says, the girl might have ignored a person she thought was of no consequence."

"Wasn't that just a mistake and a half," Cori said, as she lounged in her chair. "Let's not forget the dress from the dumpster. I know they'll find her blood on it. I can feel it in my bones."

Finn motioned to Cori's cup as he got up. She handed it to him, and he put both in the sink and rinsed them out.

"What can that garment tell us?" he asked.

"Nada, at this point," Cori said. "It was big enough to fit an average size man or woman. It was a unisex design. It could have been a dress, might be a man's tunic. No buttons, no zipper, no labels. Nothing to tell us where it came from. Nice design on the fabric, though. Kind of like a Pollock painting."

"I suppose one of the women could have worn it to the party and changed into her costume," Finn said.

"Possible, but doubtful. I've got two corroborating witnesses that say no one left the Asylum party, so none of them tossed this in the trash. There were a few coats for cover up, but everyone swears they came dressed as they were to party. Now, that doesn't mean one of them wasn't there earlier, did the deed, and tossed the tunic. Time of death isn't an exact science," Cori said.

"Did Paul give you a time?" Finn asked.

"He thought the window was no more than three hours," Cori said.

"I think it wasn't so long. The blood pools weren't congealed. We aren't talking hours," Finn said.

"There's the woman who was with Bev in the back of the room while Enver was doing his thing." Cori breathed deep, and put two fingers to her eyes. She let her head fall back as she rubbed them. Finally, she dropped her hand on the table. "Bev managed to get upstairs without officers Hunter or Douglas seeing her. It's possible the other woman could have done the same. Maybe she wrapped this dress—for want of a better word— stashed it and tossed it on her way out."

"Cori, my head's going to explode," Finn said. "'Tis the

Mad Hatter's tea party we're looking at, Alice is dead, and the Caterpillar is hiding in plain sight."

Cori clapped. "Nice, O'Brien. Very literary."

"I have my moments." Finn looked up to check the clock on the wall, but all he saw was Detective Walters, a huge block of a man, crossing their path. He poured himself a cup of coffee, and when he came back he paused to look over Finn's shoulder at the file

"That the chick from The Brewery?" he asked.

"That's her," Cori said.

The man nodded slowly, and then reached between them to shuffle the papers with one chunky finger. He came to the pictures of the crime scene, cocked his head, and considered them.

"Asylum thing, huh?" he said.

"That's correct," Finn said.

"They had some trouble in '06."

"What kind of trouble," Finn asked.

"Sexual assault," Walters said slowly. "Charges were dropped. The accused was on the Board of Supervisors. It could have been ugly."

"We'll check it out. Thanks," Cori said. Walters' head went up and down. He was still looking at the photos.

"Could be a snuff thing," Detective Walters said. "You know, a snuff thing."

With that he ambled out of the break room and headed to the bullpen. Finn raised a brow, and Cori a shoulder.

"Never crossed my mind," Finn said.

"Me neither," Cori said.

"After talking to Ali Keyes I'm not thinking it would be a consideration, but you never know," Finn said. "Not that we have time to think about it now. Bev's gentleman is allowing us fifteen minutes. Two-thirty sharp or we're banished from the lot according to the dragon who guards the man's lair."

Cori closed her computer. Finn picked up the file. He gave the picture of the victim one more look.

"Influencer." He mumbled, shook his head, and held the door for Cori. "She was very good at her job."

"How would you know," Cori said as she breezed past him.

"She influenced someone into a murderous rage," Finn said. "I'd say that's a job well done."

"Or Walters is on to something? Maybe somebody wasn't satisfied getting their rocks off the traditional Asylum way."

"Or we don't have the foggiest, Cori," Finn said. "But when we figure it out I have a feeling it's going to be stranger than even Detective Walters could imagine."

One pit stop, a phone call to Amber, a heads up to the desk officer, and Finn and Cori walked out of East L.A. Division. They got into Finn's car. Cori took shotgun. Finn got behind the wheel. Another day, another dollar. The sun was shining, and the freeways were packed. It was business as usual in Los Angeles, except the city was minus one naughty little angel. Sadly, Finn and Cori were having a devil of a time figuring who took her out.

CHAPTER 18

'Tis odd.

It's creepy.

Cori and Finn spoke out of the sides of their mouths, though there was no need to keep their conversation private. The woman leading them through the parking lot would not have known what they were talking about if they screamed it to high heaven. In fact, Mr. Stotler's secretary was paying so little attention she probably didn't even know what they looked like.

It wasn't that she was ungracious. Nor did she appear at odds and ends. She was simply more efficient than a human being had a right to be. Not a wasted gesture nor word; not an ounce of curiosity. The secretary turned them over to Mr. Stotler's assistant. He was a handsome young man who was equally efficient. Thankfully, he had a slight sparkle about him. One day he would be the man with an assistant, but today wasn't the day.

The young man took them through a building where long halls sprouted like well-placed limbs off a mighty tree. Office pods were full to bursting with agitated people.

Desks were piled with paperwork. Phones rang off their proverbial hooks. Computer screens pulsed. The group met their mark in another reception area. A woman teetering on the edge of forty whisked them to a spot outside a hangar-like building. The fortyish woman was of no consequence since she had neither name nor moniker. She waited with them, asking after their health as she scanned the lot looking for the next hand-off.

It was there, in front of the barn doors, that Cori and Finn were given over to Mr. Stotler's most important associate. She was a tall, willowy woman who looked like Beverly O'Brien's clone at first glance. Her hair was short and white blonde. She was slim of hip, broad of shoulder, and possessed of perfect posture. At second glance, this was no Bev. This woman knew the score. No hopes lurked behind her eyes, only raw ambition. She would take what she wanted even if it wasn't offered. She would learn what she could from whoever was on the rung of the ladder above her, and have no compunction about pushing them off if they slowed their climb. Finn appreciated that. He hated to play guessing games with women. That's when Gretchen crossed his mind and he smiled. He should call her and thank her for the fireworks and the rainbow.

"Gray Webster, Mr. Stotler's right hand." She introduced herself without outstretching her own hand.

"Detective Anderson and O'Brien. We have a two-thirty with Mr. Stotler," Finn said.

She checked a very large wrist watch. Her wrist was narrow and the watch hung from it, face down. She twirled it right side up.

"It's two twenty-two. I'm going to walk you through the sound stage. Don't touch anything. I'm sure you don't have to be told, but we often get visitors who want a souvenir of their visit. Please stay close to me. The set is closed today. Mr. Stotler is conferring with some of the craftsman. As you can imagine, a set like ours is incredibly sophisticated. Lots of moving parts. Any difficulties can set us back days, and that is unacceptable. Even hours can skew the production budget."

Cori and Finn walked on the heels of the Right Hand, keeping their feet on the white arrows, staying within the parallel yellow lines that defined the one path through the sound stage.

They checked out everything. They would have a fine discussion at Mick's about this place. The intricacy of the lighting, the camera's, the power cords, the touch screens that ran the production, were as intriguing as the set itself. Jeremiah Stotler's front door made sense now. This was *The Baby Jungle set*. The vines, trees, mountains with outcroppings, lakes, streams and waterfalls looked real. This was where the jungle children played.

Cori pointed out the dolls peppered throughout. Finn thought of Enver's 'companions', but these dolls were cherubic and childlike. Instead of being created to quench a man's desire, these were constructed to delight children. They frolicked in their fancy world; far away from the ugly one where young women had their faces bashed in.

"And stop. Please stand here."

The Right Hand pulled up short and Cori almost ran into her. A look communicated her disappointment at Cori's clumsiness. A thin smile spoke to her magnanimity in overlooking it. Gray Webster seemed miffed that the detectives weren't more impressed with their surroundings.

"Where will we be meeting Mr. Stotler?" Finn asked.

"He'll come here as soon as he's finished," Gray said.

"But where will we be having our talk," Finn said.

"I'm afraid with his schedule—"

"We will be as brief as possible —after we sit down," Finn said.

The Right Hand's surprise turned to annoyance. The annoyance instantly became something akin to uncertainty when Finn continued.

"This is an official investigation into a murder, miss. If we cannot find a bit of privacy here, Mr. Stotler will have to reschedule his day so we can speak at the station."

Gray Webster's taut stomach rippled under her tight sweater. It was the only sign that she was amused.

"I thought that only happened in the movies," she said. "Taking someone to the station."

"'Tis known that fiction is informed by fact," Finn said.

With that, the Right Hand did what was best for the left. She escorted them to a small, glass-enclosed room. Inside was recording equipment, but there were also four chairs.

"Wait here," Gray said.

She returned as the hands of the clock struck two-thirty. Her entrance was as impressive the second time as it had been the first. The man that came with her had, Finn was sure, been exactly like her at one time. His posture said he was still an animal on the prowl and ready to take on any challenge to his territory. Yet, having been the king of the jungle for so long, there was also a gracefulness to his manner. He did offer his hand.

"Jeremiah Stotler," he said as he shook those of the detectives.

Finn and Cori gave their names even thoughGray had probably filled him in. In fact, she probably memorized their badge numbers despite the fact that the detectives flashed them briefly her way. The important man took a seat. Gray stood in the corner. It was Finn who gave the introduction, and Cori the overview of the inquiry.

"Mr. Stotler, we're going to be asking some personal questions," Finn said when he took over.

Cori's eyes flitted to the Right Hand who looked back at her. The important man smiled. That said it all. He could count on the Right Hand. Whatever she heard, whatever sins he confessed, would never go beyond this room. She was that loyal. Her loyalty was grounded in the firm knowledge that her boss would destroy her professionally should she disappoint him. Cori's eyes went back to the star of the show.

Jeremiah Stotler was not a classically handsome man, but he did well with what he had. Bev had him beat by an inch or two in height. He was slim, but Cori didn't think it was from exercise. She had a feeling that the man was a very disciplined eater. Age? Between fifty-five and sixty-five. Who knew? His hair was thick and sprinkled with grey. It was neither too short nor too long, too straight nor too wavy. His face was clean-shaven and on the gaunt side. When he smiled, Stotler looked like everyone's favorite uncle. He was the guy you would go to with your worst problems, the man who would make it all okay with mom and dad.

His hands were narrow, his nails manicured. The clothes he wore hung so well it was a sure bet they were bespoke. And then there was Jeremiah's voice. Melodious and clear with the slightest undercurrent of a dictatorial tone.

"I'm sure you've been told that my schedule is tight. If you don't mind, I'll fill in some of your blanks right now. If I miss anything, and we still have time, I'll answer your questions." There was that smile again, but barely a breath was taken before he said, "And if you need follow-up, you can contact Gray. She will put you in touch with my lawyers. McMann, Tate and Tate. You'll be speaking to the general partner, Tom McMann."

Gray gave a slight bow as if honored to be Stotler's pack mule.

"Since that seems agreeable, let's begin. I know a young woman was killed at an Asylum event at The Brewery. Yes, I am a gold seal member of Asylum. I pay $75,000 a year for my membership. That includes all open parties. This was not an open party. I found out about the incident because the Asylum administrators are very thorough. Gold seal members were all notified by Ali Keyes, the owner of Asylum, if anything untoward happens."

Stotler turned his head as if to look over his shoulder. He never completed a full swivel. Gray stepped forward to hand each of them a piece of paper.

"This is Ali's direct number and the address of his private offices. I assume you will be discreet with this information."

Cori opened her mouth to tell him the man in question had been contacted, but Jeremiah Stotler's full attention seemed to have rendered her mute. Finn had the fleeting thought that the man must be a Svengali to have such an effect on the two women in the room. He never raised his voice, nor did it take on a harsh tone. Still, there was nothing more heady than power. He would not stop for anything or anyone, not even for a homeless man being beaten to death as Finn had. He was not a man who would ever be put upon by a crowd of haters. Poor Beverly. How she must have despised that Finn's one moment of heroism had made him a pariah. What she wanted was the hero, the conqueror, the guy in charge. Finn concluded that

Jeremiah Stotler was like the lines painted on the floor of his studio. His life was about his destination, and he never veered from his path. All the riches go to the man with the blinders.

"The evening of the incident was a private affair." Jeremiah said. "As I understand it, the purpose was pleasure while awaiting the unveiling of some new tech. It was held so close to the vest that even Gray could not find out what the product was or who issued the invitation. Beverly was there at my behest. I personally asked Ali to include her."

"Why?" Cori asked, sliding the question into his narrative.

"Because she and I are very close, and I trust her. Because I am a gold seal member. Because she is a beautiful woman who is comfortable with men of means. Because she was smart enough to know what information I needed. I wanted her to find out what was going on."

Jeremiah turned his eyes on Finn. The detective saw nothing special in them.

"Beverly told me as soon as she returned to my place, that her ex had managed to find his way into our orbit. I am assuming this does not create any problems for you or your superiors."

"It does not, sir," Finn responded.

"Very good." Jeremiah looked at his watch. Gray did the same. He continued on. "As for the lady in question. I knew who she was."

"You knew her as Cami," Finn said. His statement appeared to annoy the man.

"No, I knew exactly who she was. Roxana Masha Novika. I did not share this information with anyone, including Beverly. I pledged not to compromise any member in good standing when I joined Asylum. I did not breach that promise until Cami crossed the line. Then I found out who she was."

"So much for anonymity," Cori muttered.

"I'm fortunate to have many resources at my disposal. I can find the information I need about almost anything. A mask and an alias are flimsy defense."

"You can find out anything, except information about what was being revealed at the party," Finn said.

"Except that."

The failure was both disappointing and illuminating. Stotler inclined his head as if humbled. It was an act.

"Roxana was easy," he said. "The girl was a media whore. Her alias was ridiculous. Once I identified her, I understood how dangerous she could be. Those of us who are gold members expect anonymity as do the women who attend. Unless they agree to further interaction outside of the parties. Beverly is in full consent of our relationship, by the way."

Stotler did Finn the courtesy of actually looking his way.

"But to the matter at hand, in all the years I have been with them, that trust has never been broken until she showed up. That young woman abused Asylum members, and I was not the first."

Gray stepped forward and passed another sheet of paper over to Finn and Cori.

"These are the men she compromised. Ali did not know for a long while because these men were fearful for their futures, and retreated quietly. Society, for all its promiscuity, is actually rather puritanical. Once the media gets hold of something salacious, they work up the villagers until the only thing left is to build the scaffold. Those men paid a great deal of money to keep Roxana silent. I do not believe I am breaching a trust since these men are no longer Asylum members. It would be more embarrassing for them should you have to hunt for them," Stotler said. "When Roxana set her sights on me, I refused to be blackmail. She threatened retaliation. I am in no position to have my sexual life paraded before our stockholders. I would have plenty of money should I lose my work, but no amount of money could compensate me for the loss of my position. I have a sincere passion for what I do. I am very good at it. I create fantasy worlds for children. That I prefer a little fantasy in my private life should not enter into the equation, but it would if she followed through on her threats."

"What do you know of her interaction with Ms. O'Brien that night?" Cori asked.

"Beverly told me she confronted Roxana. She also told me she had nothing to do with murdering that woman. I believe her. If she was lying, I would have seen some evidence. When she returned home, she was angry at the situation. She was upset that she could not bring me the information I wanted because the incident curtailed whatever business was to be conducted. Beverly was also upset that you were called upon to investigate. No, Beverly did not have the demeanor of someone who murdered another human being."

"And what steps were you taking to stop Cami from outing you?" Finn asked.

"All legal, all irrelevant." Jeremiah Stotler got out of his chair, smiled and started for the door as he said: "Thank you so much for coming by."

Finn was up before the Right Hand could react.

"Mr. Stotler," Finn said. The man paused, clearly annoyed to be spoken to without permission. "With all due respect, we will call you should we have additional questions. You may call your attorney at your discretion. Thank you for your time now."

His eyes flicked to Gray who stood only steps away. Her cheeks were pale with fury.

"Thank you, Ms. Webster. We'll be seeing ourselves out."

Cori and Finn walked out the way they came in. They did not cross the carefully drawn lines; but the Right Hand and Jeremiah Stotler understood they wouldn't hesitate to do so if it were called for.

CHAPTER 19

"Fifteen minutes on the dot, O'Brien. That's when he got out of his chair. He didn't even look at the clock. And that woman. You wouldn't need air-conditioning on a hot summer night with that one. "

Finn smiled at Cori's riff. There were worse ways to pass the time, and she was right about the movie people. If he had dreams of being a star they would have been shattered when he met Jeremiah Stotler and his Right Hand. He did admire the man's forthrightness, but honesty was the privilege of the wealthy. As was leverage. As was the ability to buy your way out of a problem. As was just about everything else in the world. Still, in this instance, it was a lowly duo like Finn and Cori who had the ultimate power because they cared so little for the Stotler's of the world.

"I don't think I'd be making a trade of Bev for Gray. I'm happy to leave them both to Mr. Stotler," Finn said.

He had one arm draped over the steering wheel and the other rested on the armrest. His eyes were on the traffic. It was flowing well considering it was a few minutes after three on a Thursday afternoon. It had been a toss up to head to Roxana's house or back to the station. In the end they couldn't pass up the chance to learn more about their victim.

"Offramp." Cori pointed to the exit. Finn took it and Cori rolled right back into the conversation. "I'm counting my blessings for good old Lapinski. He chases ambulances for a living and does all right by it, but I wouldn't give one of him for ten of that guy. In fact, I have an old tape of *The Baby Jungle.* The daycare lady told me it was going to be a collector's item. I'm tossing it for sure now."

"Hollywood seems to be nothing more than business. Pity. I was hoping to find the wizard and not a man behind the curtain," Finn said.

"You don't need a heart," Cori said.

"Perhaps a brain?"

"I think you're okay there too." Cori laughed a little.

"Then let's leave Mr. Stotler and the Right Hand behind," Finn said.

"I'll red-line them," Cori said. "If Stotler had anything to do with it, he would have written a check after Gray sent the job out for bid. He would never take Roxana out himself. The man probably doesn't floss his own teeth."

"Blacker than black, that soul of his. He's in good company though. Politicians have the same playbook," Finn said.

Cori shot her partner a glance.

"And Bev?"

"Stotler would hand her over if it were expedient," Finn said. "I'm thinking to advise her to have an attorney on hand in case he turns on her."

"And I'm thinking you've lost your marbles," Cori said. "You didn't cop to the relationship up front, O'Brien. That's one strike and no matter who gets indicted, that's going to be a big deal if they call you to testify. Goes to integrity of the investigation."

"Not if Beverly was a minor player," Finn said.

"Are you kidding?" Cori barked a laugh. "I logged that video into evidence. If she says you advised her on any matter, you're toast. Besides, her beef was more than personal. It was business and you're in the same bind."

"What is it you're implying, woman?"

Finn shot her a glance and she rolled her eyes.

"Can you imagine her testimony if she's called as a witness?" Cori raised a hand and flipped her hair off her face in a poor imitation of Finn's ex. "Well, your honor, I got a great guy with a ton of money and I'm living like a queen, so I really didn't want this little girl messing with my gig. Oh, and my ex? Yeah, he gave me a heads up about getting a lawyer 'cause I guess he was worried I'd be implicated. He might have rearranged some things to protect me. Who knows? Oh, yeah, judge, he's definitely still carrying a torch. He'd do anything to protect me.'"

Finn's laugh started small and got bigger. His head shook as he navigated through Hidden Hills. A year ago Cori would have realized too late that her mimicry hit too close to home. It didn't anymore.

"I was only thinking that she should be prepared, but you're right. Watching out for her isn't my job any longer. Should the need arise, I'm sure Mr. Stotler will see to her legal needs."

"If only to cover his tight little butt," Cori said.

"Definitely. He'll cut her loose the minute it looks like she's a liability. She will understand. Sure, she will," he said."And here we are."

Finn pulled into the driveway of Roxana Masha Novika's house. Her home sat on a hill, the nearest neighbor was more than two miles away. They could see the freeway winding through the hills. It disappeared, reappeared, and vanished again like a lazy river.

Cori slid her sunglasses to the top of her head, pushing her big hair away from her face as she got out of the car. Her blue eye shadow sparkled in the sun. Finn walked to her side and they checked out the modern ranch. The front was plain, but out back there would be nothing but windows to take advantage of the view. Rock was laid like subway tiles framing flowering beds. There were no trees to cut the heat, and no grass to take away from the natural beauty of the hill. The driveway was wide. The detached garage could hold three cars.

"I must have done something wrong in my last life, O'Brien."Cori said. "Good old Roxana did okay for herself."

Finn took off his glasses too. He hooked them over the breast pocket of his leather jacket. He said:

"Except now she's lying on Paul's table, and you're still here," Finn reminded her as he headed for the front door.

Cori went the opposite way. There was a grimy Toyota parked on the side of the garage. She cupped her hands and peered through the window. Good old Roxana may live in luxury, but she sure didn't take care of her car. The interior was more of a mess than the exterior. She seemed to have a taste for Starbucks and fast food hamburgers but an aversion to trash cans.

Cori pivoted and cupped her hands again. This time she put them against the garage window and saw she had been wrong. The cars inside the garage were pristine. The Toyota was an orphan, too ugly to be in the same playpen with the other kids. She walked back to Finn who stood out of the sun under the lattice work that shaded the front entrance.

"There's a throw-away on the side of the garage that's pretty trashed. Inside the garage there's an SUV and a Porsche. There's a space for a third car, but it's MIA. If she drove it to The Brewery, it might still be there. I'll check in with the DMV and see what she's got registered."

Finn rang the bell. A chime sounded throughout the house. No one came to answer the call as expected. Finn made a fist, bent the middle finger, and rapped three times with his knuckle.

"Police," he called.

Nothing.

He rapped once again, but waited no longer than a moment before he followed Cori. They walked over the driveway and down the length of the house. It took Cori a second to figure out how the gate on the side latched, but once she had it they found themselves in a narrow walkway. It was landscaped on one side, and on the other there were trash cans. Finn opened the first can.

"Garden clippings." He replaced the lid and opened the next. "Nothing."

Cori took a gander, but all she saw was the stuff that sticks to the bottom and lives on for eternity.

"It looks like they picked up the trash recen..."

Cori paused. Above them was a window. It was too high for them to see inside the house, but something caught her attention. She put a hand out to Finn and whispered:

"Someone's in there."

She scanned the side of the house as she pulled back in hopes of catching something or someone in the window. Finn motioned and whispered back.

"I'll go 'round front door again—"

That's when they heard a click and a snap. In any other neighborhood it would have gone unnoticed, but the silence was so perfect that the sound of a door opening could not be mistaken.

Cori and Finn went around to the back of the house. There was a pergola that shaded part of a large patio, an outdoor kitchen, a large table for guests and two smaller ones next to oversized chairs.

The patio was paved with Spanish tiles. They matched the ones framing the rectangular pool. The layout drew the eye to the view. Finn's gaze went to the fruit orchards, terraced gardens, valley and the freeway beyond. It was an idyllic backyard but one thing was out of place— the man hunkered in front of the sliding door trying to pull it shut.

"Can we help you with that?" Finn said.

The question was as good as a shot. The young man threw himself up and back, stumbling into the wall of glass behind him. His eyes were wide. The color drained from his face, and his mouth opened in a prelude to a scream. He was not attractive, and he wasn't quite a man. Tops he had twenty-one years on him, but Cori doubted he'd seen much sunshine in all his days. His skin was pasty, his hair was lusterless, and he looked like he may be having a heart attack. Cori took a step forward. Finn was ahead of her by two, putting his hand inside his jacket to retrieve his badge when the man bolted.

"Hey!" Finn lunged for the man, but it wasn't going to be that easy.

The guy was fast and quick. Finn knew that those things were not one and the same. He was quick to build up his speed, and that's when it was obvious he was also going to be fast. To make matters worse, he was sure footed. That last meant little in the first hundred yards when he was flying past the pool and over the terraced lawn, but when he hit the hill Finn knew he had his work cut out for him.

Behind him, Cori sprinted past the trashcans, through the gate, and back to the car. She got inside and hit the ignition before the door closed. The tires squealed on the bricked drive and the car bucked as she shot back to the road. Instead of heading back to the main drag, Cori went down the hill, toward the freeway. Once that guy got to the bottom of the hill he had two choices: try to outrun Finn in the valley or get to civilization and lose himself. Cori bet on civilization.

The road she was on was seldom used, its only purpose was to serve utility vehicles. Cori's unmarked vehicle was no less sturdy than the black and whites. She took the bumps and grinds until she turned onto the dirt access road. There she took a hard hold of the steering wheel. When she came to a stop in a cloud of dust under the arched overpass it was just in time to see Finn give the chase his all.

He closed the gap between himself and the running man. He had discarded his jacket. His t-shirt was sweat-soaked. His arms pumped, his powerful legs pounded over the terrain as he gained an inch, a foot, and then the man made a mistake. Before he reached the hard, even ground under the freeway he looked behind him to see how close Finn was and lost his momentum to indecision. Finn had no such handicap. He saw nothing but the man ahead of him, thought of nothing but taking him down. When he made his move Cori got out of the car to help, but all she had to do was give her partner a wide berth.

As always it was something to see. Finn was a powerful man who was graceful when resolve was the final key to winning the day. He leapt, arms out, hitting the running man's back with his own shoulder for maximum impact. The man went down and Finn's arms went around him.

They rolled twice. Like the runt of the litter, the man landed on his back and put his hands up to show the alpha dog there was no fight in him. Finn straddled him, pinning his legs. Both men did nothing more than breathe hard for a moment. Finn looked over his shoulder at the hill and then back to the man on the ground.

"'Tis a long run," he said. "Wouldn't it have been easier to talk to us?"

"I don't know who you are."

Cori stepped forward, hunkered down, and held her credential up.

"We're cops," she said.

"I didn't do anything wrong," he wailed.

"Then you better tell us what it was you were doing up there because to us it looked like breaking and entering. That will put you in a cell faster than slop goes through a hog," Cori said.

Cori and Finn exchanged a glance. There was nothing like a threat with no teeth. Even if they arrested this guy, he would be back on the street in no time flat with the way the courts were backed up. The detectives didn't have to worry about being found out, the man was unconcerned. He put his arms down and balanced on his elbows, giving a nod to Finn.

"Do you mind, man? You're cutting off my circulation."

"You going to be giving me a chase again?" Finn asked.

"Naw."

"Up with you then." Finn hauled him to his feet and walked him to the piling. "Hands on. Feet spread."

"Are you kidding me? I told you, I didn't do anything."

"Do as you're told," Cori said while Finn ran his hands over the man's body, a by-the- book frisk.

"Clean." Finn pulled the man's wallet out of his back

pocket.

"What's your name?" Cori asked.

"Sam." His eyes went to Finn who was studying his wallet. "Sam Franks, and I don't think you can do that." He asked Cori, "Can he do that?"

"Darn tootin'," she said. "And you can turn around now."

Finn handed the wallet back and started with the questions.

"So what were you doing at that house? You don't live there, or you would have answered my call," Finn said.

"You know I don't live there because you saw my license. I live in Encino," Sam said.

"What's your relationship to Roxana?" Cori asked.

"Who?" Sam pulled weeds out his hair.

"The woman who owns that house on the hill," Cori said.

"Sure, can we get to your story sooner than later?" Finn said, spitting out the dust he had swallowed when he took the man down. "What were you doing? And if it was so innocent, why did you run me a mile instead of telling me up there?"

"My boss sent me to get something," Sam said.

"Lord, man! Will you speak, or do I need to pull the truth out with your teeth?"

Finn plucked his sweat-soaked T-shirt away from his body hoping to catch a breeze, but there was none. He wondered how far up he would have to hike to retrieve his jacket. Sam looked at Cori, but all she did was shrug to let him know that an upset O'Brien was his problem.

"I was supposed to pick up a computer. There's a silhouette decal of a woman on the front. You know, like the stickers you see on a trucker's mud flaps?" He put a hand behind his head and preened, but gave up when Cori and

Finn didn't find him funny. "Anyway, that's all I know. Pick up the computer with the sticker on the front, and deliver it to a place in Century City."

"Who's you're employer?" Cori asked.

"AIng Inc."

"A name of a human, if you please?" Finn said.

"I'm a virtual assistant." He held his palms skyward either in apology for his position or to indicate he existed only on the cloud. "I get an E-mail or a text, do what I'm told, and I bill the company. I don't deal with anyone in particular. In fact, I don't even do much for them. Every once in a while they have me do some research and keep up their content on their social media accounts. It's a pretty easy gig and they pay great."

Sam dusted himself off and tested his extremities. When he was assured all was in working order, he smiled at them both.

"If I thought there was anything illegal I wouldn't have taken the job, but the company sent me a key. A key, right? It's not like they told me to break in. I mean a key makes it legal."

Cori pulled her lips tight. She debated telling this kid how many ways it could be wrong. First, he had no idea who sent the key or if they had come by it legally. More than one woman hadn't changed the locks after kicking out a volatile lover. What better revenge than to steal her computer and see what could be used for blackmail. In Roxana's case that would make sense. Tit for tat.

"I'm kind of glad I didn't find it. That house was a little creepy. Super quiet. And this weird picture on the wall. I mean it was cool, but weird. Felt like a tomb in there." He brightened. "So, can I get a ride back up? I'm pooped."

* * *

Enver and Emi Cuca waited on the lawyer. They had seen him many times and yet they still did not feel comfortable. In their country, if you went to court the judge met with the lawyers separately. Whichever lawyer offered the larger bribe won. In this case, Enver and Emi knew that their bribe could never be larger than the man they were concerned about. He was rich enough to bribe God himself. And yet this was America, so they tried to believe in the goodness of justice. The lawyer's name was Mr. Thompson. His offices were modest, but he seemed an honest man. Now he was a concerned one.

"Criminal matters aren't my area of expertise," he said. "But regarding the nondisclosure agreement, it is definitely binding. In fact, I could safely say that you would open up yourself to any number of problems should you break it."

"I don't want that," Enver said.

"No, we do not want any trouble, but the police say we are under suspicion," Emi said.

"Here's the thing, I'm going to have to refer you to another colleague. A criminal attorney," Mr. Thompson said.

"But we are not criminals," Enver said. Emi's hand closed over his. She squeezed a warning to him to be cautious with his words. He shook her off. "We are not. I did not kill that woman. I didn't even know she was in the house."

"You are innocent until proven guilty," the lawyer assured them. "I'm suggesting a criminal attorney be retained in case the investigation takes a turn. The investigation is in the early stages. The man you were arguing with is a problem. You need to be prepared in case he shares something that might turn the spotlight back on you."

"Spotlight?" Enver said.

"I mean if he says something that might implicate you. Murder is a bad business. The body was found in your home. There is no way to keep you out of the mix. They will continue to have questions, and you need to be as honest as you can."

"But not about this. Not about our business," Emi said.

"No," he said. "You are legally bound by the nondisclosure unless..."

"Unless what?" Emi asked.

"Remember, while I am not a criminal attorney I am still bound by the attorney client privilege. I will protect you to the best of my ability. But if your business dealings had anything to do with the death of this young woman, it could be argued that you have an ethical obligation to tell what you know." Mr. Thompson, crossed his arms on the desk and looked at each of them in turn. "Do you know if any of the parties involved in the nondisclosure had any reason to wish this girl harm? Did any of the parties have an opportunity to injure her?"

"No," Enver said. "There was no reason to wish her harm."

"And you did not injure her?" he asked.

"No."

"And you did not know her."

"I never spoke to her," Enver said.

He turned his eyes on Emi. She looked back at him. There was a faraway look in his wife's eyes. When she realized he was waiting for her to say something, she shook her head.

"The woman? No, I had no reason to hurt this woman," Emi said, and the lawyer kept his eyes on her a second longer than was necessary. She did not waver beneath his gaze.

"Then I believe you are fine. Call me if anything else comes up." He picked up the phone on his desk and spoke to his secretary. "Marilee, will you get Mr. and Mrs. Cuca the number for Beth Bartholomew?"

He smiled as the Cucas rose.

"Marilee will give you Ms. Bartholomew's contact information. She's an excellent criminal defense attorney. It would be good to have her on your side now. If the police want to question you further, make sure Beth is with you. I'll fill her in on your residency status and the NDA, so we're all on the same page."

The Cucas left the office and drove back to The Brewery. Mitzie saw them and she waved. Pedal saw them and called out. But Emi and Enver didn't notice or didn't want to. They went into their home, closed their door, and locked it. They had lunch, and then began to work again. When work was over, before dinner, Enver left Emi and stayed apart from her. She went to bed alone. She didn't hear him come to bed because she had been asleep for a long while. But when he stirred in his sleep, she woke. Rolling over she reached for him but changed her mind. She knew where he'd been and he wouldn't want her any more than she wanted him.

* * *

Cori and Finn stood in the living room of the house on the hill. Sam was long gone. The car on the side of the garage had been his. They had taken a quick look through the mess of papers, discarded cups, and food wrappers. Finn and Cori checked out the trunk, and had seen nothing remotely interesting. The detectives sent him on his way. They had everything they wanted from Sam: the address where he was supposed to deliver the computer, the name and email contact of the company that hired him, and his home address. If they had asked for his first born, Sam would have wrapped it up and given it over. Finn gave him a warning: he was only to tell his employer that he could not find the computer. There was to be no mention of the police or the fact that they were now in possession of the key to the house.

They had bagged the key, although Cori and Finn had no illusions that they would find anyone's prints on it but Sam's. A virtual assistant who had no curiosity about who paid him or what he was doing for a client was either really smart or a total idiot. Cori and Finn had a very short discussion about entering the premises. They believed that, when finding a man running from the property, they were justified in entering the house. They could argue that they feared someone inside might be hurt. Cori and Finn left the door open behind them, calling out even though they knew no one else was inside. The house seemed to know that no one would be ever again.

"You know, guys like Sam kind of make you wonder how that generation is going to rule the world."

"I'm thinking they might not be able to push my wheelchair in my old age unless they can maneuver it with a joy stick."

"Track pads are the thing now," Cori said. She wandered the living room, two small steps at a time, careful not to touch anything.

"By then all they'll have to do is think the word 'go' and that chair of mine will be off and running." Finn stopped in front of the painting that had made Sam so uncomfortable.

"If they can do that, then they can think us dead and be done with it," Cori mused. "Nice furniture. This girl had good taste."

"She was a beauty," Finn said. Cori turned to look at the painting he was admiring.

"I'm with Sam. It's freakishly realistic. Three dimensional," Cori said.

"I wouldn't be surprised if that painting talked," Finn said. He took a step closer. "Enver Cuca. Signed bottom right as it should be."

"Well, well," Cori said.

"He is good, I'll give him that."

"Does it not strike you strange, Cori?" Finn mused. "Is it not odd, that Enver Cuca painted this portrait of a woman who died in his home. Yet he says he doesn't know who she is or even that she was in his house?"

"This is Los Angeles. The whole place is frickin' weird," Cori said.

"Mr. Cuca must have spent some time with her to paint something like this. All he had to do was look at her mail to know her name," Finn said.

"Not necessarily. If Sam was hired virtually, why not Enver Cuca? A picture is all he'd need. Or one of those programs where they do imaging? Ask Lapinski. He'll know. He knows all that stuff," Cori said. "She could have sent a 3-D image, he paints from it, and sends this thing off for delivery."

"And she dies in a room upstairs in his studio? A bit of a coincidence," Finn said.

"Stranger things have happened."

"Not many," Finn answered. He took a minute, and then said, "So I think there's only one thing to do."

"Go talk to the Cucas again?"

"'Tis on the list, right after we secure a search warrant."

Finn's phone rang. He answered it and walked away. The call took no more than a minute.

"Hot date?" Cori asked as they made their way back through the house.

"Gretchen," Finn said.

"From Micks?" Cori seemed impressed.

"One and the same," Finn answered.

"Nice," Cori said, giving her blessing.

"Thank you, Cori," Finn said. "I'm thinking so."

They got back in the car. Cori fixed her seat belt, adjusted her shoulder holster, and dropped her purse at her feet. Finn took the wheel and guided them back the way they'd come. Cori watched him. She would always love Finn O'Brien, had been in love with him for a time, but now she was happy to see him move on. She had Amber, and the baby, Tucker, and Thomas Lapinski waiting in the wings. Cori wished that one of these days Finn O'Brien would have that much happiness. But he wasn't going to have a chance to see if Gretchen the firefighter was going to be his princess. By the time they were almost back to the precinct, she called again. She was pulling double duty and would talk to him after her three day shift.

"There's only one thing left then," Cori said. "You're coming to dinner."

Finn laughed aloud.

"Sure a broken date does not make me a broken man, Cori."

"Nope, but Lapinski's coming. What say we pick his brain over a beer or two. I'd sure like to know who it was that hired good old Sam."

"Poor Thomas," Finn said. "Used and abused."

"And loving every minute of it."

CHAPTER 20

Cori pushed the button on the side of the driver's seat and rode backward three inches. She rested one knee on the steering wheel and fiddled with her phone. She was back where she started, sitting in a car parked on the fancy driveway in front of Roxana Masha Novika's house. It was another perfect day, the view was still astounding, but it was morning and there was a snake of bumper-to-bumper cars on the freeway.

She had watched the gridlock for a while, and then kicked around the garbage cans again. Cori had tried the garage door hoping to get a closer look at the cars inside, but it was still locked. For a while she sat on the passenger side of her car, door open, legs splayed as she kept an eye on the road so she could see Finn coming. After it got hot, and Finn called to say the judge was dragging his feet on the warrant, Cori got behind the wheel once again and turned the air conditioning vents her way.

The night before hadn't been what she expected. Thomas was late, Amber tired, and the baby cranky. The fried chicken and mashed potatoes were reheated. Lapinski didn't have time to research the company that hired Sam.

Cori and Finn were disappointed that they even had to ask him, but the LAPD resources were stretched so thin they would have to wait until the cows came home if they relied on their research department. With the hour late, the small group disbanded with weary good nights.

This morning she learned that theLAPD was restricted from using facial recognition software. Some group of do-gooders had sued claiming the software was culturally biased. It would be litigated for years in the courts, so Cori would rather have Lapinski take a look. If anything came of his poking around, then they'd worry about a lawsuit. Now, bored out of her mind, Cori sent the attorney a message:

Morning. I owe you another chicken dinner. Work your magic.

Tell me who this guy is.

She hit send and the video of Bev, Roxana, and the Asian man was in Lapinski's phone. Cori closed her eyes and counted her blessings. She and Finn had a lot to show for their work: victim ID, a video, a bloody dress in a bag, a patent pending intrigue, mention of an NDA, and knowledge that something was about to change the world after a tech reveal at the Asylum shindig. What she wouldn't give to know what that secret was and why Roxana was critical to it.

Just as Cori was drifting off, a small truck turned into the drive. Cori dropped her knee, sat up straight, and watched it park. A young woman hopped out of the cab and slammed the door behind her. Cori got out of her car too.

"How's it going?" Cori said.

The woman gave the detective a chin tuck and a huge smile. She was the bittiest thing with the longest hair. It swayed all the way to her butt. Her eyes were huge and brown. She wore no make-up, had the body of a teenager, and the attitude of someone who had been around the block.

"Not bad," she said, unconcerned to see someone waiting in the driveway. "You?"

"Can't complain," Cori said.

She locked her car and as she did so her sweatshirt fell off one shoulder making her look like a sexy fairy.

"Have you been waiting long?" The girl slowed as she passed Cori, but didn't stop. Instead she did a little pirouette and ended up walking backwards.

"Awhile." Cori followed along.

"If I were you, I wouldn't hang around," the girl said. "Roxana hasn't been here for a while. I hope she didn't, you know, lead you on or anything."

"Does she do that to a lot of people?" Cori asked.

"Enough." The girl laughed and turned again. She headed for the front door.

"Don't worry, this isn't personal." Cori raised her voice. The girl gave her a passing glance.

"Good to know."

She took a key ring out of the pocket of her cut-offs. She wasn't adverse to a conversation, but she wasn't especially interested either. Still, she was polite.

"So if it's not a hook up, I still think you're out of luck. She hasn't been here for a week, maybe more."

"How do you know," Cori asked.

"'Cause I clean the place." The girl found the key she wanted on her chain, and put it in the lock. She opened the front door, held onto the knob, put her hip out and smiled. "Want to come in?"

"I should tell you I'm a cop," Cori said.

"What did she do?" the maid asked.

"She died for starters."

"That's a bummer."

"Still want me to come in?" Cori asked.

"Since she croaked, I guess I'm going to have to find another gig." She pushed the door open wide. "We might as well have some fun."

* * *

Finn found them by the pool when he arrived with warrant in hand. Cori'spants were rolled up to the knees, her feet dangled in the pool, and her jacket was on a lounge. A young woman was in the pool, her arms crossed on the tile edge, her feet kicking gently as she talked to Cori. Her name was Karyn with a 'k' and a 'y', and she was buck naked. She looked fetching; water beads on her cheeks sparkled under the late morning sun, her skin was smooth and tan. Her hair was long, slicked back in front and float-ing behind her in the water. Little dry wisps curled around her brow. Under the water, Finn could just make out her bum. Given the glancing light and the movement of the water, her undress seemed quite innocent. She smiled at Finn, invited him to join her in a swim, and then took no offense when he declined.

"Karyn is an actress, but she cleans houses to make ends meet. I was invited in, but I told her I needed to wait for you outside," Cori said, knowing he was wondering if she had already made the search warrant moot.

Finn smiled at both women. He asked Karyn, "How is it in Hollywood?"

"It's a shit place, but I'll make it."

"I've no doubt," Finn said.

"So I was telling Cori that I saw the Asian guy once. The one in the video."

The girl dipped her head back, and then shook it out.
The little wisps were plastered against her head now. Finn
pulled up a chair and looked at the video Cori held out to
remind him. He needed no reminder. It was a pity to look at
Beverly demean herself, to see a man so feeble in the face
of two women and their anger. He only wished the video
was clearer. Finn would have liked to see Roxana's reaction
to the attack. Was she frightened? Angry? Disdainful. To
see her face at that moment would have told Finn so much.
Yet all he saw was the push, Bev leaning over her, the man
moving forward. Finn got the sense that should Roxana
scramble up, Bev would have gotten as good as she gave.

"And do you know his name?" Finn asked.

"What?" Her head came up. "My ears were under water."

"Do you know this gentleman's name?" Finn said.

"Nope. But I'll tell you this, it was the only time I
saw *her be* close to human." Karyn drew out the word
so that it was clear there was no love lost between her
and her employer.

"Sounds like you didn't get along?" Cori asked.

"Oh, come on. Everybody knows that stchitck. I've
seen it on *Law and Order* a zillion times. I tell you we
didn't get along, you tell me I'm a suspect." Karyn kicked
off, did a twirl, disappeared under the water, came up,
and swam back to the side. "I'm going to miss this place.
When she wasn't home for a couple days I just hung out
back here, read scripts, and recorded some auditions. It
was a sweet gig. Sometimes I thought that Roxana didn't
really live here. I know she didn't cook. She drank, but
she didn't cook."

"We'll give you a pass on the suspect thing," Cori
said, trying not to laugh. "And you tell us what you know
about this man."

"I don't know anything about him." Karyn's face was suddenly pinched as if the mere mention of him was distasteful. "He came in when I was finishing one day. Weird dude. I kind of felt sorry for him. He couldn't look me in the eye." She looked at Cori. "Did you have one of those smart kids in grammar school? The one whose mom sent them to school with their shirt buttoned all the way up? Glasses. Their pants were always a size too big, so they could grow into them?"

"I did," Cori said.

"Sure, I think I might have been that boy," Finn said.

"Oh, right." Karyn laughed and gave him a wink. "Anyway, he came in and sat down. I heard them talking a little bit and Roxana was almost, I don't know, flirty? That was strange for her because she was pretty mean to everybody. Not when she was on camera. Now there was a good actress."

"Who were these everybodies she was mean to?" Finn asked.

"Typical wanna-be-influencer types. Lots of pouty looks in the camera, lots of money or pretend money. Who knows? Anyone who came here was like that." Karyn shrugged. "The movies I'm going to be in will mean something. What Roxana did was just gross. Sometimes I'd catch her in the bathroom in her undies. She'd be looking into the mirror and putting on her make-up. Of course she was filming. She talked like the people who followed her were her very, very best girlfriends."

"Did she have a lot of them? Followers?"

"Last time I looked she had like almost a million. I have to hand it to her, she figured out how to make it work. I always wondered if people would be okay with her being such a bitch."

"Someone wasn't," Finn said.

"That's funny," Kayrn said as she put her hands palm down on the edge of the pool. She started to push up. "Fair warning. I'm getting out."

"Then Cori and I would best be going about our business."

"Chicken," she laughed.

Finn raised a hand in farewell, and left her to frolic naked in the pool without an audience.

"She'll go far in Hollywood if she ever gets a break," he said.

"It would be easier for her if she married a rich guy, and forgot about the movies," Cori answered.

"Sure then she could act happy all day long."

* * *

"Dildo." Cori held up a rather impressive toy. "It's new. And we've got some oils, lotions, and condoms. Not exactly Pleasure Palace kinky. You could probably find the same in any suburban housewife's bedroom."

"Sure, I've not met such a housewife," Finn said, more amused than wistful.

"Sure, you weren't looking," Cori said and chuckled. "Bet you're in for some surprises when you find her."

"One can only hope, Cori." Finn opened a door revealing a walk-in closet. Cori joined him.

"Wow." Cori turned little circles, nodding her appreciation.

"I'm thinking if I met a housewife who had all this I wouldn't know what to do with her."

"It even smells rich in here," Cori said.

Roxana's closet was as big as Cori's first apartment, but better turned out. There was a tufted round lounge covered in apricot velvet. Built-in storage ran from floor to ceiling. Half of it looked like an apothecary's cabinet. Drawer after drawer opened to lingerie, jewelry, and scarves. On one wall, a library of lighted cubbyholes showcased purses and bags. It shared space with rows of shoes in every color of the rainbow. High heels, low heels, strange heels that looked as if they had been carved into totem poles. Cori was like a moth to a flame.

"She's got..." Cori pointed as she counted silently. "Fifteen pairs of black pumps. Fifteen."

"I'm assuming by your tone that's excessive," Finn said.

"How many did Bev have?" Cori whipped her head his way, her blonde hair flipping over her shoulder.

"I've no idea," Finn answered.

"Well that's reason right there to leave you, buddy. You didn't notice her shoes."

"I noticed the ones she was wearing the other night."

Finn turned his attention to the clothing that hung in neat rows, coordinated by category and then by color. Jackets, jeans, suits, slacks, dresses, and evening gowns. Finn pushed them aside and looked at the walls behind.

"No safe. Nothing."

He pushed the clothes back so that they hung neatly. Cori was in the drawers.

"Nothing here. No lockbox, not even for the jewelry."

"Perhaps it's not real and not worth protecting."

"It's real," Cori said.

They left the closet and stood together in the big bedroom. The bed was wider than a normal king size. It sat on a platform that faced a wall of glass. The headboard was upholstered in blue velvet. Roxana —and whoever might be with her in the morning—would see the sunrise over the hills. At night, they could watch the sunset. If Roxana wanted privacy, a remote panel near the bed lowered the shades. The bedside tables were solid blocks of black marble . There were no drawers. Nowhere to tuck away a diary, an address book, or a calendar. The bedroom was as slick and clean as a showroom. Even the huge picture over the bed seemed generic. It was nothing but a canvas with a swath of black painted across it.

The bathroom was the same. Roxana would have lounged in a claw-foot tub, looking through walls of glass. There was a freestanding sink and a vanity. Both were very modern, very clean. It felt like a stage where Roxana acted happy and made herself beautiful for her audience.

"Did you notice there are no real pictures?" Cori asked.

"Except for the one of herself," Finn said.

"And that's a big one. But it's strange not to have something to remind yourself of family, or friends, or travel. Or what about all those magazines she's been in?" Cori said. "Wouldn't you think she would frame those tear sheets?"

"Some people are not sentimental," Finn said. "Or this is not her only home. Perhaps this is—"

"A playpen?" Cori said. "Roxana might have been bringing the Asylum men here. You know, take more pictures, more fodder for her side business."

"If she played that game at the party the other night, someone would have known her name."

"Not necessarily. They could bring the role-play home or not own up to knowing her name. Besides, when we talked to them the woman was dead. If they had an issue with her they weren't going to broadcast it. The only reason we knew about Jeremiah Stotler is because of Bev."

"True," Finn said. "Let's do a title search and find out if she owns any other property. And if it's true that her side business was blackmail, then there must be a record of deposits somewhere."

"If she used banks," Cori countered. "Bitcoin or PayPal are the thing these days. This woman was nineteen; she made her living on line. She's not going to waste her time on calendars or deposit slips."

"Then where is the computer Sam was looking for?" Finn said. "This place is clean. Not so much as a dead insect about."

"Karyn knows her business," Cori said.

"I'm a friggin' cleaning freak, don't you know."

Karyn came in and threw herself on the bed. Dressed, her hair still wet, she had the glow of someone for whom all was right with the world.

"We're admiring your handiwork," Cori said.

"To tell you the truth, it was a pretty easy gig. No parties. Nothing like that. I could scrub the whole place in three hours and she paid me for five."

"Do you know anything about her personal life? Friends you might be able to identify?" Finn asked.

"No, sorry. I cleaned the house, and it was like I wasn't even here. I get that a lot. The men always notice me, but the women act like I'm a toadstool." Karyn twirled a lock of hair and checked out the ends. "When I'm rich and famous, I'm going to be nice to everyone."

With that, the girl fell back on the mattress, spreading her legs and arms like a kid making a snow angel. She looked at Cori. She turned her head to Finn and gave him a look that he couldn't quite decipher. She wiggled her fingers, and tipped her chin up. Cori suppressed a laugh when Finn crossed his eyes.

"Oh, come on you guys. What kind of detectives are you? This is a clue."

Karen stopped wiggling her fingers and pointed straight

up. Cori and Finn looked at the ceiling.

"And we're looking at what?" Finn asked.

Karyn laughed and scrambled up. She knee-walked over the mattress to the giant picture above the bed.

"Not the ceiling, silly. The picture."

With one hand she held the side of the big, unframed picture. The fingers of the other one ran along the bottom of the canvas. The next time Karyn flashed them a mischievous grin was just before they heard a click and a whir. The click was clear and had come from inside the bedroom; the whir was faint and was coming from the closet. Karyn scrambled off the bed.

"Come on. You're not going to believe it."

Finn and Cori followed her back to the closet, but it looked different now. Some of the shoes and purses were gone and in their place was an opening and beyond that...

"Well, I'll be," Cori said. "A panic room."

CHAPTER 21

"If you see a jar that says drink this, don't," Cori said.

Karyn giggled. "I would if it made me taller."

"'Tisn't a panic room," Finn said.

They were in an eight-by-ten room. There was no bed, no food, and, something he found very interesting, no obvious way to call outside for help. The room was a state of the art studio filled with recording equipment, lights, cameras, and desktop computer. There was a full soundboard and a bank of screens. From her social media posts, it was clear Roxana recorded all around her house, not in the sterile environment of a studio.

"Did Roxana say what this room was for?" Finn asked.

"Are you kidding?" Karen sniffed. "She didn't know I knew about it, so of course she wouldn't say anything. I found this when I was cleaning, you know, dusting under the painting."

"Who dusts under a painting?" Finn asked.

"I told you she was good," Cori said. "I'd hire you if I could afford you."

"It's a gift," Karyn said. "Anyway, I almost peed my

pants when that wall opened up. Then I couldn't figure out how to get it closed, and I almost peed my pants again. I knew Roxana would fire me if she thought I was snooping—which I wasn't— but then I figured out how to close it."

"And where would that little doohickey be?" Cori asked.

"It's a button under the brown Louis Vuitton bag. It took me forever to find it."

Finn went into the closet, lifted the bag, and saw the button. Whoever had constructed this room had done an excellent job. The mechanism to close the hidden door rested in an indentation that looked to be nothing more than a flaw in the wood. He shook his head in admiration and then smiled as he imagined Karyn rummaging through the place, half out of her mind as she looked to cover her tracks. He rejoined the women just as Karyn was showing Cori how to operate the equipment.

"Is our warrant good for this?" Cori asked.

"We are in the house," Finn said. "What are you showing us, Karyn?"

"Okay," she said. "So this is like top-of-the-line recording equipment. I mean, it would cost me a fortune to do a high end audition tape if I had to pay for a studio decked out like this."

Her fingers ran over the computer keyboard. The center screen populated with file folders. She leaned across to the soundboard and adjusted the levels.

"When I figured out that Roxana was gone more than she was home in the last year, I started using this place."

She sat back and crossed her arms. Her long hair had dried into waves and curls. She smelled like chlorine and sunshine. Karyn tipped her head back, splitting her attention between Finn and Cori. Finn could see a spattering of freckles across her nose.

"I made a couple of audition tapes, and that was it," Karyn said. "I swear. I mean, what was I hurting? I didn't take anything. I was really careful."

"I don't think Roxana will be caring any now," Finn said.

Karyn smiled and he saw the girl she had been before dreams of Hollywood entered her head.

"I don't really care about her, but I wanted you guys to know that I wasn't trying to take advantage. I just work so hard, you know? She had so much."

"You're good as far as we're concerned," Finn said."Besides, if snooping was a crime, half the world would be in jail."

"What's this?" Cori held up a cap of some sort with little buttons dangling from it.

"Oh, it's for MoCap—motion capture," Karyn said. "The studios use it for like super hero stuff. Video games. You put it on your head, put those little round things on your muscle points, and it records your movements. I don't know if Roxana ever used it. Could be she was thinking about doing some sort of app of herself."

Cori put it aside. She had no idea what the girl was talking about.

"So, Karyn," Finn said. "If you've something you think we should see, now would be a good time to bare your soul."

"I already bared everything and you're interested in my soul? That's funny." Karyn giggled and then raised her hands over the keyboard like a maestro. "Okay, then. Let's get this show on the road."

Cori settled on a stool in the corner of the room. Finn perched on the edge of a desk behind Karyn. She clicked on the first file folder. It was labeled *Lips*. The screen pulled up a close-up video of Roxana Masha Novika's beautiful, naked lips. The picture was so close they could trace each delicate vertical line. There was a dusting of blonde down on her upper lip. When her lips closed in a certain way, there was a small dimple on her cheek.

Roxana formed words, silently at first and then they heard her voice when she repeated them. That voice was both sultry and innocent. It was rich the way the heady scent of a rose is tempered by the sharp thorns. Finn sat up straighter. Cori leaned forward. They glimpsed her teeth, the front ones slightly larger than they should be, but charming nonetheless. They saw her tongue as she formed each word. The languid lull of her voice was seductive. No one would ever hear her speak again, but they were hearing her now.

I...

I want...

I want you...

I...

I love...

I love you...

Finn glanced over his shoulder at Cori. It took her a moment to tear her eyes away from the screen. Karyn swiveled in her chair.

"What did I tell you?" she said. "Crazy."

* * *

"What in all the heavens is this for?"

Finn had traded places with Cori. He now sat on the stool and Cori leaned against a wall. Karyn had pushed her chair back, and put her feet up on the edge of the sound-board. She was close enough to the keyboard that she could maneuver the cursor. She had stopped clicking the file folders in order. Each represented a different body part.

Some were more interesting than others. It was Cori who had cried uncle after watching five minutes of Roxana's elbow flexing. They had fallen silent as they watched her brown eyes. Over the course of the video, as Roxana turned at different angles, those eyes became hazel and gold and then brown again. Her lashes were long and thick.

"She looks like she's doing some kind of exercise," Cori said.

She and Finn had seen the battered pulp of this woman's face at the crime scene. For Cori it was hard to reconcile what she was seeing on the screen with the horror of Roxana on the coroner's table. They both started when Karyn snapped them out of their trance.

"It kind of is."

"What?" Finn said.

Karyn turned her head so the detectives could see her move her eyes in the same way Roxana had. Her gesture was at once mechanical and graceful. She stopped after a second.

"It kind of is like an exercise. It's for the editor," Karyn said. "This way he can choose a different angle, or a different look when he edits the film."

"So you think she was making a movie?" Finn asked.

"I don't know." Her fingers tapped out a little tune on the arms of the chair. She tipped her head one way and then the other. "Honestly, I've never seen anything like this. The lips I get. The eyes. But elbows? Toes? Fingers? She has a good ten minutes on her kneecap. That's just over-the-top."

"This whole thing has been weird from the beginning," Cori said.

Karyn dropped her feet and pulled the chair up close.

"You haven't seen anything yet," she said. "But I'm not sure you want to see it."

The cursor hovered over a file labeled *vagina*. Karyn waited for their decision. Cori shook her head, and held up her hand. Finn said:

"Sure, we've seen enough for now."

They would open each file eventually, but screening something this intimate in Roxanna's own house didn't feel right. For Finn it was hard to reconcile the physical beauty of this woman and her lovely voice with the person she was in life. He would have been led astray by her as would any man. But there was a difference between being led astray and being overwhelmed by such passion that you would want to destroy her. What was it that drove such a person to kill? The discovery of her callousness? Or was it that Roxana shared herself with millions of people she didn't know? Perhaps it was her greedy heart? Or maybe it was rejection? Rejection was the greatest human hurt of all.

"I've got something interesting here," Cori said.

Finn turned to see her pulling a metal box from a desk drawer.

"You want me to shut this down?" Karyn asked, as Finn joined Cori.

"Unless there's something else besides her body parts on there," Cori said. "Any other files? Ones that aren't video or audio?"

"Like emails and stuff?" When Cori nodded Karyn said. "Sorry, she had a laptop for that."

"With a silver decal of a woman on the front?" Finn asked.

"Yep," Karen said. "That's the one."

"Can you see if you can find it?"

"Sure, but I've gotta run in about twenty minutes. I've

got an audition for a soap."

Finn and Cori thanked her for her help and had her write down her contact information. She went off to search for the computer, as Cori opened the fireproof box.

"Bingo." She smiled. "Paper trail."

Cori handed him a packet of paper. It was folded in thirds, and bound in pale blue cover stock. White string wrapped around the pouch and was secured around a grommet. Finn opened it and started to read while Cori continued to sort through the other contents of the box.

"I've got a key, and I've got codes," she said. "I told you she wouldn't use banks. She's got a code for ADA, Ethereum, and Bitcoin."

"And I've got a contract," Finn said. "It is drawn up by the same corporation that sent Sam on his errand. And look who else is mentioned in such a fine legal document. Mr. Enver Cuca."

Finn held out the papers for Cori to see. Before she could react, Karyn was back.

"Hey you guys I'm out of here. Been really good to meet you."

Before she took her leave, she cast them a naughty look and pulled the computer from behind her back. She gave it a merry little shake.

"Look what I found."

On the front of the tablet was a shiny, silhouette decal of a naked woman, the kind of thing you'd see on a trucker's mud flap. Roxana Masha Novika was about to start talking.

CHAPTER 22

"My eyes are going to fall out of my head if I have to stare at this computer screen one more second, O'Brien."

Cori threw herself back in her chair, stuck her legs out in front of her, and let her arms dangle by her sides. Her head lolled, her eyes closed. When no sympathy was forthcoming, she opened one eye. Finn hadn't heard a word, so intent was he on his own research.

"Lot of fun you are."Cori pushed herself upright, picked up her mug, and saw that it was empty. "Want me to bring you back some coffee?"

"What?"Finn spoke but it took him a second to tear his eyes away from his screen."I'm sorry. I'm getting nowhere with this. That corporation on Roxana's contract has ten different iterations in as many countries. It's a circle I can't close. We're going to need to go back to the cybercrime folks."

"We'll be lucky to get in the queue a year from now." Cori picked up his mug and held both in one hand as she perched on the side of his desk. "What about Lapinski?"

"He's got his own work," Finn said. "Besides, it's a fine

line asking him to be so deeply involved. You've already sent him the video."

"It's no different than getting a statement from a witness, place of employment, blah, blah, blah," Cori said.

"Except that we've provided him evidence."

"A video recorded by a Ring doorbell that he could have gotten the same way I did?" Cori rolled her eyes.

"All I'm saying is we need to be cognizant, Cori," Finn said. "And wouldn't the contents of that computer be just a bit over the line?"

"I wasn't going to give him free rein. Just a few tidbits. Geeze." She chuckled. There was no mistaking her weariness for the job or her fondness for the subject that was Thomas Lapinski. "But it would be cool if we could pull him in on this fulltime. He's kind of amazing isn't he? That man is so darn smart and. . ."

Finn laced his hands behind his head ready to listen to her sing the praises of the attorney, but Cori came to her senses, smoothing over the hint of affection she had for the man.

"Still, you're right. We don't have a darn thing for all his work on that Ring image," she said.

"He explained it was a problem with the quality of the video. Sure the man can't work miracles," Finn said.

"Say it ain't so." Cori leaned over Finn's desk to peruse the mess of papers and the image on his computer screen. "Are you finding anything in the phone records that will help?"

"Not what I had hoped for," he said. "I've six months of Roxana's records, and not one call to the Cucas' numbers."

"Do you have all their numbers?"

"Two cells and a land line. If there's another it would have to be a burner."

"Entirely possible," Cori said. "The little miss was involved in some pretty rotten stuff. Burners wouldn't be out of the question. Look at the poor reverend she dug her claws into. He nearly had a heart attack when we showed up on his doorstep."

The interview with the man of God had been a hoot. From his bad dye job to his brood-mare caps and matchy-matchy leisure outfit, he was everything Cori knew he would be. The minister would look great on television with the right lighting—he might even look sexy and diabolical in a mask and tuxedo at an Asylum party— but without his girdle and make-up there wasn't much to recommend him.

"Did you catch his reaction when we told him she was dead?" Cori chuckled. "I swear his soul flew straight up to heaven to thank the good Lord."

"At least the missus wasn't there to hear," Finn said, unable to hide his smile "From what I gathered, he was being beaten up by women on all sides."

"Only one lady in his life now," Cori said. "He isn't an Asylum guy anymore."

"But we do know he's a man of great faith," Finn said.

"How's that?" Cori asked.

"He had faith that Roxana had no duplicate files of the incriminating photos," Finn said.

"It was an act. That guy was going to go to his own grave sweating that. Now he can kick back and enjoy his millions 'cause she beat him to that fancy box," Cori said. "But you know what? I've got me a ton of faith that you'll find something in those phone records that will lead us right back to the Cucas. My money is still on good old Enver."

"I'm of the same opinion." Finn sat up. Cori slid off the desk. "But we'd have to tie ourselves in knots to convince a D.A. to bring charges with what we have now. So much and so little all at the same time."

"This thing has more layers than a wedding cake," Cori said. "We just got to cut through the paste and get to the yummy stuff."

"It's early yet," Finn said. "And I've a long list of questions for Mr. Cuca. The picture he painted of Roxana, the NDA we've heard of, his mention in the contract. I want to know who arranged the party, and how the girl was in his home, and yet no one saw her come in. That bothers me more than a howling wind. How could he never have met her?"

"You want to bring him and the little woman down here tomorrow?" Cori asked.

"No. We'll go to them. I want another look at that upstairs room." He inclined his head to a roll of blueprints he'd put aside. "I've got those from the city. They've records of the building going back to when it was built in 1918. There was a redo in '47, and then some minor changes when it became a work/live space. There are tunnels and doors indicated on the plans that are confusing. We should find out if they still exist."

"And you're counting on the building department to have kept accurate records? Now who has the faith?" Cori laughed and headed for the door.

"I try to keep the flame burning bright," Finn said.

Cori waited because she knew there would be more. Indeed, Finn's brow was furrowed, his fingers were tapping on the desk, and his mouth was still moving.

"You would think these fancy people would be wanting to talk to us instead of hunkering down in a foxhole. I've never seen such scurrying for cover, and no care for justice."

Cori sighed as she sauntered back toward Finn and put the heel of one hand on the desk. The mugs she was holding in the crook of her finger clunked against her thigh.

"You really gotta get rid of those rose colored glasses, O'Brien. Roxana was a huge pain in their pampered little rears. Dropping her body in a pauper's grave, and forgetting her will make them happy. Until that happens, they are going to circle the wagons."

Finn chuckled. "Sure it's you who should have been a preacher, Cori."

"Not quite fire and brimstone, but you get my drift." She stood up. "We're the only two who give a rat's ass about finding the truth. When we're shooting some tequila at Mick's we can ask Geoffrey why we even bother. Just remember, we have the advantage. The only skin we have in this game is that we're good cops."

"'Tis uplifted I am by that thought," he said, before taking on a cop's other role. Devil's advocate. "But explain this to me. If the money she makes as an influencer is so good, if her shakedown has brought her even more money, why sell out for this?"

Finn picked up a copy of the contract they had found in her home. Yellow marker highlighted passages, and asterisks dotted the page.

"A million dollars up front, and a yearly royalty of a quarter of a million dollars. In return, Roxana agrees not to appear in any public forum. That includes print, TV, or social media until such time it is determined by the other party that the exclusivity clause is terminated. At that time she will receive another payday of five million."

"I'd take it," Cori said.

"But she's a young woman, wealthy in her own right. Why trade the business she built for a flat sum? Not to mention, she can be terminated at any time. This is asking her to trade her body and soul, and to disappear. 'Tis like being a stock girl after you've owned the department store," Finn said.

"The only way to know is if we analyze what she was making versus this payout. We can't do that until the computer folk can finish their hack. We have her digital banking codes so we should be able to access her financials. Our Roxana seems to have a ton of money, a bunch of enemies, a zillion followers, and no friends. We've got our work cut out for us." Cori rapped the desk. "Coffee, coming up."

Before she could take a step, two phones rang: Cori's cell, and Finn's desk phone. Finn picked his up; Cori answered hers. She mouthed the word *Lapinski.* Finn waved his hand to keep her attention.

"Yes, Captain. Detective Anderson also?" He listened for a moment. "We'll be right there."

Cori dismissed Lapinski with 'call you back', stashed the mugs on the desk, and pocketed her phone.

"Trouble?" she asked.

"I've no idea. Captain Smith unhappy is the same as the Captain Smith happy."

"Good point," Cori said as Finn stepped back and let the lady through the door first.

CHAPTER 23

Captain Smith's happiness was not in question. What she had to say was business as usual; just not business that would please Cori and Finn. The meeting was about a glitch, an oversight, a wrinkle. It was about the search of Roxana's house. Cori and Finn had done a good job, but it wasn't good enough. Roxana Masha Novika's lawyers filed a Return of Property request. The request covered her computer and all electronic devices registered to the young woman not covered under the search warrant.

"The warrant was good," Finn objected. To which the captain responded:

"Do you know Karyn Drago?"

"She's the housekeeper," Cori said. "She arrived before Detective O'Brien came with the warrant. I remained outside the residence with her during that time. If she says different then she's telling a tall one, captain."

"No, nothing like that," Captain Smith said. "It's the warrant itself. Once you ID'd the victim, next of kin was advised. Her father is in Russia, but the man is represented by Oxfam & Damelir in Los Angeles. Hence the expedited Return of Property order."

"Even with that firm, someone has got to be sleeping with the judge to get an order that fast," Cori muttered.

"Anderson."

Finn had the fleeting thought that this captain would have made an excellent nun. She had silenced Cori with one word and a disapproving look. But that was only a detour. She was still on track.

"They sent one of their attorneys to the house along with administrative staff. Their intent was to do inventory, and seal the home until the victim's father made arrangements. They found the copy of the warrant you left."

"Then all above board, captain," Finn said.

"Except not," Captain Smith said. "You did not find the computer according to Ms. Drago. She did."

"Agreed," Finn said. "She knew where it was, retrieved it, and handed it to us. We had apprehended a man who had been sent to take it from the house. We had to assume it was a crucial piece of evidence. "

"It appears that you did not ask Ms. Drago where she found it," Captain Smith said.

"There was no reason. The cars, the garage and the house were all covered by the warrant," Finn said. "If you're trying to tell us there is some sort of error, we'll need to revisit with the court."

"The warrant for the house and the attached buildings was in order, but it seems there was a small gardening house in her orchard. Your victim worked there on occasion. That structure was detached and, as such, is not covered under the parameters of the warrant."

Captain Smith's lips pulled tight to show she was not unsympathetic to the situation. Cori glanced at Finn. His color was high, his jaw tight. He took a deep breath, and asked:

"When must we hand it over? We're so very close to. . ."

"It's already gone, O'Brien." Captain Smith's chest rose and fell under her uniform. The only sign of her disappointment. "Next time let's be more specific on the warrant. Cover all structures and open property, and for God sake don't send anyone else to do the chore. Go with them, take it into evidence with your own hands."

Cori and Finn offered apologies; the captain had one more piece of business.

"I've read over your initial report, detectives. A Beverly O'Brien was interviewed and released. Any relation?"

"Captain, I was the one who—" Cori began, but Captain Smith cut her off without so much as a glance.

"This question is directed to Detective O'Brien."

"My ex-wife, captain."

Finn spoke clearly knowing the consequences could be dire. He regretted not having told her before. Especially now when he had been remiss in securing evidence. A small mistake here, an omission there, and Finn O'Brien would bear watching. This was a prospect he didn't relish, but he would accept that if it were to be his reprimand.

"Are you good with that?" she asked.

"Yes, captain" Finn said. "We've been divorced for some-time. I carry no grudge."

"No unfinished business of any kind?" The captain pressed him.

"No," he answered.

Captain Smith held his gaze, and he didn't flinch. Finally, she looked at Cori.

"Detective Anderson, should there be a need to discuss anything with Ms. O'Brien, you will handle it." Those eyes went back to Finn. "Detective O'Brien. I do not think you are a troublemaker, but it is now clear that you can rub people the wrong way. I am one of those people who have been so rubbed. I do not appreciate being kept in the dark. Even the smallest thing that could compromise you, me, your partner, or my department is better communicated sooner than later. I overlooked your comments to our officers, I will let you slide on this. One more problem, and I will send you packing. I promise it won't be back to Wilshire Division."

Captain Smith raised an eyebrow. Cori and Finn stood at attention. There was nothing to say given the clarity of her message. When she was satisfied they understood, she said, "Dismissed."

Finn turned on his heel and left the office; Cori was right beside him.

"You don't put yourself between me and a slap on the wrist, Cori," Finn said.

"You're welcome," she answered, more than a little miffed by his attitude.

Cori moved on ahead. Behind her she heard Finn palm the swinging door that led to the mens room. Fine, let him put his head in the toilette and flush if that was going to make him feel better. Cori hit the bullpen at top speed. Detective Walters looked up from his late afternoon snack of a bagel and cola.

"What are you looking at?" Cori snapped as she passed him.

"Lover's quarrel?" he snickered.

Cori rolled her eyes and plopped herself at her desk. She was glad her back was to Walters because the other way around and she might have to bare her teeth and go for the jugular. Cori sniffed once. Twice. She thought to return Lapinski's call, but decided to calm down first. With that criteria, it might be a week before she talked to him. Cori yanked her keyboard closer, and began to scroll through Roxana's list of Instagram followers. She was looking for a connection that seemed more personal than most, sponsors, anything to piece together some idea of the girl's business and personal life. Her eyes kept cutting to Finn's empty chair. He was wrong to be angry with her; she was wrong to be angry with him. They should be angry with Bev and all the people who were making it so hard for them to do their job.

Her gaze went to the white board where they were laying out their case. On the left was Roxana's 'family tree'. A picture of her in life was at the top of the grid. Three branches radiated from her photo. Those branches represented the men she had blackmailed. Jeremiah Stotler was the only one who hadn't been vetted to Finn's satisfaction. The other two men had alibis for the night of her murder, and neither had the will to do anything but keep their heads down when it came to Roxana. Jeremiah's alibi was a phone call to Gray, the Right Hand. Hardly an alibi that sat well with Finn and Cori. On another branch, there were Roxana's business contacts. Ali Keyes was a nice guy who, according to Finn, was able to separate his squeaky clean personal life from his unusual professional one. Cori wondered about him. He may not have a violent bone in his body, but did he have a vindictive one? Cori thought not. In fact, for all the indecent aspects of his business, he seemed the least interesting person on the board.

From Ali there were lines connecting him to Jeremiah Stotler. From Jeremiah there trailed another line to Bev O'Brien. They had also added a line for the Right Hand. Stotler's associate was a curiosity. The detectives did not put it past her to have tried to permanently solve her boss's problem, but that was a long shot. And there was a line for the Asian man. There they had put a grainy picture of him and three question marks. Business? Pleasure? Wrong place/wrong time?

Finn had drawn two more lines. One was for assumed personal male friends and the other was for Roxana's family. If she had lovers, they had seen no sign of them yet. Her family seemed casual about their involvement with her. This was underscored by the fact that lawyers secured her computer but did not claim her body. The faceless corpse still rested in Paul's cold storage along with four hundred other stiffs. The thought of that −of a young woman left naked and alone—softened Cori's mood. She made a note to see if that had changed in the last few days.

On the right side of the boardthere was another circle. This one was marked E/EC, Enver and Emily Cuca. Their 'family tree' included Roxana (question mark), Asian man (question mark). The business lines were blank except for Ali Keyes. But Ali wasn't really a connection. One of his associates had booked the Cuca space at the behest of a corporation. Instructions were specific as to food, time, number of guests, and the fee paid for use of the Cucas' living area. The artist and his wife had no relatives in the United States. The relatives in Albania were few, and the Cucas had not spoken to them since they had immigrated.

The Cucas' clients were not listed. They had created more than 1500 companions. They dealt in cash, the names and addresses of their clients were sketchy. These folks preferred keeping their predilection for silicone over flesh private. Cori requested the Cucas' income tax returns. The Cucas' accountant was on it.

There was a third bubble. This one bore no picture, only the title AIing Inc. Roxana had a contract with this corporation, agreeing to stop her career as an influencer in return for a large sum of money. The same one that barred Enver Cuca from reproducing Cami's image. This was the same corporation that contracted with Sam to retrieve Roxana's computer. The legal name of the corporation was Action Intelligencing Inc. It was a multinational concern. Its subsidiaries and ownership interests stretched from small towns in the Midwest to villages in Sri Lanka, and chic addresses in Hong Kong, London, and Paris. The subsidiaries each had their own map of influence.

Cori and Finn only wanted to know who the human being was who set the wheels in motion that led to Roxana's death, not the history of the corporation. They would do a deep dive into AIing Inc. if it became necessary, but they believed the web that needed unraveling was closer to home. It was spun by someone who had caught up Asylum, the Cucas, and Roxana. Somewhere in the mess was one person who knew exactly what happened that night and why that girl had to die.

Cori put her elbow up on the desk. She rested her head in her upturned palm, curling a stray hair around one finger as she looked at the board. Her eyes were pulled back time and again to the pictures of the Cucas' unit. The first room. The tables. Sofas. Chairs. The knife and the mutilated companion.

The second landing. Nothing but a locked closet and bare walls.

The third. Cori shivered as her gaze lingered on the workroom. Even in a photograph that place looked like a portal to hell. Then there was the 'house' room as they had come to call it. But it wasn't a house at all; it was the stage for a brutal crime. So clean. So useless. Cori dropped her hand. She bit her bottom lip. The pictures told a story that Cori didn't understand.

She let her gaze linger on the yellow plastic markers where blood traces had been found. Some had been so microscopic that she and Finn missed them. The forensic team identified them at the entrance to the 'house' room, and then again near the worktable. The person who beat Roxana walked through the workroom, paused at the table, and —what? The microscopic blood drops had ended there. Where had that person gone? Where had they put the murder weapon? Where...

Cori looked back at the photographs of the 'house' room. The closer the camera moved to the curtains surrounding the bed, the more prevalent the markers were. Near the platform on which the mattress sat there was only yellow tape. No need to mark a spot, there was blood everywhere. The pictures that had been taken after the mattress, curtains, and pillows were removed and sent to the lab caught her interest. The tape was still there. The platform was still there but without the curtains it was more interesting. Cori looked at the bathroom area and the freestanding tub. She cut over to the mock up of the living room. Her gaze traveled to the meticulous arrangement of the outdoor furniture.

She sat up, and leaned forward. Cori closed her eyes, and then opened them again. She was concentrating so hard it took her a moment to realize that Finn was beside her. She didn't bother to acknowledge their tiff; she didn't want to talk about warrants or what they had lost.

"What do you see?" she asked.

"A well put together but incomplete evidence display." Finn said. "What do you see?"

Cori got up. She walked to the board. She pointed to each of the 'house' room pictures: living room, bathroom, dining room, patio.

"I. See. Roxana's. House."

Cori turned her head. Her big blue eyes were wide; the shadow above them sparkled prettily in the ugly bullpen light. Finn's lips tipped. He moved to her side, nodding. His fingers traced a path over the photographs. He saw it too. The 'house' room was built for Roxana. It was a home away from home.

"'Tis a gilded cage," Finn said.

"Why?" Cori wondered. "Why would she want to stay in a place like that?"

"She sold her soul to some devil," Finn said. "The contract says she is to cut off from her world. Someone bought her, Cori, and this is where they would put her once she signed the contract."

"Pedal could be right. Maybe Roxana was a slave." Cori pointed to the pictures. "That was going to be her doll house once they hooked everything up. Lord above, could Cuca be as sick as all that?"

Cori turned toward her partner. In her eyes was a flash of horror. Finn saw that look when a case hit too close to home, when a woman was mistreated and powerless to control her own destiny. Being doomed to exist in a world of a sick man's making frightened Cori most of all.

"Remember, Cori, she entered into this agreement of her own free will," Finn said. "That doesn't make it right, but I promise we'll find whoever is responsible. It won't happen to anyone else."

Finn held up a piece of paper he had brought with him.

"They found DNA on the piece of clothing from the dumpster. Sweat stains under the arms where the water hadn't reached. It wasn't washed in a machine. They've identified the DNA as a woman's."

"The victim's?" Cori asked.

"No," Finn said. "We'll want swabs from all the women at the party."

"I'll call them," Cori said. "Bev may refuse."

"They all may," Finn said. "And won't that be telling?"

Cori's eyes flickered to his other hand. Between his thumb and forefinger was a flash drive.

"And that?"

"Roxana's life."

CHAPTER 24

"And I thought cyber techs were lazy. Shame on me," Cori said.

"The tech told me it was a matter of course to back up the drive. Like making a copy of a report," Finn said. "She said it wasn't hard to get in to the computer. Roxana was not as sophisticated as we believed."

"We should tell the captain," Cori said.

"I stopped in to do just that, but she's left for the day." "I'll tell her in the morning. I think she'll agree that a case can be made for splitting hairs. If they are calling a little garden house separate from the main property, we can make a distinction between the hardware and the content it held."

"Bring on the popcorn."

Cori settled into a conference room chair while Finn did the honors. Roxana's desktop appeared on the big screen at the front of the room.

"Lord have mercy," Cori breathed as the tiny files popped up on the screen for a full ten seconds. "That girl was busy."

Finn grinned and clicked on the top left file folder. Three hours later pizza boxes, soda cans, water bottles, paper, Post-Its, and pens littered the table. Cori and Finn had scrolled through correspondence, financial information, pictures, and videos. Within the first hour they decided to focus on one thing at a time. Sponsorships were the current topic.

"What's our count on companies keeping our girl in clover? " Finn asked.

"Twelve so far. L'Oreal, Revlon, Wet 'N Wild, Stila, Sephora, Bite, to name a few," Cori said.

"I had no idea there were so many things women could put on themselves," Finn said.

"That's because you lived with a woman who didn't need all that stuff. Next time you're at my place I'll show you my stash," she said.

"I'm thinking I'll pass, Cori."

Finn put his back to the screen and one hand to his neck, rotating and stretching to get the kinks out. He and Cori had run through fifty of Roxana's tutorials. She was mesmerizing to watch. Her face, skin, and hair were flawless; her movements naturally sensual. They were more convinced than ever that the attack was one of passion and regret as the ME had suggested. Who could not regret destroying something so lovely? The evening was getting on and there was still much to do.

"Okay, let's start adding it up," Finn said.

"Roxana pulled in five hundred and fifty-five thousand a year from L'Oreal. That includes advertising and new product roll out. Then it drops to three seventy five for Sephora, and a hundred and fifty thousand for Stila. According to the contracts, Stila is in for another fifty K each time they do a new product roll out." Cori did a quick accounting. "Right now we're looking at a total of fifty to a hundred thousand a year just from Stila. Advertising spots and product placement look to be at a different rate."

"What's the difference between the two?" Finn said.

"The jars and bottles on her bathtub or on her sink? That's a placement. She doesn't have to say a word about it, just position the label so it can be seen."

"'Tis a sweet deal," Finn said.

"Someone sees the magic. Not me." Cori said as her partner came to look at the figures she was adding up. "So what is she looking at for a year?"

"Almost a million-one a year."

"She's got a personal appearance agent, too." Cori scrolled through and found the email she wanted. "He's pitching her at twenty-five thousand. For that she walks into a party, waves, has a drink, and walks out with five figures. I think twenty-five is on the lower end for something like this."

"I'm not seeing the AIing Inc. deal as enough to shut down her work."

Finn sat across from Cori. Her hands were on the table, her fingers entwined. She had grown quiet and thoughtful. She opened her mouth to speak, thought better of it, and then decided to say what was on her mind.

"Do you think it could be love, O'Brien?"

"Cori," Finn said, and shook his head. "Seriously?"

"Think about it. We've got a draw on the money. She's doing great on her own. Her family's rich. She's been a bad girl all her life. What if she fell hard ass in love, and is giving it all up for some guy." Cori smiled, opened her hands, and shrugged her shoulders. "It happens. It might be a thrill this girl never had before. Maybe she was all in for love and money."

"I won't discount it," Finn said. "It might be as you say. Bev left for love of money. She sold her soul to Jeremiah Stotler, did his bidding, protected him. Perhaps love is not a bridge too far."

"But which man?" Cori said. "I doubt Enver has that kind of money. And if he does, how does he keep this arrangement from his wife if he's going to house her upstairs?"

"Maybe Emi is the one paying for it," Finn said.

Cori's hands unlaced. She picked up a piece of cold pizza and put it down again.

"I don't see it," she said. "This is an obsessed guy thing. Emi would have to be deranged to put up with that."

"Why not just kill the wife and install the mistress? Better yet, divorce Emi. Easier still," Finn said.

"Unless the money was coming from Emi's invention. If he divorced her before the patent was approved she might argue he deserved no profit." Cori knew the brainstorming would lead somewhere, so she kept thinking. Suddenly she sat up, excited by her ephiphany. "Roxana was backing out. That's it. A chick who blackmails rich guys would be a major tease. Enver builds her this home away from home, promises the world, she comes to her senses, and she screws him. That would be enough to send any guy over the edge. She has a Russian passport. What does she care about contracts? Walking out on Enver would be fun."

"True. And he could have gotten her upstairs because everyone was busy in the big room. But how did he get her in? And why that night with all those potential witnesses?" Finn waved all this away. "Not that it matters. Until we can tie him to AIing Inc. we've got nothing."

"Now that we have a contact name over at AIing Inc., the connection may come sooner than we think. George Nye signed the contract as a proxy." Finn referred to his notes. "And we need to talk to Roxana's lawyer."

Cori considered the list of directives. They would divide up the chores in the days to come. They would try to run down the pixels that made up the picture of Roxana's life. Cori had no doubt it would be interesting once it came into focus.

"Okay, let's move on" Cori said.

Finn clicked on the folder labeled Asylum. Inside were four subfolders. Photos were in the first. The other three were labeled with the names of the men she blackmailed. They opened *photos*.

Roxana was fond of selfies. She looked stunning and seductive in each one. She favored a mask of black lace with silver ribbons tied in bows at the side of her head. The ends of the ribbons trailed down her cheeks. She piled her long hair atop her head in a way that made her look as if she had come from bed. There were other photos that were reflections in her bathroom mirror. In one she was naked under a sheer gown that fell from her shoulders to her silver-sandaled feet. Another showed her in a thong and bra, this time with a mask shaped like golden wings.

Bev was in one photo. The background did not suggest Roxana's home, for which Finn was grateful. To have caught his ex lying about a friendship with the girl would move her up the list of suspects. It was one thing to cavort with Roxana at the same Asylum party, quite another to be preening in the girl's house. Still, it didn't seem that Beverly was disliking their moment. They would ask her where this picture was taken. If, as she said, cameras were forbidden at Asylum events then Bev was no better than Roxana.

"She looks good," Cori said, knowing her partner needed a prompt to bring him back to the here and now.

"That she does, Cori."

He didn't say what was on his mind. Beverly's beauty could not compete with Roxana's. There is nothing like a young girl's blush, the sparkle in her eyes, and the luster of her hair to make a man's heart race. By comparison— while lovely—Bev looked old.

"I don't see any men in these pictures," Cori said.

"As it should be, according to the rules," Finn answered.

They clicked through sixty or seventy pictures until they hit the mother lode. There were ten pictures of one of Roxana's marks: the preacher. Naked and in a position of subservience to a dominatrix, he proved to be even less than attractive than he already was. Given some of the things Finn and Cori had seen in Hollywood this was mild. However, in the context of a man of God it was damning.

"I'd rather cuddle," Cori said, and Finn chuckled.

"We've got Mr. Normand, the banker. Father of ten," Finn said.

This time it was a *ménage a trois* that had ruined the man. They knew he had paid Roxana a hundred and fifty thousand dollars to keep these pictures from his wife. Finn wasn't certain if the man loved his wife so much that he was willing to pay a fortune to protect her feelings, or feared she would take more than that in the divorce.

Finally, they came upon photos of Jeremiah Stotler in bed with a woman and a young girl. The woman's face was turned away as she straddled him, but there was no mistaking Bev O'Brien. The girl looked to be no more than fifteen. Cori reached over and clicked through.

"We get the idea," she said. "I'll find out who the girl is. If she was at an Asylum party, Ali Keyes is going to have to prove her age. We can shut them down if she's as young as she looks."

"I'm thinking Mr. Keyes is too smart for that and too

ethical," Finn said. "This could be a private matter that Stotler set up on his own."

"Then how did Roxana get the photo?" Cori asked. "Bev said she didn't hang with her."

"And Bev has been known to stretch the truth," Finn reminded her. "But there are other ways. Roxana was resourceful. She could have paid someone else to take the picture."

Finn moved on, clicking through more images. Jeremiah Stotler appeared in more than one surreptitiously taken photograph. These weren't centered, the subjects seemed completely unaware, and many were unfocused.

"The man does seem to have a preference," Finn muttered. "Blonde, tall and—"

"Young," Cori said, needing no other word to state the obvious. Bev was the odd duck.

"True. But he is cohabitating with my ex-wife. That is some sort of commitment," Finn said. "Man does not live by sex alone."

"Coulda fooled me." Cori snorted. "So what is it about Bev? Maybe she's his intellectual equal and the sex stuff is the side job."

"She's his beard more than likely," Finn said. "His public woman."

"That's a lousy position to be in. Do you think she knows?"

"I wouldn't think so. Beverly has a certain romantic self-image," Finn said. "What is it these people are looking for, Cori? I truly want to know."

"The men are still those insecure little boys on the playground. The women are still the girls who didn't get asked to the dance," Cori said. "Now it's the big boy's playground, the ladies have proof they're desirable. We're all children, O'Brien. It's as simple as that."

Finn shook head as he closed out of that folder.

"On my childhood playground we only hurt feelings with our mean words. These people ruin lives with their shenanigans."

"I've got to call Lapinski." Cori stood up and stretched.

"Go on, then," Finn said as he clicked the next file. "I want to take a quick look at this one."

Cori had her phone in hand. As she dialed she did a speed read of the correspondence file Finn was scrolling through.

"Curt little thing on paper," Cori said, as she listened to the phone ring.

"She knows what she wants. No hard copies. Email threads only," Finn said.

"She loves to ask for free stuff. Look at this one. She wants a car."

"Did you see a Porsche in the garage?" Finn asked.

"I did," Cori said.

"Then it looks as if it doesn't hurt to ask," Finn said.

"He's on a conference call." Cori pocketed her phone. "He says meet him at Mick's because he has something important for us."

"And I've found something important too."

Finn got up and pointed to the big screen and the long text displayed on it. Cori read, and then re-read the letter.

"'Twasn't love that was taking her out of the world, Cori. It was survival." Finn went back to the computer and ejected the thumb drive.

"Looks like Jeremiah Stotler called her bluff and then some," Cori said.

"Chalk one up for the biggest boy on the playground," Finn said.

CHAPTER 25

Mick's was quiet. Geoffrey was busy trying to fix the espresso machine, so that meant he was quiet too. More to the point he was verbal about the machine, but had no time to chat with Cori, Finn, and Thomas .

The lawyer had beat them to the pub, and was half way through a Long Island Ice Tea by the time the detectives arrived. They had settled at the big round table near the window, as far away from the bar as they could get. Geoffrey delivered their drinks, and left them alone. Before Thomas could share his news, Cori filled him in on theirs.

"Stotler was calling in favors. He convinced every single one of Roxana's sponsors to drop her, and managed to get her buried on Google too. She didn't show up 'till page four. That's the kiss of death for her business. Twitter had flagged some of her stuff as prurient. It was the smoothest take down I've ever seen," Cori said. "That chick had it easy with the banker and the preacher, but Stotler was on a whole different level. He was squeezing her hard. God, what a game."

"Much as I appreciate your enthusiasm, Cori, it gives the important man no reason to want Roxana dead. He had taken care of the problem," Finn said.

"True, unless he wanted to make sure she stayed down. I doubt it though. Still it brings up another question. Did Bev know about his 'solution'?" Cori said. "What if she still thought Roxanna was a threat? She could have taken matters into her own hands to save her relationship with Stotler. You saw her that night—"

"Stop. Stop."Thomas pushed aside his glass. " I think there's something going on that's way deeper than some movie producer and his problems."

Thomas reached into his briefcase and came up with a sheaf of papers.

"So, Cori sent me that video from the Ring doorbell camera, the one that your tech people said was too grainy to get a good read? Well, it wasn't easy, but I got something."He put an eight by ten picture on the table. It was of the Asian man who had fluttered around Roxana when Bev pushed her. "That, my friends, is Ding Xiang."

Thomas sat back, crossed his arms, and beamed. Finn scooted his chair up and poked at the picture.

"Sure, Thomas, that's the name I've been meaning to tell you," he said. "That boy at The Brewery— Peter?—he told me that he had seen him. He said he is an important man in computers."

"Oh Finn, Finn." Thomas waggled his finger and his tone became weighty. "He is so much more. Ding Xiang is a ghost. He is a legend. He is almost as legendary and ghostly as Satoshi Nakamoto."

"And that is the other name," Finn said.

"You lost me, boys." Cori picked up her bourbon on the rocks and took a swig. "Want to fill me in?"

"With pleasure," Lapinski said, as he blocked off a piece of air with his parallel palms. "Over here, is

Satoshi Nakamoto the father of Bitcoin. It is the mother of all cryptocurrency. It can be purchased with any currency, no middlemen, no banks. International payments are easy and cheap because bitcoins are not tied to any country or subject to regulation. It all bypasses normal channels of finance and it is giving Wall Street and governments fits. Right now the market is trading one Bitcoin at five figures, U.S."

Cori whistled. He had her attention. Finn was not far behind.

"But I don't think that has anything to do with that girl's murder. I'm just saying that we can rule out that these two guys are one and the same," Thomas said.

"And why would that be, Thomas?" Finn asked.

"Because Satoshi Nakamoto has never ever shown his face. There is no record of him. He could be an urban myth for all anyone knows." Thomas moved his hands to frame another imaginary box. "Over here is Ding Xiang's box. It is filled with evidence of his existence."

"Thomas, might we just open Ding Xiang's box and see what's got you so excited," Finn asked.

"Sorry." He took Cori's hand and gave it a squeeze, as if to say she was going to be very proud of him. "You aren't going to believe this."

She put her elbow on the table and rested her chin in her upturned hand.

"Amaze me," she drawled before putting a major dent in her bourbon.

"Ding Xiang was—is— a wunderkind. Twenty years ago he was responsible for a huge leap in Chinese tech. He was maybe twenty-five at the time. The People's Republic of China said he was fifteen when he first advised the government, but that's suspect. Anyway, his claim to fame is that he figured out how to wire Beijing. He gave the government a way to gather reporting data on every citizen, every minute of the day. It was a thing of beauty. Actually, it's terrifying from a social standpoint, but from a tech point of view it was way ahead of its time."

"A few years go by and we're doing our thing over here. We've got Gates and Zuckerberg and all the rest of them weighing in. We've got all sorts of discussions going on about privacy. Congress is being all hysterical that we don't want to be China. At some point someone realizes Ding Xiang is out of the picture. No one knows what happened."

Thomas looked at Cori. He looked at Finn. He looked over his shoulder at Geoffrey, twirled his finger for another round, and got a 'oh yes, mon' in response. Thomas didn't miss more than one beat.

"Only computer geeks would have noticed—"

"Or computer geek lawyers," Cori said.

"Thomas, can we get to the pot of gold at the end of your rainbow. A computer expert helping our victim up off the ground is not seeming to be earth shattering news."

"Okay, okay."

Thomas took a deep breath. He rifled through the papers and laid out some articles for Cori and Finn to peruse.

"Bottom line, our guy disappeared from the world stage. No one knew where he went or if he's really gone. If the Chinese government took him out, they aren't saying; if he defected, whatever country he's in is not claiming him."

"Then we get the dark web. After all the sweetness and light of the Internet, it turns out there's a parallel universe operating that isn't so nice. Ding Xiang resurfaces on the dark web in a big way. No one knows where he is physically, but he speaks about his work. He has segued into cyber security and spyware that is not sanctioned by any government."

"Where can we hear him?"

"I'll send you the file. It's not the clearest but it's interesting. The guy is definitely some kind of social mutant. It's painful to watch him talk. Worse to hear him."

"And..."

"And here be your drinks."

Geoffrey interrupted with another Guinness, bourbon, and Long Island Ice Tea. Thanks were given. The man read the room and left them to their work. Thomas leaned over the table. He lowered his voice.

"Ding Xiang has his mark on everything in the tech world. Word has it he's made billions selling his spyware to countries on blockchain platforms. Nobody can prove exactly who has it, but there's circumstantial evidence. More than one country has been caught flatfooted after some deep secret reveal that has no other explanation than Ding Xiang software."

"Think Julian Assange on steroids?" Cori asked.

"Double steroids," Thomas agreed. "But he's branched out. He's got his finger in medical R &D, communications, farming, just everything. His empire is so interwoven it's hard to tell who owns what and who does what. But if you take the time you can trace a lot of it directly back to him."

"So he moved off the dark web and back into the mainstream?"

This time it was Finn who huddled, hunching his shoulders, taking up some of the press Thomas had brought, reading as the lawyer talked.

"Yes, but I doubt he's left the dark web behind. That's where the fun stuff is. Some of his interests are too controversial for the open market. He's got a hand in cyber warriors, bots that can be put into water supplies. The bots are particularly scary. I mean, you could use one of those things to inoculate a population, but on the other hand you could kill everyone with a turn of the tap. Then again, Ding Xiang has done amazing things with hydroponics, surgical robots, prosthetics..."

"Whoa, there," Cori said. She turned to Finn. "Emi's patent?"

"Could be," Finn said, not wanting to jump ahead. "Go on, Thomas."

"Here's the bottom line. Ding Xiang believes technology can run the world better than human beings. He's the original matrix guy, and right now he's the Bigfoot of technology. Except that with this photo we have proof that he was in Los Angeles, at The Brewery, on the night your victim died."

Thomas finished. All three of them took a drink. They considered the papers spread over the table. Ding Xiang was a mysterious and worrisome addition to an already sticky problem.

"But this isn't the Matrix, guys." Cori was the first to speak. She disliked the darkness, and the tech, and the sci-fi story Thomas was peddling. The explanation was simpler. "If he was at an Asylum party he's just another dick head."

"But one interested in our dead girl," Finn added.

"Or not," Thomas said. "He went to her aid. Nobody saw him with Roxana. All you know is that he was in the same place as the Asylum people. The video was taken outside. I could destroy you in the courtroom if you tried to pin a murder on him and that's all you brought."

"But we know he was inside. Enver Cuca admitted they

were arguing by the stairs," Finn said. "And the Cucas' stories matched. They agreed that he went upstairs where the body was found, but we searched that unit top to bottom. There was no way for him to leave that room."

"You yourselves said that the layout of that place made no sense. Did you look outside the unit? You know, work your way inside instead of trying to get out," Thomas suggested. He took up his drink again. When he put it down he said, "We are also talking about a ghost. If Ding Xiang doesn't want to be seen, he won't be seen. Given what he does, given his money, given his ability to disappear from the world stage, he could take out a baby influencer and you'd never lay a hand on him."

"If you can do all that, why care about being outed? And if you did care, why not have someone else do the job. If your work is on an unregulated platform and governments can't touch you, then the law can't," Finn said.

"There's always something a human being cares about," Cori said. "Maybe Roxana had more than a sex thing on him. Maybe she got some government secret from him. Governments have disappeared a person without anyone knowing, and they've done it just on the suspicion that someone was going to scam them. The woman is Russian. Don't forget that."

"Holy mother, you've got us in a conspiracy now?" Finn laughed. "I'm not James Bond nor are you—"

"Don't go there, O'Brien," Cori warned.

"It's not like that. No, no. It's about humanity," Thomas said. "Tech can't substitute for the basic human responses: jealousy, anger, revenge. Ding Xiang might be socially backward, but he is human."

"And this is speculation," Finn said. "We know he was near Enver Cuca's unit the night of the Asylum party, and we also know he was inside at least twice before that night. We know he was at Roxana's house. We know that Enver Cuca painted a portrait of Roxana. She was in his home at least once because that is where she died. It all circles back to Enver Cuca. All of it."

Cori's eyes flitted to Thomas. He raised a shoulder as if to say 'why not'. Cori looked back to Finn.

"I have a funny feeling we're going to be pulling some overtime," Cori said.

"Aren't you wanting to close this circle, Cori?"

In answer she finished her drink, took a few bills out, and put them on the table.

Finn got up, put on his jacket. He gathered up the papers. He took one last look at Ding Xiang's picture and put some money on the table too.

"Yours is on me, Thomas, for all your hard work."

"My pleasure," the lawyer said. "All I ask is that if you find Ding Xiang, you call me so I can have him sign my autograph book."

"We'll do our best," Finn said.

"Thanks, Lapinski." Cori gave his shoulder a squeeze. Lapinski's hand covered hers briefly.

"Stay safe," he said.

"Always," Cori answered.

A few minutes later they were on the road to The Brewery.

CHAPTER 26

The cowboy still rode his white steed, his hat was still held skyward. He grinned and grinned, but in the coming dark he looked sad and lonely. He could wave his hat in welcome all he liked, but Finn and Cori could not get through the gate. The guardhouse was not manned, no one came or went to allow them to drive in on their pass. If they had been on foot it would be no easier; the pedestrian gate had a coded lock.

Finn dialed his phone. He listened to it ring. Cori watched the street. A block or two down she saw the twinkle of Christmas lights on a hamburger/taco stand where she had pulled in for fries and a drink after her dunk in the garbage. She could see the glow of lights from the artists' lofts and the common area fixtures, but the place was buttoned up.

"Yes," Finn said. "If you would. Thank you, Mitzie."

"The fabric artist?"

"She'll come and let us in," Finn said.

"How did Hunter and Douglas get in the other night?" she asked, making small talk while they waited.

"The man who called it in opened it," Finn said, and

then: "There she is."

Finn put his eyes on the gate, and released the emergency brake when it pulled open. Mitzie stood back waiting. Finn stopped the car alongside her.

"There's a visitor spot over there."

Finn followed her directions. She met them half way when the detectives got out of the car.

"You must be psychic," she said. "I was thinking about calling you."

"Are you okay?" Finn said.

"Me? I'm always fine." She waved away his concern. Her blue hair had turned to green. Finn preferred the blue. They walked slowly toward the compound. "It's probably nothing, but there's a delivery still on Enver and Emi's steps. It's not like them to leave anything out. You know how it is here. If it's on the steps it's fair game."

"Perhaps that was their intent," Finn said.

"All wrapped up in a shipping box? I don't think so," Mitzie smiled at Cori. "When it's just stuff on the stoop we don't wrap it up. We leave it outside our units or put it in the park. I met Detective O'Brien in the park."

"So he said," Cori answered. "Have you seen the Cucas recently?"

"Once when a policeman brought them home. I was going to check in on them, but I'm a chicken. I don't want to get involved. No one does now. It's like there's a black cloud over them."

They walked as far as the Cucas' unit without interruption. This night there were no spectators, because there was nothing interesting to see. Porch lights were on. Most units had no windows, and of those that did only a few were covered. They could see one man painting and another soldering.

"I always thought a place like this would be hopping at night," Cori said.

"The murder was as much excitement as anyone wants for a while." She looked from one detective to the other. "Do you want me to come with you?"

Finn shook his head. "No, thank you, missus."

"God I love the way you talk." Mitzie put a hand on Cori's arm. "Don't you love the way he talks?"

"It's pretty awesome," Cori said. "But you kind of get used to it."

With that, they sent Mitzie on her way promising to stop for a nightcap before they left. They forgot the promise the minute she was out of sight. Finn cut away from Cori and went to the side of the building. Cori checked out the front steps. When he came back Cori said:

"The delivery is from Art World. Looks legit."

"There's a light on up in Roxana's room," Finn said.

"Anyone up there?" Cori's eyes went up even though she couldn't see the windows.

"No idea."

Finn picked up the package and put it under his arm. Cori walked ahead of him, up the stairs toward the front door. The bronze ladies still held their crackle glass globes high, but those fixtures were dark. Still, there was a sliver of light to show them the way and it came from inside.

Cori knocked.

The door opened a little. Finn took hold of the knob and pushed it further still.

"Mr. and Mrs. Cuca? Detectives O'Brien and Anderson," he called.

All was silent.

He knocked again. He called once more. And once more after that.

"I'm not liking this," Cori said. "It's too quiet."

"Agreed."

Finn took the package from under his arm, and put it down inside the door. He and Cori were thinking the same thing. Those under a black cloud of suspicion followed many paths. Some stood strong and let the process take its course. Others turned their anger against the system. Still others raged against those they loved, and sometimes destroyed themselves in the process. Enver and Emi Cuca might have fallen into the last category.

Fearing for their safety, Finn and Cori drew their weapons and went through the great room. The couches, chairs, and tables werein place. The crack running down the huge glass table had given way and part of the edge was broken off. The floor gleamed. Cori listed this way, Finn took a few steps that way. Their eyes moved, the hands that held their weapons swept in front of them. Cori made her way to the back of the room. The kitchen was spotless. She used her foot to nudge the bathroom door open. She looked into the bedroom. Both rooms were empty and the bed was made. Finn looked for any sign of disturbance as he went toward the alcove and the stairs. He found none.

Cori was back with him, shaking her head, confirming that she had found nothing untoward. There was an eerie silence in the room, a staleness that had not been there before. The place felt abandoned.They moved on, going up the familiar staircase. As before, Finn went onto the landing and Cori hung back. This time the closet door was open. It was dark inside and empty except for a chair in one corner.

They went up the next flight of stairs, and stood at the mouth of the short hall that led to the workroom. Though they had seen it before, the sight of the body parts and finished companions was jarring.

Finn moved forward with purpose, emboldened by the emptiness of the first two floors. In his heart, he hoped there was a fourth option: the Cucas had simply left. He would much rather hunt them down as fugitives than find one or both of them dead. That proved to be wishful thinking. He motioned to Cori. Pointing to the 'house' room. When she joined him, she heard Emi and Enver Cuca arguing. They spoke in their native language. Enver's voice raised an octave. Emi shut him down. Her words were like bullets spitting from a machine gun.

Finn went through the workroom, silently pushing through the companions. Cori caught one and set it aside carefully as she followed her partner. The 'house' room was exactly as they had first seen it. The white curtains around the bed had been replaced. They were more opaque than the originals. They hung high and the fabric pooled elegantly on the floor, but these replacements were panels and not cut from one length of fabric. They parted enough so that the detectives could see a new mattress was on the box springs, but housekeeping was not their concern. They only had eyes for Enver and Emi Cuca.

Enver's back was to the curtains. He looked drawn and grey as if he had neither food nor sleep in the days since the murder. His clothes were rumpled, his hair unwashed. Emi Cuca faced him, a piece of metal in one hand and a gun in the other. She pointed the gun at her husband's head. If she pulled the trigger, the bullet would enter above the bridge of his nose. Neither of them knew Finn and Cori were watching. Enver because he was transfixed by the sight of the gun; Emi because she only had eyes for her husband.

"*Largohu. Largohu tani.* Get away. Leave now."

Emi's voice was harsh. Finn could see her profile. Her

face was puffy, there was a catch in her throat as she tried to control her words.

"*Jo. Jo*, Emi," Enver said, and Finn knew he was pleading with her.

She took a step forward, he took one back. That's when Enver saw the detectives.

"*Ju lutem*, Emi, *Policia është këtu*. The police are here, Emi."

He held one hand toward Finn and Cori, begging his wife to see the truth of what he said. A shudder ran up Emi's spine. Her arm shook, but she doubled down and gripped the gun tighter. Her head swiveled toward them and back again, so that she could keep her eye on her husband. They had seen enough to know that Emi Cuca was now made of grief and hatred and that was a dangerous combination.

"You go. You go until this is done." She growled at Cori and Finn without looking their way again.

"Missus. Missus."

Finn repeated the word over and over as he moved into the room. He held his arms wide, and let his weapon dangle from one finger. There was no risk to him. Cori had her gun trained on Emi Cuca's back. The woman would go down before she could pivot, and squeeze the trigger on her gun.

"Missus, I am putting up my weapon. Look. See. I wish you no harm. Whatever it is, we are here to help."

Finn's voice was lilting and soothing, but Emi Cuca held her ground.

"Look. Look here at me." Finn made a great show of holstering his gun. "Mine is away. Now, yours. Please. You don't want to hurt your husband."

A great sob welled up from Emi's gut, and nearly doubled her over. Finn was close enough to see the tears begin to fall from her eyes. The polished floor became wet with them. He thought it sad that they had tried to make this place more than it was. The floor was only cement, common and cheap. The room was no better than a storage unit.

"I don't want to hurt, Enver. I do not," she cried.

"Then give me the gun so there's no mistake."

Finn moved in on her, but she shook her head violently. He paused before moving another step. Three more and he would put himself between husband and wife. Finn saw Enver's eyes tracking Cori's movement. Emi Cuca was so distraught she didn't notice what her husband was doing; she didn't sense Cori closing in.

"No. No. No," Emi sobbed. "I do this for Enver. I do this so we can live. It's the other one. The other one—"

In the next minute Cori went for Emi Cuca, taking her down fast. Finn was on Enver, pulling him out of the way. Enver collapsed to the floor, done in. Finn lost his balance and went down with him.

"Emi. Emi," the big man whimpered. "I'm sorry."

Enver's face was on the ground. He cried as he watched his wife. Emi Cuca lay on the floor, curled into herself, sobbing and mumbling words only she and Enver understood. Whatever was between them was soul searing, and Finn had the awful feeling that he was watching two people die. But it was more than the brutal death of Roxana Masha Novika that caused this. Finn imagined this was the pain of a betrayed woman trying to be faithful to a murderer.

"You good, Cori?" Finn asked.

"Yeah."

Cori was up and holding the piece of metal in one hand as she looked around for Emi's gun. She spied it on the floor in front of the curtains. Knowing the woman had nowhere to go, Cori took a tissue out of her pocket and went to retrieve it.

As Cori crouched down to reach for the trigger guard, she froze. Emi Cuca's sobs were loud, but not loud enough to drown out the whispers that came from behind the curtain. She looked for Finn, and pointed to them.

With the utmost care, she reached inside her jacket for her gun as she carefully put the metal piece on the ground. Righting herself, Cori used her foot to move Emi Cuca's gun out of the way. Finn stood. The Cucas stayed where they had fallen, exhausted, and surrendered.

"This is the police. Come out," Cori called.

Behind her, Emi Cuca raised her head like a snake: aware, deadly, waiting for the moment to strike. Her nostrils flared. Her rage had only been resting.

"Come out. Show them. Show yourself," Emi howled.

"Shut up," Cori yelled.

"Stay down," Finn ordered.

Crazed with anger, Emi Cuca sprang to her feet. Before anyone could stop her, she dashed across the floor. Slipping once, she was still fast enough to take up the metal rod. She rushed past Cori, wielding the thing like a bat.

"Guns will do nothing. Nothing," she screamed. "You don't know."

With her free hand, Emi pulled aside the curtain surrounding the bed. Now Enver was up too. Wringing his hands, dancing as he watched his world shatter.

"Don't hurt her. Don't hurt her," he cried as Emi lunged for the man cowering on the bed.

"O'Brien," Cori called, but Finn needed no direction.

He was on Emi Cuca, putting her to the ground, disarming her so swiftly that she lay stunned and unmoving on the floor. Emi blubbered, begging them to understand.

Her voice rose briefly and then fell to a plaintive muttering. Enver Cuca continued to beg for restraint, but the detectives had had enough.

"Everyone. Stay put," Finn ordered.

He took hold of the curtains and tore one off the hooks. It fell to the floor, revealing the bedroom in full. Cori trained her weapon on the bed, Finn was frozen where he stood. Half reclining on the mattress was Ding Xiang. Neither young nor old, he looked exactly as he had on the video. His shirt was buttoned up to his neck. His pants were belted high on his thin frame. He wore soft shoes. His eyes were moist and myopic behind his thick glasses. Here he was. The genius. The ghost. The dark web God was staring back at them, but something was wrong. He wasn't cowering in fear hoping to save himself, he was protecting someone.

"Move," Finn said.

The man blinked.

"Move away now."

Finn pulled his gun and raised his gun until the barrel pointed at the man's heart. Ding Xiang pushed his glasses with one finger. With great effort he moved aside, so they could see who was hiding with him.

"Holy Mother Mary," Finn breathed.

Lounging on the bed was Roxana Masha Novika. She wore a linen shift so sheer they could see the outline of her body. The breasts, the nip of her waist and the length of her legs were all too familiar to the detectives. Her luxurious hair hung over her shoulders. Her eyes were bright and beautiful. A twin, was Finn's first thought. The fingerprint analysis had been a mistake, not detecting the minor differences between this woman and the dead one. He opened his mouth, but she spoke first.

"Ding and I are so happy to see you. Would you like something to drink?"

It was Roxana's double who moved off the bed like she was rising from the dead, but it was Emi Cuca who wanted to send this one back to hell. With her last ounce of strength, she scrambled up and ran at the woman, screeching a cry of despair and rage. Roxana saw her coming and put her arms up to ward off the attack. The woman's fear meant nothing to Emi Cuca.

"Kill her," Emi cried. "Kill her."

Ding Xiang rolled off the bed, and scrambled away. Enver was on his feet. He too cried out in horror. Cori and Finn were quick, but Emi was superhuman in her resolve. Roxana's twin fell back on the bed, throwing her arms up to protect herself.

"Help me. Help me," she begged.

Emi hurled herself onto the bed, covering the woman with her own body. Her hands clawed at the woman's face as the woman threw her head from side to side trying to thwart the attack. Emi put her hands around Roxana's neck and dug her big, strong fingers into the soft flesh. Unable to talk, unable to move, the twin Roxana lay beneath Emi Cuca and ceased to struggle. Finn, closer than Cori, was on Emi, gathering her into his arms, yanking her away from the other woman. But Emi Cuca struggled against him. She dug in, holding her ground.

Finn saw the soft skin give, he heard a crack as if bones were breaking. With a huge cry, he pulled Emi Cuca up and back until she released her hold. Together the detective and the artist's wife tumbled across the bed and slid onto the floor. Exhausted, Emi didn't fight him. She lay in Finn O'Brien's arms, captured and subdued. Finn closed his eyes and lay with his face turned toward the ceiling until he heard:

"Oh my Lord."

He turned his head to look at Cori, but she was looking at the thing in Emi Cuca's hand. It was Roxana Masha Novika's face, wide eyed and full lipped. Finn set the woman aside. She rolled over, clutching the face to her chest as Finn got to his feet. His eyes went to the bed. His breath was labored as much from exertion as revulsion of the abomination he was looking at. Cori moved to his side, her hand touched his. He understood the need for human contact, and he understood the tremor of disgust that ran through his partner.

On the bed lay a body —not a twin but a doll. A companion.A thing. The metal jaw still moved as if gasping for breath; the eye sockets clicked left as if searching for a savior. Everyone in the room looked from Emi Cuca to the body; everyone except Ding Xiang.

He was gone.

CHAPTER 27

"What have you done? What have you done?"

The detectives were so focused on Emi Cuca, they were startled when Enver called out and rushed toward them. Finn stepped in front of the woman, but there was no need to protect Emi from her husband. The man rushed past them, threw himself on the bed, pulled the faceless body to him, and keened as he rocked it.

"Enough!" Emi's scream was piercing as she made an end run for her husband.

"Enough both of you," Finn countered.

He caught Emi's arm and pulled her close. He took hold of the plastic face, but Emi fought mightily for it. Finally, he ripped it out of her hands and twirled her to Cori. Tossing the thing aside, Finn stormed to the bed. At another time he would have had some sympathy if this were a distraught man with a woman caught up in his arms, but this was no woman. The man wept for his own creation, and from what they had just witnessed it was an abominable thing to lament. It certainly was not something to kill for.

Cori put Emi on the couch while Finn wrested the companion from the man, pulled him off the bed and dragged him, stumbling and whimpering, to the sofa. He threw Enver down beside his wife.

"Do not move an inch," Finn roared, his voice crashing against the concrete walls and bouncing back again.

Enver wept and so did Emi, but hers were tears of outrage and his were of pain. In front of them, Cori stood watch. The thing had stopped moving and Finn barely gave it a glance as he swept the room. He moved the bed and tore off the curtains. He went to the bathtub and fell to his knees, running his hands across the floor. Frustrated when he found nothing, he scoured the perimeter of the room, and when he was done he went to Enver Cuca.

"How did he leave here? Ding Xiang. Where did he go?"

Enver shook his head. "I don't know."

Finn took him by his shirt and pulled him upwards, but before he could do more Emi Cuca stopped him.

"Leave him be," Emi commanded.

Finn hesitated. It was Enver Cuca he wanted to hear speak, but Emi was determined to be heard. She swiped at her tears with the back of her hand.

"The man comes and goes. We don't know how. We receive a message when we are to stay away from this room."

"'Tis late. I've little patience," Finn said. "Show me the texts."

"They are gone," Enver said.

Finn and Cori exchanged a glance; they were not surprised.

"Do you know who he is?" Cori asked. "Do you?"

"Not at first, but now. Until he came it was good, Enver." Emi looked at her husband. "All you had to do was give him what he paid for."

She looked away from her husband, her eyes darting between Cori and Finn.

"No one can paint like Enver, but I created the socket and it made the companion move exactly as we move. We didn't need that man. We should have stopped long ago."

"Stop what?" Cori asked.

"Stop what we did for him. The other companions, those were art and engineering. We didn't think about them once they were gone, but this time..."

"This time you played God," Cori said.

"It wasn't that way," Emi snapped. She swung her head toward her husband. "Tell them, Enver. Tell them how it happened."

Emi started to stand up, but Cori put her hand on the woman's shoulder and kept her down. When her husband stayed silent, Emi shook her head.

"Fine Enver. I will say." She swallowed hard and composed herself. "We didn't see what was happening. First a portrait was ordered. Enver painted it from a video and pictures. We sent it away. We thought nothing of it. One day a contract is sent saying Enver may not use that image. Enver signed it. What did we want with the girl's face? There are many beautiful girls he could paint. One portrait didn't matter."

"Then Ding Xiang came and asked for a companion. It was the same girl, but this time he had many things he wanted. He told us how to make this room. He paid the rent for six months. He ordered a companion with the face of the girl Enver had painted. We signed an agreement to speak of none of this. He paid so much we didn't care what he did here."

Emi's shoulders fell. She put her palms to her cheek.

Enver never moved, but he spoke as if remembering a long lost love.

"All of her," he said. "I knew all of her, every shade of her."

"When did you first meet her?" Finn asked.

"She came only once to see the room," Emi said. "We saw her with Ding Xiang then. We spied and saw them. She never came back. We did not meet her."

Suddenly she stood up and began to pace, needing to move even if there was nowhere she could go.

"We put her to bed every night in this room, as we were told. I didn't know why Ding Xiang didn't want us to send her to him. Then I thought he was like the other men, eccentric, odd. Enver finished painting, but I had not sealed her. A package came for me. Inside was a chip, and a wiring schematic. I knew what this was. I was to make her move."

"But there are moving dolls, missus? This is nothing strange," Finn said. Emi looked at him and her eyes darkened, her voice lowered.

"Not like this one." Emi's steps slowed. She wrapped her arms around herself as she wandered in and out of the light that came through the big windows. "I followed instructions. I wired her. I embedded the chip. Soon only Enver put her to bed. He said it was so I did not hurt myself lifting her. She was beautiful in the moonlight. She was the best we had ever done. One night Enver did not come back so quickly from this room. I went to see what was wrong. Enver was stroking her hair. He came away when I called. He was embarrassed. I thought he was only admiring his work."

She turned and looked at Cori and Finn, sighing when she realized they did not understand what she was telling them.

"Ding Xiang came and went. I don't know what program was in her head but each day, each week, he did something to make her more human. Sometimes we were still working in the night, and we could hear her moving. At first she was like a child, stumbling, hitting things. I would find her leg chipped, and I would repair her skin. Enver would repaint her. For months we did this. Then we heard them together. She spoke."

"We couldn't understand her words," Enver said, as if that was an excuse for something.

"Did that matter, Enver?" Emi said.

"She cried," he said, his voice tight as he remembered the moment "I heard her crying."

Emi uttered a sound, guttural and primal. She went for her husband, but Cori stopped her. Emi raised her hands and backed off.

"You made this happen. You are shamed," Emi said, her voice dripping with disdain.

"Missus. Look at me. Look at me," Finn said. Reluctantly she did as she was told. "Did you not fear for yourselves knowing this man could come as he pleased?"

"He needed us." Emi shrugged away that concern. "And money makes you think unreasonable things are reasonable. You cut off your arm. Enough money tells you it was never there, so you learn to use the one you have left."

"Emi." Enver roused himself with a warning to his wife. "We can be sent away if you speak of this. We have a right to a lawyer. We ask for a lawyer."

Emi's voice rose, her neck stretched as she looked around Finn.

"I want no lawyer. I want this to end."

She pushed past Finn. She cast a withering glance at Cori. Emi Cuca took a high backed chair and waited until she had their attention. Enver could not look at her, but he would hear and that was enough for Emi.

"That girl is dead because of Enver," she said. "Sometimes he didn't hear me speak. Sometimes he did not come to bed, and I would find him asleep holding *her* hand after Ding Xiang was gone. Enver brushed her hair. Only Enver touched this one unless I was adjusting her wiring or her joints. Sometimes I found her in the closet, locked inside instead of in this room as she should be. Enver wanted to be alone with *her*; he wanted to hide *her* so that I couldn't see them."

"Then one day Ding Xiang came through the front door to thank us for our work. He invited us upstairs. She was on the bed as instructed. I was happy that Ding Xiang would take her away."

Emi fell silent, thinking about the hope she had harbored; remembering the moment when she thought Ding Xiang would be gone from their life.

"But he didn't take her, did he?" Cori spoke.

"No. We stood just there." Emi pointed to the dining room table. "Ding Xiang opened the curtains around the bed. I looked at Enver. I thought it was funny this sad little man was so dramatic, but Enver was hardly breathing. He knew what she was. You should have told me, Enver."

Enver Cuca turned his head as if his wife had slapped him. Emi looked triumphant. The edge of her lips tipped up.

"Ding Xiang called to her. 'Roxana' he said. The doll stirred as if she had been sleeping. She got off the bed, and smiled and spoke. 'Hello, Ding. I've missed you'. Ding said 'we have guests'. The thing said 'Enver. Emi. How nice to see you. Sit down.' He did not say it was us in the room. He didn't have to. She saw us. Then Ding Xiang asked her how she was. The thing said 'a little tired'. How can a thing be tired?"

Emi shivered. The pride she had felt in her accomplishment was gone leaving her with a mix of disgust, terror, shame, and grudging fascination. Now that she'd begun she was determined to finish the story

"She thought. She saw. She cried. What Ding Xiang gave me—what I put in her head— made her a woman. Ding Xiang loved her. Enver loved her. What was left for me who made her?"

Emi hands were clenched so tight her knuckles were white.

"Ding Xiang went away again. He told us when the people came and saw her they would want many more companions like this. He told us to be ready, as if we should be happy to make more. I did not want a world of those companions. My husband was sick with love for this one thing. He did not want anyone to have a companion like her. I knew what had to be done."

Tears rolled down Emi's cheeks. They were hot, angry, tortured tears that spoke of human pain.

"I heard you speak to her like you used to speak to me. You made her look like a goddess. I made her move like a woman. It was him, Ding Xiang, who made her wicked. I had to do something to stop it. I wanted you back for me, Enver."

"You killed Roxana." Finn said, his voice flat.

"I did not mean to." Emi buried her face in her hands and sobbed only once before hands fell away. She looked at Finn and confessed to him. "I didn't know the woman was upstairs. I didn't know Ding Xiang's plan to show the companion and the woman together. It was always just the companion on the bed. Always."

Emi shook her head, her hands clasped and unclasped.

She gasped for breath as her eyes went from Finn to Cori, searching for some understanding.

"You saw her eyes. You heard her voice. Would you know? Even if it wasn't dark, would you know the difference between that thing and the woman?" With one great breath, her shoulders rose and fell. She looked at Enver, but spoke to them all. "Don't you see? She wasn't real. None of this is real."

CHAPTER 28

"The DNA on the dress from the dumpster is Emi Cuca's," Cori said. "And the blood she tried to wash off was Roxana's. And Roxana's blood was on the inside of the smock where the dress rubbed against it. I can't believe I missed that extra layer when I patted her down."

She swiveled her chair and filed the report in the box she would be sending to the D.A.

"I wouldn't have known that smock wasn't her dress, and I sure cannot make sense of these contracts. I think the Cucas handed themselves over to Ding Xiang completely." Finn tossed his reports to Cori for filing. "Access to their unit, their bank accounts, their computers, and all with the threat of deportation hanging over them. Ding Xiang came pretty close to getting everything he wanted."

"Except love," Cori laughed. "Too bad making a woman was the only way he was ever going to get that."

"'Twas about more than love, Cori. That man knew the value of his software and Emi's socket joint. He was on the verge of realizing a new world order," Finn said. "And there were four men from Asylum who were going to be in on the ground floor."

"The whole Asylum thing seems like a lot of drama for nothing," Cori mused. "Why not just call the guys with money and go for it?"

"I doubt Ding Xiang really needed investors. I think what he wanted were men who were powerful, embedded in the mainstream, and shared his vision. They also had to possess a certain unhealthy attitude toward the fairer sex. Asylum members had already proved themselves open to indecent pleasures and a willingness to pay for them. In that context it makes all the sense in the world."

"Too bad Stotler didn't make the cut."

"I'm thinking Mr. Stotler is a bit cold for Ding Xiang's liking. The man actually tried to protect the companion Roxana, after all. Stotler has no such soft spot," Finn said.

"Yeah, but in the end Ding Xiang saved his own butt," Cori reminded him as she held out a piece of paper. "Speaking of which, there's a message for you."

Finn reached across their desks, took it, read it, and tossed it.

"Bev is back in her apartment," Finn said, half smiling as he glanced at Cori. "But I've a feeling you knew that."

"Someone's got to have your back," Cori said without apology.

"I'm one lucky man to have you," Finn said. "Still, I am sorry she has been banished from Shangri-La."

"Stotler will snap his fingers for her now and again," Cori assured him.

"And I'm sure if Mr. Stotler snaps, Bev will be happy to jump." Finn shook his head, not in dismay but in confusion. His ex was a mystery these days. "Still, I'm happy she had nothing to do with the murder."

Cori thought she should tell her partner that she was

glad too, but she answered her phone instead.

"Lapinski's here." Before the phone was on its cradle, the man himself appeared.

"Hello, folks. Ready to call it a day?"

"Five minutes," Cori said. "Finn, is Gretchen meeting us at Mick's?"

"She is, and I've only to rearrange the files to send off tomorrow. It won't take long."

Finn turned back to his computer screen. Thomas settled himself on the edge of the desk, keeping one foot on the floor for balance. He unbuttoned his jacket.

"Take your time," Lapinski said as he leaned over Cori's desk. She gathered up the final reports to keep them from prying eyes.

"You know everything you need to know," she said.

"And some things you may not." He tapped his nose and grinned. "I took a look into AIing Inc. The place has a subsidiary of its own. A very elite cyber security firm in Switzerland that's heavy into R&D on Artificial General Intelligence."

"Like the Alphabet project?" Finn asked as he clicked on one file and then dragged another across the screen. "Feeding books and such into a machine and the machine learns to think?"

"Kind of, but you're talking about simple pattern recognition. AGI is more intuitive. If I read it right, this place is working on breaking down and then recreating the connection between human emotions, actions, and reaction. I thought all that was something light years away. There's work in Germany that associates sensory information from the nervous system and connects it with environment. Another one called NLP—natural language process—is also fascinating. If Ding Xiang was able to combine all these disciplines, your doll could have appeared to be alive and thinking. She would be both proactive and a reactive. "

He shook his head, becoming uncharacteristically somber.

"I can't imagine the programing it took to incorporate all those videos of Roxana. That woman spent hundreds of hours moving her body and mouthing words, but it had to take thousands to make it all work seamlessly in the program."

"That explains the studio in her house. I get that," Cori said. "What I don't get is the fake apartment."

"It appears the place was a training ground." Finn looked up from his work. "People reported seeing a woman moving like she was drunk, but it was the companion learning. Emi said they had to repair her when she bumped into things. I think once they put the thing to bed each night, Ding Xiang would either remotely activate her or pay the companion a visit. He wanted to test her in a duplicate of the real woman's environment."

"I agree," Thomas said. "They had six months to watch her learn. If Ding Xiang didn't like a certain outcome, his team referred back to the files of the real woman and reprogrammed the fake one. It sounds like he wanted her to be as natural as possible, not just some sort of robotic handmaiden."

"Roxana was just as sick as Ding Xiang," Cori pointed out. "What normal woman would agree to have herself duplicated?"

"Why not when the payday was so good?" Finn said. "Stotler had ruined her career, so she would be out of the spotlight anyway. Once Ding Xiang tired of his companion Roxana, he would release the real woman from the contract and she could go back to doing whatever she liked. Living a quiet life might be difficult for someone like her, but he wasn't holding her prisoner. "

"She would still know that doll existed," Cori insisted.

"And that would mean nothing to her. She might even have taken some perverse pleasure in it. Ethics are in short supply these days," Thomas said. He turned to Finn. "Is someone working on breaking into that chip?"

"Certainly they are," Finn said. "But I won't hold out much hope. Ding Xiang is as brilliant as you say. Destroying the chip is child's play."

"I'd love to know what makes that guy tick," Thomas said.

"Whatever it is, I hope he takes it somewhere else." Cori picked up the blueprints and gave them over to Finn.

"And how did the great man come and go?" Thomas asked as he watched the hand-off.

"Years ago a portion of The Brewery was sold off to small manufacturers," Finn said. "The one closest to the property line still had a grain chute that went directly to the Cuca's place. When Ding Xiang identified them as the only ones who could build his girl, he had to figure out how to protect the project and not draw attention to himself. He did his homework, bought that building, secured the lease with the Cucas, and had his team reopen the passage way. The man is meticulous in his planning."

"But where was the door?" Thomas asked.

"In the wall behind the bed area," Cori said. "From inside it looked like a crack in the concrete that's why we didn't notice it. We had to open it from inside the chute to figure it out."

"I imagine the same people who camouflaged the mechanism in Roxana's closet also created the hidden door. It was a thing of beauty." Finn hit send and smiled. "Done."

"Good for you." Cori put her hands together for her partner, and then veered back to the topic at hand. "Ding Xiang made all these grand plans, but Emi trumped him with a simpler one: destroy the companion. She was going to bash its head in, but Ding Xiang decided to be a showman and parade the real girl and the companion in front of the Asylum crowd. Emi didn't know that he'd sent the real Roxana upstairs or that Enver put the fake in the closet. She assumed it was the companion on the bed just like it had been for six months."

"Wow," Thomas said. "When you think about it, it's amazing what that man accomplished. The idea, the execution, the cooperation. Incredible."

"Just not admirable." Finn reached for his jacket. "Because you can doesn't mean you should."

"That's a conversation you should have with Ding Xiang. A man of faith versus a man of science. Aren't you even the least bit curious where the world can go with all this, Finn?" Thomas asked.

"I only want to go to dinner," Finn said. "I've a real stomach that needs real food."

"Actually," Thomas said as he helped Cori on with her jacket. "There is one more thing. Why this specific girl?"

"I know the answer to that because Roxana backed up all the messages she got from Ding Xiang before she opened them." Cori reached for her purse. "The very first time he contacted her, he proclaimed his love and it never let up. The poor guy was totally awkward but he was smitten. They were a perfect match. Neither of them worked in the real world. Crazy, huh?"

"Crazy complicated and simple all at the same time. He loves her, she loves money, the Cucas love a challenge, and then Emi Cuca ruins everything because her husband fell in love with the thing he created," Finn said.

"Can we all say Frankenstein," Cori drawled as she put the top on the evidence box.

"That woman must have freaked when she realized her mistake." Thomas put out his hand and Cori went ahead. Finn fell in step behind the lawyer.

"Emi was a nut bag too," Cori said. "I think she was so fixated on that doll that the murder registered as a messy mistake. She said she had no idea what she was going to do with the body, she just wanted the companion gone."

"Don't give her too much sympathy, Cori. She was smart enough to clean her hands and face and to put that smock over her bloody clothes," Finn said. "Not to mention the fact that she was very smart about the murder weapon."

"Which was what?" Lapinski said as they funneled into the hall.

"A metal femur. Emi sealed it into the leg of a companion after she did the deed," Cori said. "That's why we didn't find blood after that one point in the workroom. We would have never found it in that doll unless she told us where it was."

"And after all that, the Roxana companion was still in the house," Finn said. "The body had no face, so Officers Hunter and Douglas didn't know that they were looking at a duplicate of the victim when they opened that closet. If they had, this investigation would have been over before it was begun."

"And good old Enver can't keep his hands off the thing, so Emi goes off the rails," Cori said. "Do you guys think Enver knew his wife killed the real Roxana?"

"I don't know." Finn sighed. He shook his head. "He hated Ding Xiang so much, he probably thought he'd done it. "

"But there would be no reason," Lapinski said.

"Is there reason to any of this? It's the D.A.'s problem now, thank goodness."

Finn stepped out of the way to let an officer pass in the hall. That's when he heard Captain Smith call to them. Lapinski went on alone as the detectives detoured into the captain's office. She spoke without preamble.

"The mayor wants to know when you'll complete The Brewery file."

"All of it is going off tomorrow," Finn said. "The lawyers will have their work cut out for them."

"Not really. The D.A. is planning to plead Emi Cuca out if only to keep a whole lot of important people from being dragged into this," Captain Smith said. "A public trial is in no one's best interest, and the circumstances make a murder conviction iffy. The woman's attorney would argue that her intent was to destroy property not take a life. Intent is what the law is all about."

"Inventive defense," Cori said.

"And a true one," Finn added.

"And none of our concern," the captain said. "We did our jobs. Let's move on. Dismissed and good work."

The detectives took their leave, allowing themselves a fist bump on the way out of the building. Lapinski was leaning on the hood of his car. He pushed off and met them half way.

"Problems?"

"A pat on the back," Finn said.

"Well deserved." Lapinski grinned and took Cori's arm to guide her to the curb.

"We couldn't have done it without you, Lapinski." Cori kissed him on the cheek when he opened the door for her.

Finn added 'many thanks' as he zipped up his jacket.

L.A. was finally feeling a bit of a chill. He said, "You know, there is something about this that all those rich men will never understand."

"What's that?" Lapinski asked.

"If they had thrown in with Ding Xiang, money would flow into their pockets and they would have perfect sex with perfect, ageless women. Yet for all their grand plans of populating the world with manufactured people, all they did was expose the raw power of humanity. Love, jealousy, the protective instinct," he said. "It was all those real things in Emi Cuca's heart that brought them down."

"Ain't love fantastic." Cori chuckled and swung her legs into the car.

"It could be," Thomas said. Cori rolled her eyes as he closed the door. Finn put a hand on the attorney's shoulder.

"Sure, she'll come around," he said.

"Darn right. Thomas Lapinski never loses a case. See you at Mick's."

Finn walked to his car. When Cori and Thomas drove past, he raised a hand. Traffic was light in East L.A. What there was of it rolled leisurely past the small houses and sad strip malls. A mother pushed a stroller down the sidewalk while two small children skipped beside her. The sun was going down. The day was ending. People would eat, and make love, and kiss their children, and sleep. They would wake up and do it all over again the next day and the day after that. Most people would never know that living among them were men who dressed up like goats and treated women like animals. They could never imagine anyone wanting to substitute metal and rubber for the warmth of a living, breathing human being.

As he got behind the wheel of his car and started the engine, Finn thought of Gretchen. There was nothing more exciting than a woman who spoke her own mind and moved by virtue of her own free will. Then his Irish heart corrected itself. The only thing more exciting was a grown woman who could do all that andstill make room for rainbows and unicorns. That was a woman he didn't want to keep waiting.

Finn pulled into traffic, leaving behind any thought of Emi and Enver Cuca. He was no longer curious about Ding Xiang, the man who would be God. He didn't wonder if the body of Roxana Masha Novika would ever be claimed, and Finn O'Brien even forgot the faceless doll that lay, not on a bed of fine linen, but in an evidence room, a thing of no use to anyone.

A LOOK AT: BEFORE HER EYES

READER'S CHOICE AWARD – BEST MYSTERY

In a remote mountain community, the execution of a grocer and the abduction of a world-renowned model leave Sheriff Dove Connolley searching for a connection, two killers and a woman who is running for her life. Obsessed with finding Tessa Bradley before it's too late, Dove's investigation leads him into a shadowy world where nothing is as it seems, hope is bought and paid for and death has many faces.

She runs, death follows.

"This is one of the most haunting stories I have read…"

AVAILABLE NOW

ALSO BY REBECCA FORSTER

ABOUT THE AUTHOR

Rebecca Forster started writing on a crazy dare and is now a *USA Today* and Amazon bestselling author with over 40 books to her name. She lives in Southern California, is married to a judge, and is the mother of two grown sons.

CPSIA information can be obtained
at www.ICGtesting.com
Printed in the USA
LVHW041636280421
685863LV00013B/2219